Tiger Thief

Tiger Thief

Michaela Clarke

nosy crow

First published in the UK in 2013 by Nosy Crow Ltd
The Crow's Nest, 10a Lant Street
London, SE1 1QR, UK

Nosy Crow and associated logos are trademarks and/or registered trademarks
of Nosy Crow Ltd

Text © Michaela Clarke, 2013
Cover illustration © Dominic Harman, 2013
Cover and inside pattern and typography © Sarah Coleman, 2013

Printed and bound in the UK by Clays Ltd, St Ives Plc
Typeset by Tiger Media Ltd, Bishops Stortford, Hertfordshire

Papers used by Nosy Crow are made from wood grown in sustainable forests.

ISBN: 978 0 85763 137 4

www.nosycrow.com

This book is dedicated to my beloved
Mama and Papa

Chapter One

JINNI

Emira paced backwards and forwards in her wooden cage. Each time she turned, her tail flicked in irritation against the bars. Behind her, a tatty orange circus tent rose up into the evening sky, silver limelight shining through cracks in the canvas. The air was hot and still, and hungry bats flitted overhead, feeding on the insects that flew up from the parched earth.

Sharat pulled on a pair of white trousers. He was naked from the waist up and a dark braid hung down his back.

He paused to look across the river. For days they'd been trudging through the heat and dust of the southern plains towards the City of Jewels. Now they were here, but instead of the glittering streets he'd been expecting, the land lay cracked and bare, and ragged slums clung

like a scab to the outskirts of the city. The only sign that this was the capital of the richest empire in the world was the fortress that rose up at the centre of the old town, its forbidding, stone walls dominating the streets below.

Sharat shivered in excitement. Shergarh. Tomorrow they would be performing there for the Emperor himself.

Emira made an impatient noise at the back of her throat.

Sharat glanced back at her. "I'm coming!" he said. Stepping towards the cage, he fished around behind one of the wheels and pulled out a key.

The tiger watched him with unblinking blue-green eyes as he unlocked the door. Her tail twitched. She had been restless all day.

"Don't blame me," grumbled Sharat. "The cage wasn't *my* idea."

Emira growled as she lifted one of her great paws and pushed the door open, jumping down to land silently next to him. Her fur shone with an unearthly glow in the twilight, pure white with tracings of ebony.

Sharat put out a hand to stroke her, but instead of stopping to purr as she usually did, she slid straight past him and padded towards the circus tent.

"Hey!"

Frowning, Sharat dropped the key back in its hiding place as he hurried to follow her. Together they slipped through a gap in the canvas to wait in the shadows.

This was the circus's first night in the city and it was a full house. The air was heavy with the smell of incense that was burning to keep the mosquitoes away, and

2

the audience sat on cushions and blankets on the floor. Farmers rubbed shoulders with shopkeepers and their wives, while their children jostled for space at the front. Many of the women kept their faces covered, but a few shimmered like exotic birds in brilliant silk saris as they whispered to each other. By the door, a group of soldiers stood watching, silently, their swords glinting by their sides.

Sharat glanced up. Overhead, his cousin Risa glittered in her silver costume as she twisted her body around a rope that was hanging from the roof. With perfect control, she slid down until she was suspended by one of her ankles. For a moment she struck a pose, arms outstretched. Then, slowly, she began to swing.

Sharat had seen the show a thousand times. He knew Risa was getting ready to fly towards the trapeze.

"Ready?" he said, glancing at the tiger as he pulled on a pair of leather gloves.

Emira's tail quivered as she watched the acrobat. A low growl played in her throat.

Sharat bent down to pick up his long leather whip. "Calm down!" he muttered. "It's only Risa."

Instead of giving him her usual friendly meow, Emira snarled and lurched forward.

Sharat stumbled as she pushed past him.

"What *is* it?" he snapped.

Emira's eyes darted across the ceiling. This time her growl was more insistent.

Puzzled, Sharat looked up as Risa passed overhead in

3

a graceful arc.

Then suddenly he saw it! There was something up there, something small and dark crouching in the rigging. Squinting, he craned his head, but before he could make out what it was, it scurried towards the trapeze and began to fiddle with the knots.

Catching his breath, Sharat ran forward.

"Risa!" he cried. "Don't let go!"

It was too late. With a flick of her foot the acrobat unwound the loop around her ankle. She was already flying through the air when one side of the crossbar fell.

There was a gasp from the crowd. Risa's outstretched hands were reaching into empty space.

Without thinking, Sharat threw himself into the ring. Cracking his whip, the leather cord caught the wooden bar just in time to swing it towards the acrobat's flying body.

"Catch!" he shouted.

By some miracle, Risa managed to grab the pole with one hand as the whip clattered to the floor. She looked terrified.

Jabbering with excitement, the audience surged to their feet and pushed forward to get a better look, but Lemo, the ringmaster, got there first.

"Loosen the ropes!" he boomed, sprinting into the ring. "Bring her down!"

Lemo was Sharat's father. His naked torso rippled with muscles and his dark eyes flashed with authority as he called out his orders.

Risa's own father and brother had already appeared out of the shadows. Quickly, they lowered Risa to the ground and carried her away.

Sharat's heart was pounding as he scanned the ceiling. What was up there? A monkey? A bird? He caught a glimpse of shining eyes, but before he could get a proper look there was a shiver of wings, and the creature disappeared through a hole in the canvas.

Emira had seen it too. She leapt forward, her teeth bared in a terrible growl. With a gasp, mothers snatched their children and the audience swerved back in terror. All at once the soldiers drew their swords and began to advance. Lemo didn't miss a beat. With a crack of his whip he cut Emira off from the crowd. Then he spun to face all sides, his arms outstretched.

"Ladies and gentlemen!" he cried. "Please show your appreciation for our final act: Tiger Boy and Emira, the White Princess!"

Before Sharat could object, someone pressed a flaming hoop into his gloved hand and pushed him into the ring. Right on cue, Emira let out a terrible roar and lunged towards him, eyes blazing and claws outstretched. This time, the children in the front row shrieked with pleasure.

Sharat had no choice. Snatching his whip from the floor, he slipped into his routine. Dodging Emira, he proceeded to put her through her paces. To the audience it seemed that the tiger would surely rip him to shreds, but somehow he always managed to bring her under control until, at last, it was time for the grand finale.

With a flick of his wrist, Sharat threw the hoop of fire into the air. Then, as Emira leapt through the flames, he flipped backwards, landing just in time to snatch the spinning hoop from the sky.

The audience rose to their feet with a roar of applause.

Emira snarled menacingly at the crowd while Sharat took his bows. Then, with a final crack of the whip, they ran out of the ring.

Sharat's heart was hammering with excitement as he led the tiger back to her cage.

"What was that thing in the rigging?" he demanded as he pulled off his gloves.

Emira growled and lashed her tail.

Sharat laughed as he ruffled her fur. He and Emira usually understood each other perfectly, but this time even *she* couldn't tell him what she'd seen. His mind was racing as he remembered the small, dark creature. Was it a monkey? A bird?

"I'll have to ask Risa," he said.

Quickly, he reached for the key and opened the cage door.

The tiger turned to fix him with a disapproving stare.

Sharat sighed; Emira hated being locked up. In the countryside she was allowed to roam free, but it was dangerous in the city.

"Go on," he said. "Lemo's orders."

Emira bared her teeth in scorn as she lifted one of her paws and pressed it against his chest, flexing her claws just slightly to prick his skin.

6

"Ow!" complained Sharat, brushing away her paw. "I know you can look after yourself," he said. "*I'm* the one who will get into trouble." He gave her a push. "Just get in!"

Emira grumbled, but she climbed in with a swish of her tail.

"We can go out hunting tomorrow," promised Sharat, as he threw her a hunk of mutton.

With a growl the tiger caught the meat, but she turned her back on him to eat.

Sharat went down to the river to wash. The water was brown, and the current sluggish this far south, but it felt good to splash his body clean. Afterwards, he filled a bucket of water up for Emira and put it in her cage.

"I'll be back soon," he said.

Emira flicked her tail in disdain.

The show was over and the crowds were already pouring into the night as Sharat made his way around the circus tent towards the campsite. For as long as he could remember, the ringmaster's caravan had been his home, but now his father's new wife, Mohini, lived there.

Tonight, she was sitting on the brightly painted steps, brushing her long, black hair. When she saw Sharat coming she smiled, her eyes green and knowing.

Sharat scowled. Mohini had been at the circus for less than a month, but she was already acting like she owned the place. Flushing angrily, he hurried past.

His father was standing nearby with the acrobats, Pias and Ram. Pias was Lemo's brother, but his body was wiry

7

and his face was pinched and narrow. He was holding the crossbar of the trapeze.

"Where do you think you're going?" he snapped as he caught sight of Sharat.

Sharat was surprised by the tone of his voice. He stopped short to catch his breath.

"I'm looking for Risa," he said.

Pias frowned. "What do you want with Risa?"

Sharat hesitated, wondering why his uncle looked so angry. He glanced up at his father.

"I want to talk to her about the accident," he said.

Lemo looked serious. "I think you'd better talk to us first."

Sharat felt a pang of anxiety. "What's the matter?" he asked. "Is Risa all right?"

Pias leaned forward, his small eyes mean with fury. "Risa's fine," he said. "No thanks to *you*."

"What do you mean?" said Sharat. "I just saved Risa's life. Didn't you see?"

"I'll tell you what I saw," said Pias, his voice heavy with threat. "I saw you watching the trapeze before it came down. It was as if you *knew* it was going to fall."

Suddenly Sharat understood. "Surely you don't think *I* loosened the trapeze?" he said in disbelief.

Pias's lip curled. "That's exactly what I think."

Sharat shook his head. "Don't be stupid," he said. "I would never do something like that." He turned to his father.

"There was something up there," he explained.

8

"Something messing with the rigging."

Ram, Risa's brother, was only a year older than Sharat, but he was already bigger than his father. His broad mouth twisted in disdain.

"What are you talking about, Ratty?" he sneered.

Sharat threw him a dirty look.

"I suppose it must have been a monkey," he said. "I didn't see it that clearly."

Pias snorted. "No monkey could untie one of *my* knots."

"Well, maybe it wasn't a monkey," said Sharat, "but it was small and black." He frowned as he thought of the dark figure he'd seen crouching on the ropes. "I think it may have had wings."

Ram rolled his eyes. "Maybe it was a *jinni*," he suggested sarcastically.

Sharat's heart leapt. "A jinni?"

"That's enough," snapped Lemo, shooting a warning look at his nephew.

There was a sulky expression on Ram's face, but he bit his lip.

Lemo glanced at Sharat. "This is no time for one of your stories," he said.

"It's not a story," protested Sharat. "There *was* something up there. Emira saw it too, that's why she went so wild."

"What nonsense," said Pias. "Emira went wild because you don't know how to control her."

Sharat glared at his uncle. "That's not true!"

Before Pias could answer, Lemo stepped in. Putting his hand on Sharat's shoulder he glanced at his brother.

"Leave him to me," he said quietly. "I'll make sure he gets the punishment he deserves."

Pias looked annoyed, but he didn't dare argue with Lemo. He jerked his head. "Come on," he told Ram, "let's go back and check the rigging. We'll soon be able to tell if it's been tampered with."

Ram followed obediently, but he flashed Sharat a scornful look as he left.

When they were gone, Sharat turned to confront his father. For the first time he noticed that Lemo's face was tired and lined with worry.

"I'm not lying," he said. "I would never loosen the trapeze. Pias blames me for everything."

"Pias is … difficult," Lemo admitted.

Sharat scowled. "He's jealous because I've got Emira."

Lemo sighed. The boy was right. When Emira had first come to the circus, Pias had wanted Ram to have her, but the tiger had never obeyed anyone except Sharat. They had grown up together.

"Leave Pias to me," he said. "But promise me you won't talk about what you saw tonight. I don't want the crew getting nervous."

Sharat shook his head. "They wouldn't believe me anyway," he muttered.

Angrily, he turned away, ignoring Mohini, who was watching silently from the caravan steps. He had been so excited about saving Risa's life. He should have known it

would somehow get him into trouble. But there *had* been something up there. He was sure of it. Emira had seen it too. His heart quickened as he remembered those glinting eyes. Could it really have been a jinni?

Sharat shivered. He'd heard stories about jinnis, but he'd never really paid much attention – it was considered bad luck to even talk about them at the circus.

Quickly, he hurried back towards Emira's cage. As he passed the campfire, he could hear the rest of the circus laughing and joking. He considered joining them, but he knew they would be sure to ask him about the accident. Instead he stuck to the shadows, skirting the circus tent until he was facing the City of Jewels.

The night was still and the moon was not yet risen. All he could see now were cooking fires glowing in the slums. For a moment he stopped to look at the menacing shape of the fortress at the centre of town, a silhouette against the stars.

Just then he heard a growl behind him.

"Emira?"

He glanced over. Then he stiffened. There was a man standing in the darkness next to the tiger's cage.

"Hello?" he called out. "Who's there? Is that you, Pias? Ram?"

As he spoke, Sharat felt something shift in the night air and his skin became clammy despite the heat. Just then he saw that the figure in front of him was dressed from head to foot in black. This wasn't one of the circus crew. This was a stranger.

Trapped in her cage, Emira had drawn herself up to her full height with her ears pulled back. She bared her teeth and snarled. Sharat clenched his fists.

"Who's that?" he called again, ready to fight.

There was no answer, but as the man turned, Sharat saw him more clearly. His hair was swept back in waves from his forehead, he had no beard and his face was deathly white, but even more frightening were his pale eyes, their colour indistinguishable in the starlight.

Sharat felt his stomach contract in fear. He stepped forward.

"What do you want?" he demanded.

The man in black didn't reply. Instead, his mouth opened in a ghastly smile and the gap between his lips became as wide and black as the gates of death. He raised his staff.

A blast of scorching air engulfed Sharat. Wind whipped the hair around his face, and his limbs were pinned to his sides. For a horrible moment he thought he would be lifted off his feet, but just then Emira's terrible roar shattered the whirlwind. In a flash, the man in black disappeared.

Sharat spun around, staring into the darkness. The harsh cry of a bird sounded overhead. For the briefest moment an enormous shadow blacked out the night, but nothing stirred on the ground.

Emira hissed. Her ears were flattened close to her head and the hair along the length of her spine bristled. She was frightened.

Sharat's heart was pounding. This wasn't the first time they'd had trouble. There had been other occasions when gangs of children had come to taunt Emira. Then, he'd been able to see them off with his whip. This stranger was something else.

He reached through the bars to stroke the tiger's flank. "Did he hurt you?" he demanded.

Her growl was low and threatening.

With a quick glance to make sure the coast was clear, Sharat unlocked the cage and Emira jumped out to stand by his side, her tail trembling in fury as he wrapped his arms fiercely around her neck.

Sharat slowly relaxed, but he had no intention of putting Emira back in her cage.

"I don't care what Lemo says," he murmured into her fur. "You're spending the night with me."

Chapter Two
ROOKH

As his feet touched the ground, Rookh's wings disappeared and were replaced by a robe that fell in dark folds to the floor. He had landed in an open courtyard, but with a few long strides he stepped over the threshold into a dusty apartment and swept down a flight of stairs to an underground chamber.

It was as dark as a tomb, but at the click of his fingers flames sprang to life in the candelabra overhead, casting a thousand shadows on the vaulted ceiling above.

In a niche against one wall was a great stone urn. Rookh reached out to touch it. It was still warm.

"Casmerim."

The name was soft and magical on his lips.

There was a portrait on the wall of a dark woman,

shaded by the spreading branches of a tree. He almost felt his heart ache. *Trapped in the dark, like a dead thing.* The thought rose unbidden in his mind.

He shuddered.

"So you thought you could trick me, did you?" he whispered, pressing his clenched fist against the unyielding stone of the urn. "Thought you could *escape*?"

There was no reply of course. Casmerim was asleep – would remain asleep for as long as Rookh required it. He couldn't kill her. He'd tried. All he could do was make sure that she never woke to see the light of day.

Fury gnawed at his belly. Of course he knew he shouldn't feel betrayed. What else could he have expected? That she would thank him for kidnapping her and making her his queen? No. She'd been a queen already. Queen of the Forest. Queen of the Jinnis. Queen of Aruanda. Until he'd taken her power and made her his slave. His prisoner. His wife.

Drawing back his shoulders, his eyes flickered by the light of the flames. He thought he heard a sigh from deep inside the urn, but he didn't open the lid in case she woke and looked back up at him with pity in her eyes.

"You'll never escape me now," he warned the woman in the picture. "Not now I know your plan."

It had been the Queen's fragrant handmaid who'd told him. Taunting him with her secret.

"You think you're so powerful, enslaving all the jinnis," she'd said. "But you didn't get us all. There was one who escaped you."

Rookh had stiffened. "Who?" he'd demanded.

"He's called the Prince of Jinnis," whispered the slave. "Nobody knows where he is. Some say he lies sleeping deep below the city. Others claim he still lives in Aruanda. Or it may be that he walks the earth, protected by magic from knowing eyes. But wherever he is, when the time is ripe, a white tiger will lead him back to the City of Jewels to free the Queen of the Forest. And when that happens, the Empire will fall, and you will fall with it."

A prophecy, spells, jinni magic. Rookh was a stranger in this land, but he was inextricably tied up in it all. After all, it was he that had enslaved the Queen and her people, but he was also a man of science, of reason. Surely he could change his fate. Why should he wait until this jinni prince came to destroy him?

"Is there nothing I can do?" he'd asked.

The handmaid's eyes had glittered. She was no friend of the Queen of the Forest.

"To keep your empire safe you must find the tiger," she'd said. "Only then can you stop the hidden prince from fulfiling his destiny."

In perfumed whispers she had told him what to do. Sweetening her words with kisses. He'd almost forgotten Casmerim.

Now, he looked at the picture again. Such beauty. Such strength. Such innocence. And yet, to him, she'd been as cold as ice. He felt his heart contract.

"I'll catch this hidden prince, just like I caught you," he swore. "He'll be my slave like all the rest."

And what then? whispered the voice that came from deep inside him. *You already own the Empire.*

A familiar hunger gnawed at Rookh's heart.

"Then I'll conquer the world," he hissed in answer to his own question. "Every jewel, every ounce of gold, every man, woman and jinni that walks the earth will be mine!"

Chapter Three

HUSSEIN

Sharat woke early the next day to the sound of holy men calling the faithful to morning prayers. Next to him Emira lay purring in her sleep. Yawning, he squeezed his eyes shut and burrowed his head into her soft fur, but it was no use. Before long a rooster began to crow and soon a pack of dogs joined in with the dawn chorus.

Sharat opened his eyes. Grey light had started appearing through cracks in the tent. With a sigh he wriggled out from between Emira's paws, wrapped a cloth around his waist and slipped outside.

It was a cool morning, but the sky was brightening fast and the sinister events of the previous night seemed unimportant in the light of day.

There was a trumpeting noise, followed by the sound

18

of splashing. The circus elephants were washing while the rest of the crew still snored in their beds.

Hacking open a coconut, Sharat gulped down its juice and scooped the meat into his mouth. Then, tossing aside the shell, he went down to the river to wash.

Tara the she-elephant lay on her side with her eyes blissfully shut while Hussein, the *mahout*, scrubbed her down with a stiff brush. Nearby, Baba the bull-elephant wallowed in the shallows, waiting for his turn. Next to them lay the last of the bananas.

Hussein had been an army *mahout* for years, training elephants for the old Emperor, but tiring of battles and blood he'd left the army long ago to join the circus. He was Lemo's oldest friend.

"Good morning!" called Sharat as he reached out and stole a banana.

Baba trumpeted, and Tara opened her eyes to wink at him.

The *mahout* looked up. He was bald and stocky, and his scalp was dented with scars. A slow smile spread across his face.

"There you are!" he said. "What happened to you last night? I wanted to congratulate you. You saved Risa's life!"

Sharat grinned. "I'm glad *somebody* noticed."

"It was difficult to miss," replied Hussein. "Risa owes you one."

Sharat gave a short laugh. "Tell that to Pias," he said. "He thinks *I* was the one that untied the trapeze."

Baba blew a raspberry.

Hussein laughed, but there was a look of concern in his eyes. "Did you?" he asked.

"Of course not," said Sharat, rolling his eyes. "Pias is an idiot."

Hussein sat back on his heels as he studied Sharat. The boy had a wide face and his hair hung carelessly over his skinny shoulders. In many ways he looked like a typical circus child, and yet there was something different about him – something about his eyes.

"In that case, what did happen with the trapeze?" he asked.

Sharat hesitated, wary of his promise to his father.

"It's all right, you can tell me," said Hussein. "Lemo told me you saw something in the rigging."

Sharat couldn't help feeling relieved. "I did see something," he admitted. "But I'm not sure what it was."

"What did it look like?"

Sharat frowned. "It was small and black," he said. "At first I thought it must be a monkey, but it didn't move like a monkey. It didn't *look* like a monkey either." He paused. "Ram said it might be a *jinni*."

He was expecting Hussein to scoff and dismiss the suggestion, but instead a look of worry crossed his face.

"A jinni?" he said. "Of *course*."

Sharat looked at him in surprise. "Do you think it really *was* a jinni?" he asked.

Hussein nodded slowly. "It could well have been. After all, this place was once called the City of Jinnis."

Sharat felt a thrill of fear. "Why was it called *that*?"

Hussein lowered his voice. "They say that long ago, before men took over, jinnis ruled this land," he said. "Then when people began to live here the name stuck. It was only changed when they cut down the forests to mine for jewels."

Sharat nodded. He knew about the jewels. Thanks to the mines, the City of Jewels was the capital of the richest empire in the world.

"But why would a jinni want to untie Risa's trapeze?" he asked.

Hussein hesitated. "I can't say for sure," he said, "but there are dark forces at work in this city. It was very different the last time we were here. The old town used to be famous for its gardens, and there were forests as far as the eye could see." He shook his head sadly. "Now look at it."

Sharat glanced at the wastelands surrounding the city. For the first time he noticed that there wasn't a single tree on the horizon.

"What happened?" he asked.

"All I know is that there was some kind of revolution," Hussein told him. "I just hope we didn't make a mistake coming back."

Sharat shifted uneasily. "What do you mean?"

Hussein shook his head. "It's an old story," he said. "Perhaps it's best not to talk about it."

"You have to tell me now!" protested Sharat.

Hussein sighed. "I suppose it does concern you," he

21

said. "It's about Emira."

"Emira?" Sharat frowned. "What's she got to do with it?"

"Emira comes from the City of Jewels," explained Hussein. "Someone gave her to Lemo the last time we were here."

Sharat shrugged. "So what?"

"When we were given Emira for the circus, it was on one condition," Hussein told him. "Lemo had to promise never to come back."

Sharat felt his skin prickle. "Why?"

"I'm not sure," said Hussein. He hesitated. "I have to admit that I've always wondered whether Emira was stolen."

"*Stolen?*" Sharat looked at Hussein in alarm. "What makes you think that?"

"Emira came to the circus at the beginning of the revolution," Hussein told him. "It's possible she may have belonged to one of the noble families who were in power before the Empire. A prince maybe, or a princess. They like to have exotic pets."

Sharat felt the stirrings of fear. It had never occurred to him that Emira might have belonged to anyone else.

"So do you think that what happened in the rigging was some kind of revenge?" he asked.

"Perhaps," said Hussein. "Or it could have been a warning." He shook his head. "Either way, I don't like it."

With a shiver, Sharat thought about the man in black.

Was *he* Emira's real owner?

"Why did Lemo break his promise?" he asked.

"Money," Hussein told him. "We can make more in one night performing for the Emperor than we'd make in one week on the road."

"But why do we need so much money?"

Hussein sighed. "Lemo's a great showman, but he's not the best businessman," he said. "Recently Pias threatened to take Emira and give her to Ram, unless Lemo found a way to pay him."

Sharat felt fury rising up inside him. "Ram can't take Emira, she mine!" he said.

Hussein nodded. "That's what Lemo told him," he said, "but Pias disputes your rights."

Sharat pressed his lips together. He knew Hussein was referring to his birth. Lemo hadn't been married to his mother, and Pias never let him forget it. Not that it mattered. His mother had died in childbirth.

Feeling anxious, he stood up. "I think I'd better go and check on Emira," he said.

"Good idea," said Hussein. "I'm sure things will be fine if you keep an eye on her. After all, it was a long time ago."

Bending down, he started scrubbing Tara again. The elephant's ears flapped appreciatively. Then she lifted her trunk and reached back, gently caressing the top of his bald head. The *mahout* pretended not to notice, so Tara lifted her trunk and blew Sharat a noisy kiss instead.

Sharat couldn't help laughing. Still, Hussein's words

had disturbed him. He'd better put Emira back in her cage before Lemo found out she was missing.

He hurried back up towards the campsite.

"Get up, you lazy beast!" he called once he reached the tent. But, as he stuck his head through a flap in the canvas his heart dropped. There was no sign of the tiger.

He spun round in alarm.

"Emira?" he called, his voice sharp. "Emira! Where are you?"

There was no reply.

Trying to stay calm, Sharat ran swiftly around the campsite, whistling and calling as he checked the tents and caravans, but Emira was nowhere to be seen. With a growing sense of panic, he stopped and looked out at the city and beyond. His tiger *always* came when he called her. Where could she be?

Chapter Four

AYA

Aya squatted by the river with a look of fierce concentration on her face as she slid her hand into the water, fingers wriggling. Moments later, she was rewarded by a cold, muscular body moving in towards her palm and she felt a surge of excitement. It was a big one.

"Tickle, tickle, little fish," she sang under her breath, waiting for the creature to settle into her hand. Then, with one swift move, she grabbed its tail and slammed it against a rock.

"Gotcha!" she cried in triumph. The fish lay dead, killed by the blow. A grin of satisfaction lit her face. "Breakfast!" she whispered. Her stomach grumbled in anticipation.

Quickly, she gutted her catch, trying not to grimace as she tossed the waste into the river. She was just building a fire to cook it, when suddenly she heard a low growl behind her.

For a moment she froze, the skin on the back of her neck prickling in warning. Then, slowly and carefully, she turned around.

She stifled a gasp. She was looking into the face of an enormous white tiger.

Too shocked to be afraid, Aya just stared. Then, with a steady hand, she reached out and picked up the fish.

"Do you … do you want it?" she offered, lifting it towards the beast.

For a few seconds, the tiger examined her with interest, but instead of bounding over to take the fish, or indeed to eat her, it just sniffed the air and growled once more. Then, to her relief, it turned its tail to carry on upriver.

Aya remained frozen as she watched the great cat make its way towards the temple. As soon as it had disappeared, she dropped the fish and allowed herself to breathe again. Her heart was pounding with excitement. She'd just seen a white tiger!

A nursery rhyme her mother used to tell her ran through her head:

Earthbound, breathled, firefound and watermet,
Brought to his fate by tiger white, and called by name
from death to life,
The Prince of Jinnis will come again,

To overthrow the rule of men,
And save our queen from slavery,
So all her creatures can be free.

The Prince of Jinnis.

Everyone else thought jinnis were wicked and dangerous, but Aya's mother had always told her otherwise.

"This place was called the City of Jinnis," she'd said. *"It used to be ruled by a beautiful queen called the Queen of the Forest. And when the jinnis were free, the people were happy and the land was fertile and green."*

Aya knew those days were gone. Nowadays the land was barren, the trees had been cut down, and all the jinnis that used to live here had been enslaved. With a beating heart, she turned to look up at Shergarh. Even from the outskirts of town the fortress seemed to possess some sinister power.

And yet she had just seen a white tiger.

Her heart leapt in hope.

The Prince of Jinnis will come again, to overthrow the rule of men...

"Long live the Prince of Jinnis!" she whispered.

Sharat was furious with himself for leaving Emira on her own. He looked around the bleak landscape wondering which way she'd gone. To the west he saw nothing but empty fields, nowhere for a cat to hunt or hide. To the east was the river. The tiger loved to swim,

but only in lively mountain streams where she could fish. Here the water was sluggish, muddy-brown, and crossed by boats and barges, too deep and dirty for the fastidious Emira. To the south was the city. She hated cities. She must have gone north – back in the direction of the mountains.

Praying that nobody would see him, he ducked away from the circus camp and ran along the river. Soon he passed a travellers' inn. Here, a group of traders sat in the shade playing dice while their mangy camels dozed in the sun.

He stopped in front of them, panting. "Have any of you seen a white tiger?" he gasped. "She's escaped from the circus."

A leathery little man glanced at his companions as if he'd just won a bet. Then he smiled at Sharat with a flash of gold teeth and pointed towards the river and the north.

"She went that way," he said.

Sharat felt a rush of relief. He was on the right track.

"Thank you!" he called, as he dodged past the camels and continued upriver.

Further along, he saw a little girl in a ragged dress lighting a fire next to the skeleton of a banyan tree. About seven or eight years old, she was crowned by a mop of unruly curls and there was a look of concentration on her face.

Sharat stopped again. "I'm looking for my white tiger," he blurted out. "Have you seen her?"

The little girl's head shot up with a look of excitement. "Is she *yours*?" she said.

"Yes," said Sharat. "She's run away. We're from the circus."

The girl's face dropped. "The *circus*?" She sounded disappointed, but Sharat barely noticed.

"Did you see which way she went?" he asked. "I've got to get her back or I'll really be in trouble."

The girl studied him for a moment, then she picked up a small bag and slung it over her shoulder. "I think I know where she's gone," she said. "Follow me."

Running lightly on bare feet, she led him along the cracked mud pathway that wound around the huts and down towards the riverbank. Soon they stopped next to a stone staircase that led down into the water. A majestic, tiered temple, covered in carvings of voluptuous goddesses, mighty warriors and marching elephants, rose up further along the bank. Nearby, several bonfires smouldered, their smoke rising straight to heaven in the stillness of the day. A cloying smell hung heavy in the air; the smell of roasting flesh.

Sharat shuddered. He knew that smell. They'd reached the burning *ghats*, where the bodies of the dead were cremated so that their ashes could be scattered into the holy river. Those weren't just bonfires. They were funeral pyres. Covered in garlands of paper flowers, they were tended by grieving relatives, or by the silent, ghostly men who spent their whole lives at the crematorium, scrabbling through the ashes for golden teeth and anything else of

value that the dead had left behind.

The girl glanced back at Sharat. "I'm pretty sure your tiger came this way," she said. "There's an old woman living at the temple called Uma. She'll be able to help you."

"Thanks!" said Sharat.

He was just about to run off when he felt a pang of pity. The girl seemed so small and ragged. He wondered what she was doing all by herself on the banks of the river. He paused.

"What's your name?" he asked.

She held his gaze with clear, serious eyes. "Aya," she said.

Aya. It was an unusual name. Sharat hadn't heard it before. "Have you ever been to the circus?" he asked.

Aya shook her head.

For some reason Sharat wanted to make her smile. "Come tonight!" he said impulsively. "It's a special show. We're performing inside Shergarh."

To his surprise Aya shot a dour glance at the fortress. "I'm not going in *there*," she said.

Sharat didn't have time to ask her why. "Come tomorrow, then," he said. "We'll be doing another show."

Aya hesitated, but there was a look of yearning in her eyes. "I've always wanted to go to the circus," she admitted.

"Just ask for me and they'll let you in," said Sharat. "I'm Sharat."

For the first time a shy smile crossed Aya's face. "Will

your tiger be in the show?" she asked.

Taking a deep breath, Sharat turned to face the cremation grounds.

"Only if I can find her," he said.

Chapter Five

UMA

The smell of charred flesh grew stronger as Sharat picked his way towards the temple. He passed a group of *sadhus*, holy men, with long, tangled locks of hair and serene eyes. They were naked apart from their ragged loincloths and they sat meditating in a circle around one of the funeral pyres, while vultures wheeled overhead and a pack of wild dogs lay waiting for the remains of the dead to be thrown into the river. Behind them, the carved stone temple rose up silently to the sky.

As he hurried past, Sharat glimpsed a rigid arm, partly burned, with a claw-like hand reaching out from a woodpile. He bit his lip and reminded himself that the dead couldn't hurt him. Their souls were long gone, journeying on to be reborn into their next life.

"Emira?" he half called, half whispered.

Only the vultures cawed in reply.

"Emira!" he cried again, louder this time.

One of the dogs lifted its head and barked, but there was still no sign of the tiger.

"Emira! Where are you?" shouted Sharat as loud as he dared.

"What are you looking for, boy?" demanded a creaky voice nearby.

Sharat spun around. The most extraordinary old woman was coming towards him.

Small and thin, with high cheekbones, leathery skin and a halo of white hair, her full red skirts were covered in mirrored discs, and circles of light danced around her in the morning sun. Despite her frail appearance an aura of power surrounded her.

"What's the matter?" she demanded. "Can't you talk?"

Sharat stared at her. "Are you Uma?" he asked.

"I might be," said the old woman, narrowing her eyes. "Who are you?"

"I work at the circus," said Sharat. "Aya sent me. I'm looking for my tiger."

The old woman's eyes softened as she peered into Sharat's face. "What took you so long, circus boy?" she said. "I've been waiting for you."

Sharat's heart leapt. "Have you found my tiger?"

"It's more like she found me," said the old woman.

Sharat looked around eagerly. "Where is she?"

Uma turned and hobbled quickly away, her skirts

scattering light as she moved. "Follow me," she called over her shoulder.

Sharat hurried to catch up with her.

The old woman led him to the high wall surrounding the temple.

"Quickly! Quickly!" she hissed as she opened a narrow, wooden door that had been coated with mud to become almost invisible against the wall. Without thinking, Sharat bent down and went through.

As he straightened up he felt a change of temperature and moisture in the air. Then he heard the beating of wings followed by a sudden, raucous caw. A big bird circled him twice in a flurry of gold and green, before landing on the old woman's shoulder. It watched Sharat with beady, black eyes.

Sharat looked around in amazement. It was as if he had stepped into another world. Surrounding them was a jungle of trees, vines, bushes and flowers, all planted willy-nilly, but surprisingly lush compared to the barren plains outside, and completely hidden by the high walls. In the middle of this garden was a small mud hut.

Just then there was a growl and Emira shot out of the undergrowth, almost knocking him down as she bounded towards him.

Sharat threw his arms around her. "Where have you been?" he crooned, too relieved to be angry.

Emira rubbed her head against his, but then she stiffened as she caught sight of the bird on Uma's shoulder.

The parrot clicked his beak. "Easy, tiger!" he cawed.

34

Emira let out a low growl.

"She must have jumped over the wall," said Uma. "I just turned around and there she was."

Sharat glanced at the greenery all around them. "Maybe she was looking for breakfast," he said. "She's used to hunting in the forest."

Uma's face tightened. "She won't have much luck around here," she said. "This is the last garden in the City of Jewels."

For the first time it struck Sharat how strange it was to find this oasis in the middle of the desert. "How do you keep the plants alive?" he said. "It's so dry outside."

A secretive look crossed Uma's face. "Oh, it's not so hard if you know how," she said. "All you need is the help of the elements ... and a little bit of magic."

As she spoke a breeze lifted, and the trees shivered. Then, to Sharat's surprise he felt a sprinkling of rain. Glancing up, he saw that the sky was still clear and that the sun burned as brightly as ever.

With a feeling of unease he stared at the old woman. "Are you a witch?" he demanded.

Uma reached out to pluck a few leaves from a nearby tree. "What do you think?" she said.

The bird on her shoulder cackled, then took off and landed on a flowering sapling.

"Mad! Old! Witch!" it cawed. Sharat watched as it shivered its brilliant feathers. In the blink of an eye they changed colour to match the emerald leaves and crimson flowers on the tree. He could hardly see the bird now,

unless it moved. It winked at him.

"Shut up or I'll wring your mangy neck," muttered Uma.

Nervously, Sharat glanced at the tiny door in the wall. He realised nobody knew he was here.

"Well, thank you for finding Emira," he said, stepping back. "But I'd better be getting back to the circus. They'll be wondering where I am."

"No!" Uma glared at the bird. "Don't pay any attention to Ripiraja," she said. "You can't go yet. Emira may be in terrible danger."

Sharat felt a pang of fear. "What makes you say that?" he asked.

Uma lowered her voice. "You may not know this," she said. "But Emira comes from the City of Jewels."

With a start Sharat remembered his conversation with Hussein. "How do you know?" he said sharply.

"I know because I was the one that gave Emira to the circus," Uma told him.

Sharat's eyes widened. "Were you the one that made my father promise not to come back to the city?" he asked.

Uma nodded. "That's right," she said.

Sharat thought back to what Hussein had told him.

"But why?" he asked. He paused. "Is ... is Emira *stolen*?"

"No," said Uma, "she's not stolen."

Sharat frowned. "Then what's the promise all about?"

Uma glanced around. "You'd better come inside," she

said. "The walls have ears in this city."

Sharat really didn't want to go into this strange old woman's hut, but as Uma turned to lead the way, Emira pounced on the reflections that spun from her mirrored skirt. Then, without waiting for Sharat's permission, she slipped through the door.

"Hey!" cried Sharat, as he hurried to follow her in.

Inside, the hut was a big room divided into separate areas for cooking, sitting and sleeping. In the corner was a cauldron bubbling over a fire.

"We can't stay long," said Sharat, standing by the door.

Uma tipped the leaves she had gathered into the cauldron. "Don't worry, circus boy, I won't *eat* you," she said impatiently. "Sit down!"

The tiger was already lying on the floor. Reluctantly, Sharat sat next to her and put his hand on her back.

"So what *is* the promise all about?" he asked.

Uma brushed her hands on her skirt and hobbled over. "It's a long story," she said as she squatted down next to him. "How much do you know about the City of Jewels?"

Sharat shook his head. "Not much," he admitted. He hesitated as he thought of the creature in the rigging. "I heard it was once called the City of Jinnis."

Uma nodded. "That's right."

Sharat swallowed, but he couldn't help feeling curious. "What *are* jinnis exactly?" he asked.

Uma's eyes shone. "Jinnis are the spirits of the forest," she told him. "Every tree has its own spirit, but unlike human beings, these spirits can leave their bodies and

take on other forms."

Sharat thought of all the forests he'd travelled through with the circus. "If that's true, why haven't I ever seen one?" he asked.

Uma shook her head. "Nobody can see jinnis any more," she said. "Long ago, they drew a veil between their world, Aruanda, and our own. Now the only thing that connects the two worlds is the trees."

"But there are no trees in the City of Jewels," Sharat pointed out.

Uma sighed. "Not any more," she said, "but it hasn't always been like this. There was a time, not so long ago, when the city was surrounded by forests. In those days there was a walled garden at the centre of town, where Shergarh is now. They say that this garden was the home of the Queen of the Jinnis, the Queen of the Forest."

Sharat felt himself being drawn into Uma's story despite himself.

"What happened?" he asked.

Uma's face darkened.

"About twelve years ago, somebody found a way into Aruanda and unleashed the forces of evil," she told him. She shuddered. "For one day and one night, demons over-ran the city, cutting down the trees. And once they had finished with the gardens they started on the forests."

"But why?" demanded Sharat.

"To enslave the jinnis," Uma explained. "Without their trees, the jinnis have no way of returning to Aruanda. That's why the Empire is so rich. Only jinnis know how

38

to find the jewels that are buried under the city."

Sharat didn't know what to think. He'd always heard that jinnis were evil, malicious creatures, but Uma was painting quite a different picture.

"What's all this got to do with my tiger?" he asked.

"In the middle of the upheaval I was called in to help a woman who had gone into labour," Uma told him. "After she'd given birth she gave me a tiger-cub and asked me to smuggle her out of the city."

"Emira!" exclaimed Sharat.

Uma nodded. "Yes, Emira," she said. "That's when I gave her to Lemo. I had travelled with the circus and I knew he would take good care of her."

"But why was she in danger?" asked Sharat with a frown.

Uma lowered her voice. "Aruanda wasn't just home to the spirits of the trees," she told him. "There were other creatures that lived there too – magical creatures with mysterious powers. I believe Emira is one of these."

Sharat stared at her. "Are you trying to tell me Emira's a jinni?" he asked.

Uma tilted her head. "Something like that," she said.

"But Emira can't be a jinni," protested Sharat. "She's been with me since she was a cub. I would know if she had any special powers."

"Really?" said Uma quietly. "Are you sure?"

Sharat hesitated. He looked down at Emira. She looked back at him, her wild eyes burning with a strange light, and suddenly he wasn't so sure at all. He swallowed.

39

"Do you think she's still in danger?" he asked.

Uma's face was grim. "I'm sure of it," she said. "The demons are determined to wipe out any trace of Aruanda. If they find out about Emira, they'll want to destroy her too."

Suddenly Sharat thought of the creature in the rigging. "I think I've seen a demon!" he said. "Last night, at the circus."

Uma's eyes flashed. "In that case there's no time to waste," she said, getting to her feet.

"But what am I going to do?" said Sharat in alarm.

Uma hobbled over to the door. "Go back to the circus and tell Lemo you have to get out of the city," she said. "It's your only hope."

With a growl, Emira jumped up to follow her into the garden.

Sharat's heart sank as he thought about how his father would react if he came back talking about demons and jinnis. "He'll never believe me," he said as he hurried after them.

"Yes, he will," said Uma. "Tell him you've seen me. Remind him of his promise. He'll remember me."

For a moment she hesitated. Then she untied a necklace from around her neck and handed it over.

"Here," she said. "You'd better take this."

Sharat looked down at his hand. Lying on his palm was a golden bee with an enormous blue diamond at its centre.

"What is it?" he asked, frowning as he turned over the

40

amulet.

"It belonged to the woman who gave me Emira," Uma told him. "She said it would protect my garden, but by rights it should be yours."

Sharat glanced up at her in surprise. "Why?"

Uma's eyes glinted. "Because *you* were the baby I delivered that night."

Sharat could hardly believe his ears. "Are you saying Emira's owner was my *mother*?" he gasped.

Uma nodded. "Yes."

Sharat felt a rush of emotion. Lemo had always refused to talk about his mother. All he knew was that she'd died when he was born. He clutched Uma's arm.

"Who *was* she? Where did she come from? What did she look like?" he blurted out, unable to hide his excitement, but before she could answer a single question, a terrible shriek broke the air.

"Uma! Uma! UMAAAGGHHHH!" Above them, Ripiraja blazed scarlet as he circled the garden like a flying banshee.

"What is is?" demanded Uma as the parrot landed with a flurry of feathers.

"Lickers!" cried the bird. "Run away! Run away!"

A look of panic crossed Uma's face. Quickly, she hobbled over to the doorway in the wall, gesturing urgently for Sharat and Emira to follow.

"There's no time for questions," she said. "If they find you here they'll kill us all!"

Sharat and Emira hurried to catch up.

41

Sharat was desperate to find out more about his mother, but no sooner had he passed through the hidden door when he heard a metallic buzz and lifted his eyes to see a shimmering cloud of gold rising up over Shergarh.

"What is it?" he demanded.

Uma's face was ashen. "Never mind what it is," she gasped. "Just go!"

"Go! Go! Go!" The parrot's raucous cry echoed overhead.

Emira growled at the golden cloud. It was approaching fast and soon the noise became more distinct, like the sharpening of a thousand knives.

Sharat didn't need any more convincing. Heart pounding, he swung himself on to the tiger's back.

"You heard the witch," he said. "Let's get out of here!"

With a growl, Emira began to run.

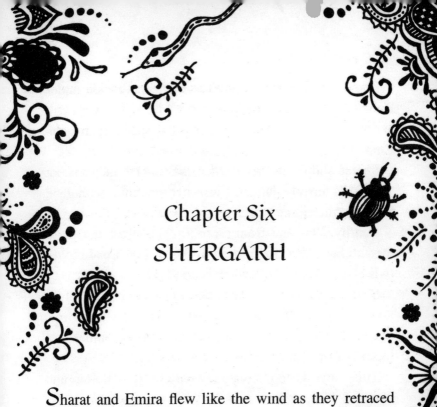

Chapter Six

SHERGARH

Sharat and Emira flew like the wind as they retraced their steps back to the circus. By the time they arrived, the encampment was alive with activity as the crew got ready for that evening's show. Sharat glanced over at Shergarh, but whatever had been heading for Uma's garden had disappeared. Quickly, he locked Emira up in her cage and ran to find Lemo and Hussein. They were with the elephants, preparing for the procession into town.

Lemo frowned as he caught sight of him. "Sharat!" he said. "Where have you been? We've been looking for you everywhere."

Gasping for breath, Sharat seized his father's arm. "Cancel the show!" he said. "We have to get out of the city."

Lemo brushed off his hand to tighten a buckle under Baba's belly. "Don't be ridiculous," he said. "We can't cancel the show. We're just about to perform for the Emperor."

Sharat shook his head. "But we *can't*!" he insisted. "We're in terrible danger. I just met the witch who gave Emira to the circus."

Nearby, Pias and Ram were hitching their horses to the acrobat's cart. Ram lifted his head. His broad mouth twisted in a sneer. "It's witches now, is it?"

Sharat ignored him as he appealed to his father. "Surely you must remember," he insisted. "Her name was Uma. She said she knew you. She told me you'd promised not to bring Emira back to the City of Jewels."

This time Lemo stopped what he was doing and frowned. "Promise?" he said. "What promise?"

"Your promise to Uma," said Sharat impatiently.

Lemo still looked confused. "The name does sound familiar," he admitted.

"Oh, for God's sake, stop pandering to the boy," snapped Pias. "Can't you see it's just another one of his stories?"

Sharat ignored him. He had no time to lock swords with Pias now. He turned to Hussein. "*You* remember the promise," he said. "You were the one that told me about it. Tell him we have to get out of here!"

Hussein's face wore a shadow of concern, but he shook his head in regret. "It's too late," he said. "The Emperor's guards have already arrived to escort us to Shergarh."

44

Sharat turned to look. There they were. Soldiers. On horseback.

"Of course we're not going to leave," said Pias impatiently. "Have you forgotten how much gold we're getting for tonight's show?"

"Nobody has forgotten, Pias," said Hussein sharply, but then he turned to Lemo.

"The boy is right, perhaps we shouldn't have come back," he said in a low voice. "I remember your promise, even if you don't."

Lemo eyed Hussein thoughtfully. The *mahout* was his right-hand man. He trusted him completely. With a sigh he passed his hand across his forehead. "My memory hasn't been its best since I got married," he admitted. He glanced at Sharat. "Well, there's nothing I can do about it now," he said. "But let's make tonight our last night in the City of Jewels."

Pias didn't dare object.

Hussein smiled down at Sharat. "A day can't make that much difference, can it?" he said, trying to be reassuring. "Now go and get your things while we hook up Emira's cage."

Sharat hesitated, but he could see that this was the best that he was going to get. For a brief moment he considered taking Emira and escaping to the mountains by himself, but he didn't quite have the courage. After all, he had no idea what kind of danger he might be facing and he would feel a lot safer travelling with the circus … tomorrow.

Reluctantly, he gathered together his props and pulled on his new white trousers. Then, with trembling fingers he reached for the amulet. As he looked down at it in wonder, he felt an unfamiliar tugging on his heart strings. Who *was* his mother? What had she looked like? And why wouldn't Lemo ever talk about her?

With a sigh, he slipped the amulet into his pocket. He would show it to his father later – perhaps it would jog his memory – but first they had to perform for the Emperor.

The circus made a colourful procession as it wound its way through the cobbled streets of the old town towards Shergarh. Both elephants were painted with bold designs. Baba the bull-elephant led the way, pulling Emira's golden cage, and Tara the she-elephant followed. On their backs sat Lemo and Hussein, looking majestic in their turbans, while Sharat rode proudly on Tara's neck, guiding her with movements of his feet and a special language used only by *mahouts*.

Behind them, the rest of the troupe – magicians, fire-eaters, contortionists and acrobats – trundled along on their painted carts, while Lara the horsewoman brought up the rear, her dark curls decorated with brightly coloured feathers as she looked down from the back of her Arabian stallion. Only Mohini wasn't there. She'd gone on ahead to help with preparations at the palace.

Sharat glanced down at the people that lined the streets as they processed through the City of Jewels. By the light of day he thought he could see a look of desperation in

46

their faces and once or twice he caught sight of fights breaking out in the crowds as they jostled for position.

Up ahead loomed the walls of Shergarh. Beyond those walls it was possible to catch a glimpse of a dome here and a spire there, gleaming in sharp contrast to the grubby streets below.

Sharat kept his eyes on the tiger's golden cage as Emira sat staring stonily into the distance. He still felt anxious as he remembered Uma's warning, but there was nothing he could do about it now. The Emperor's soldiers were riding alongside them, and soon they were crossing the drawbridge over the moat that surrounded the fortress.

The gateway into Shergarh was cast in the shape of a dragon's head with bulging eyes and pointed fangs. Flames spouted from its mouth, but as they approached, the fire subsided and the jaws of the mechanical monster opened to let them in.

"Uh oh," said Hussein. "Looks like there's trouble up ahead."

Sure enough, Baba, the old war-elephant, was refusing to go through and, moments later, even sweet-natured Tara bellowed and came to a stop while the whole circus procession ground to a halt behind them.

"You'll have to let me take over," Hussein told Sharat.

With a nod, Sharat was about to change places with him when a flurry of horses drew up beside them – the Emperor's soldiers. Dressed in smart brown uniforms and white turbans, they were armed with steel hooks – cruel weapons that were used to train

47

elephants to fight in battles.

"Stop!" cried Sharat when he saw the gleaming metal, but it was too late. With a harsh shout, one of the soldiers had swung his hook into Baba's backside. Then another came flying towards Tara's head.

The metal pierced her flesh, drawing blood, and she let out a trumpet of pain, but she moved forward with a jerk. Sharat regained his balance and glared at the soldiers. He was about to say something, but Hussein put a hand on his arm.

"Leave it," he warned, in a low voice. "There's nothing you can do."

Sharat controlled his temper and leaned over to whisper comfort into Tara's ear as she was driven through the gates into the fortress grounds.

Inside Shergarh, the Imperial Guard continued to escort them towards the palace. On either side they passed the mansions of noblemen and public squares that were decorated with tiled fountains and impossibly perfect flowerbeds.

Sharat looked around in awe, then he frowned. "I thought there weren't any gardens left in the city?" he said, remembering what Uma had told him.

Hussein shook his head. "Look closer," he murmured. "Those plants aren't real; they're made out of precious stones."

Sharat peered down. Sure enough, the flowers gleamed and sparkled in the sun, their leaves and petals painstakingly sculpted out of jewels to mimic the real

48

thing. Then something else caught his attention.

"What's that?" he asked, pointing at a small shape that scuttled along the paving in front of them. As he watched, the creature lifted its wings with a metallic buzz and took off, flying straight at them. He snatched it out of the sky. A golden beetle wriggled in his hands.

"It looks like some kind of toy," he said, looking down at it in fascination, but as he leaned closer the creature lashed out with razor-sharp legs.

"Ow!" Sharat dropped the beetle and sucked his finger. It had drawn blood.

The mechanical creatures were crawling over every jewelled leaf, bringing the artificial gardens to life. Sharat wanted to jump down and catch another one, but they had arrived at the royal palace.

It was a magnificent building made of white marble. At each corner rose an onion-shaped dome carved in intricate designs. Armed guards led them through an archway into a square courtyard where a pavilion had been set up for the performers and their audience.

"That must be where the Emperor will sit," said Hussein, pointing out an area lined with priceless carpets and strewn with cushions of brilliantly coloured silk. In front of them a low table was laid with golden plates and jewelled goblets.

Next to the Emperor's pavilion Sharat noticed a smaller enclosure, screened to hide whoever was inside. Just then he saw a flutter of movement and heard the sound of laughter. Despite his misgivings, he felt a thrill

49

of curiosity. This must be part of the Imperial *Zenana*, where the royal women lived, protected from the eyes of strangers.

The elephants were led into a grand stable with vaulted ceilings. Hussein whistled, impressed.

"They say Suleiman loves his animals," he told Sharat.

Lemo had dismounted already and was calling out instructions. He caught sight of Sharat still sitting on Tara's back.

"Are you ready?" he demanded.

Sharat slid down the elephant's neck and jumped to the floor. "Yes, Father," he said.

Lemo nodded and was about to turn away when Sharat caught his hand.

"Father. Wait!" he said.

Lemo frowned. "What is it?"

Sharat pulled out the amulet Uma had given him. "Do you recognise this?" he asked.

Lemo looked down at the golden bee. "I've never seen it before," he said, frowning as he glanced up at Sharat. "It looks valuable. Where did you get it?"

"The witch gave it to me," Sharat told him. He studied his father's face. "Are you *sure* you've never seen it?"

"Of course I'm sure," said Lemo impatiently. "Why are you bothering me with this now? We'll be on any minute. Go and check on Emira."

Sharat felt a strange mixture of disappointment and relief. Surely his father would have recognised the amulet if it had belonged to his mother? And if Uma was a liar,

50

perhaps he wasn't in any danger after all. Still, once he reached Emira's cage, he tucked the bee safely away with his things.

Just then Risa flounced past, dressed in gold. He grabbed her arm.

"Hey! How are you?" he asked.

Risa stopped. "No injuries, thanks to you," she said with a satisfied twirl.

"I wanted to see you after the accident, but they said you were resting," Sharat told her.

"My father thinks it was all your fault," said Risa.

"It wasn't me!" protested Sharat.

Risa rolled her eyes. "Of course it wasn't you," she said. She leaned towards him. "I heard you saw a jinni," she whispered. "What did it look like?"

Sharat was about to reply, when Risa was whisked away by a scowling Pias and he found himself facing Mohini. He stepped back to avoid the smell of her heavy perfume, but she just moved closer.

"Ah, Sharat," she said. "Don't run away. I have something for you."

She passed him a new hoop and whip.

Mohini's scent was making Sharat feel sick. With a grimace he reached out and took the unfamiliar equipment.

"Why are you giving me these?" he said.

"They're gifts from the Emperor," Mohini told him. "They're for you to use in the show."

Sharat cracked the whip once or twice. He had to admit

it was better than his old one.

"Not bad," he said.

Mohini smiled. "The Emperor also left something for Emira," she said.

She lifted her hand. A ruby collar glistened against her white fingers, like drops of freshly drawn blood.

Sharat stared at the glittering rubies. He knew he should be overjoyed to be given such a valuable gift but for some reason he didn't want to touch them.

"Go ahead, put them around Emira's neck," whispered Mohini, stepping forward to envelop him in a cloud of her perfume.

Numbly, Sharat took the jewels and turned towards Emira's cage. She was pacing angrily, but as he opened the door she turned to face him with a stony glare.

"Come on, Emira," he said gently as he reached out to grab the fur on her neck.

She let out a yowl of protest as Sharat hooked the rubies around her throat.

Mohini was waiting for him to finish. "Beautiful," she said.

"I'm taking them off after the show," muttered Sharat.

Mohini bowed. "As you wish," she murmured.

Just then Lemo hurried past. "The Emperor's coming," he called out. "Take your places, everyone!"

Despite his sense of foreboding, Sharat felt a flutter of excitement. He hurried to find a dark corner so that he could watch.

Bare-chested servants stood by, lighting the way with

flaming torches. Golden lanterns hung from the ceiling of the royal pavilion, casting complex shadows in the twilight. As night fell, a flock of crows appeared from nowhere and darkened the sky, wheeling above the palace.

Two of them, heavy, black birds with cruel beaks, flew down to perch on the supporting pillars of the pavilion. Blinking their yellow eyes, they turned to look down at Sharat in his hiding place. He shrank back with a shiver.

Just then Emperor Suleiman arrived, surrounded by his courtiers and bodyguards. He was a stocky boy, not much taller than Sharat, but far more muscular. He wore linen trousers and a white shirt, and a curved sword hung from his belt. He was too young to grow a beard, but an enormous emerald sparkled at the front of his turban and his face was stern.

He sat down with his courtiers. When they were ready, he clapped his hands.

"Let the performance begin," he commanded. His voice was high, but carried authority. Sharat was surprised; he had been expecting to see a spoilt, arrogant boy, but Suleiman had power and dignity and, if the rumours were true, the fearsome weapon around his waist was no toy.

The flares sprang to life, casting a silver glow on to the circus ring. For a few moments Sharat watched the performance begin, then he went back to Emira's cage. She let out a reproachful growl.

"Only one more show," Sharat told her. "Then we'll be out of here."

Emira tossed her head impatiently. As well as the rubies, she had a lead around her neck. After what had happened the night before, Pias had insisted on it.

"I'll undo it when we get to the ring," Sharat told her as he opened the cage door.

Tugging the lead, he led her to the back of the circus pavilion. Hussein was waiting in the shadows.

"How is she?" he asked.

Sharat shook his head. "Not happy," he said. "Calm her down while I undo this."

Again, Emira growled low in her throat.

"Steady, girl," said Hussein, putting a firm hand on her back as Sharat undid the knot. Emira lashed her tail, but there was no repetition of the previous night.

Sharat let out a sigh of relief. From the corner of his eye, he saw Risa fly though the air towards the trapeze. This time there were no accidents as she spun gracefully through her routine and, at last, Lemo introduced Tiger Boy and Emira, the White Princess.

"Here goes," muttered Sharat, running into the ring as he flicked his whip. Right on cue, Hussein released Emira. With a roar, she bounded in after him.

At first Sharat's stomach was tight with nerves, but Emira behaved perfectly, and as they went through all their familiar moves, he was pleased to see the Emperor himself lean forward, his face alive with excitement. After that he lost himself in the act and soon it was time for the grand finale.

With a crack of his whip, he tossed his ring of fire into

the air and did a backwards flip, landing neatly on his feet. But this time, as the tiger leapt up to jump through the spinning hoop, the impossible happened. For a moment, Emira and the hoop seemed to hang, frozen in mid-air. Then, before Sharat even had time to blink, there was a flash of light and they both disappeared.

Confused, he stared up at the empty space above him. Where had Emira gone? Had she landed behind him? Was she hiding? He spun to look around the ring.

"Emira!" he called out harshly. "Emira?"

There was no reply.

"Bravo! Bravo!" cheered the young Emperor, a grin of delight lighting his face at this unexpected illusion. His courtiers joined in with whistles and applause.

Sharat stopped in the middle of the ring.

"Don't clap!" he cried. "That wasn't part of the show." He stepped towards the royal pavilion.

At this the Emperor's guards glanced at each other and drew their swords.

Lemo ran out into the ring, closely followed by Hussein. They grabbed Sharat's arms.

"What are you doing?" hissed Lemo. "Do you want to get us all killed? Bow down! Bow to the Emperor!"

Lemo and Hussein threw themselves to the floor, dragging Sharat with them. As they bobbed up and down with their heads touching the dirt, the guards relaxed. At a signal from the Emperor, his men threw bags of gold into the ring. Sharat forced himself to bow, but he continued to scan the room. Where *was* Emira?

Just then one of the courtiers caught his eye. Unlike the others, he wasn't cheering or clapping. Instead he stood behind the Emperor, watching silently through colourless eyes. Perhaps once he might have been handsome, but now his cheeks were hollow and there was a haunted, hungry look on his sallow face. Suddenly Sharat's heart skipped a beat. This was the man who'd been waiting by Emira's cage. The man in black.

As he stared, Sharat heard the beating of wings and two crows dived down to rake their claws through his hair, cawing in triumph as they flew by. Then, as he ducked, he saw the man in black lift his hand and the crows landed heavily on his arm. One hopped up on to his shoulder, and the other jumped over to perch on his staff.

Sharat wanted to cry out in alarm, but Lemo and Hussein had finished their bowing and grovelling and were dragging him out of the ring. In desperation he twisted his head for one final glance around the room. With a jolt of fear, he saw that the man in black was looking straight at him. The gaze from his pale eyes was cold and piercing.

Quickly, Sharat dropped his head, but at the same time he clenched his fists.

That man knows where Emira is, he thought. *I'm sure of it!*

Chapter Seven
CONSPIRITORS

Rookh and Mohini stood in Casmerim's shrine. In front of them lay Emira, tightly bound in spirals of golden wire – Mohini's treacherous hoop.

With a look of triumph in her eyes, Mohini waved her hand, and the wire hoop thickened and grew to form a golden cage. Inside, Emira looked stunned, her eyes as red as the rubies around her neck.

Rookh eyed Mohini with approval. "Well done," he said. "Not bad for a *handmaid*."

With a swish of his robes he lifted her hand to his lips and shivered as he inhaled her scent.

A faint smile twisted Mohini's lips, but she bowed her head in submission. "Thank you, master," she whispered.

Rookh eyed her with fascinated suspicion. *Playing*

the subservient jinni, he thought. He knew Mohini only too well. Thankfully she couldn't disobey him. "Tell me, how did you do it?" he asked.

Again, Mohini bowed her head. "It was easy," she said. "They were already fighting over money, just like humans always do. All I had to do was mention the Emperor's gold and Lemo's promise was forgotten. As for the tiger, the circus brat did most of the work. He even put on the collar." She glanced at the rubies that glittered against the tiger's fur.

"May I?" she asked.

"Certainly," Rookh told her.

At a word from Mohini, the rubies unhooked themselves and flew to land in her hand. With a snarl Emira threw herself against the golden bars. The candelabra flickered overhead, but the cage didn't budge.

"Good," said Rookh. "Now we just have to make sure she doesn't get away."

He snapped his fingers and two dark little men with hunched shoulders, hooked noses and scrawny legs appeared out of the shadows and bowed. As they lifted their heads their eyes glittered, uncanny replicas of their master's.

"Take the tiger to my workshop," Rookh ordered.

The servants' eyes shone with approval. "Yes, master!" said one. He glanced at the tiger and licked his lips with a maggoty tongue.

Rookh gave an involuntary shudder. "Quickly!" he snapped. "I don't have all night."

Sniggering, the servants approached the golden cage. As they did so, Emira lunged again, roaring in fury, but the bars held as solid as steel. With cackles and jeers they wheeled her away.

Once they were gone, Rookh looked over at Mohini again. She was waiting, demurely as ever, for his command.

"Now what?" he asked.

Mohini's eyes were shielded with secrets. "To keep your Empire safe you will need to kill the tiger," she said. "But first you must find the Prince of Jinnis."

"Where do you think he is?" said Rookh.

Mohini shook her head. "I don't know," she said. "The Prince of Jinnis is hidden by a spell that not even I can break. All I know is that he's bound to come looking for the tiger, and when he does, we will be ready for him."

Rookh almost smiled. He admired Mohini immensely, but he trusted her less than a snake in the grass. "Why are you doing all of this?" he demanded. "You're a jinni. Don't you want your queen to be restored to her throne?"

Mohini tossed her head. "I don't care about the Queen of the Forest," she said. Her eyes flashed as she glanced at him, quickly, flirtatiously. "I would rather be *your* queen."

Rookh drew her closer. "You would make an excellent queen," he agreed. "Ruthless, ambitious and dangerous. We can discuss terms once we've dealt with the tiger and her prince."

He glanced up at Casmerim's picture. He would show

her. He didn't need her.

Mohini saw his glance.

"Forget her," she said. "Am I not just as beautiful?"

Rookh's laugh was harsh. Seizing her long, shining hair, he wrapped it twice around his hand, and pulled back her head.

"Show me!" he hissed, cupping her pale face with his other hand.

In an easy moment Mohini's face had changed, darkened, modelling itself on the face in the picture. Even the hair was thicker. Only her eyes remained the same.

"Very good." Rookh lowered his voice. "Now close your eyes!"

Mohini obeyed, lashes trembling on her cheeks.

"Beautiful!" he sighed. "*Now* you are my queen."

Mohini's mouth curved in a smile. "Yes, master," she said.

Losing himself to the moment, Rookh leaned down for his kiss.

For a moment there was silence. For a moment there was peace. Even the voices inside were still.

Afterwards, he held her close, as if relieved. There was no denying it. Mohini might be poison, but her lips were as sweet as Casmerim's.

Chapter Eight
RUNAWAY

Sharat felt sick with shock as he watched Emira's empty cage bouncing along the cobbles. His guts twisted in regret. Why hadn't he listened to Uma?

Behind him, Hussein kept a protective hand on his shoulder.

"Maybe she'll find her own way home," he ventured, but his voice sounded hollow even to his own ears.

Sharat twisted to stare at him in disbelief. "Emira's not *lost*," he said. "She *disappeared*." He turned to look back at Shergarh. "Let me go back and find her," he begged.

Hussein shook his head. "I'm sure Lemo's doing all he can," he said.

The ringmaster had stayed behind to talk to the Emperor's men.

"It won't do any good," said Sharat angrily. "Emira's been stolen." He glared at Hussein. "You knew about the promise. Why didn't you stop my father from coming here?"

Hussein looked down unhappily. "Believe me, I tried," he said. "But he hasn't been himself since he married that woman."

Sharat grimaced. He didn't want to think about Mohini right now. All he wanted to think about was Emira. "If he doesn't find her, I will!" he swore.

They continued their journey in silence.

Back at the camp, the troupe gathered around the fire, their faces weary in the flickering light. After a big show they usually liked to sing, dance and swap tales, but tonight everyone was subdued as they waited for Lemo to return with news of Emira.

As Sharat stared miserably into the flames, Bhim the magician tried to cheer him up with a new trick.

Sharat pushed him away. "Leave me alone!" he snapped.

Risa came to sit next to him, murmuring words of comfort, but he didn't want to listen to her either. He felt furious with everyone around him but, most of all, he was furious with himself. Emira was gone. He didn't know how he would bear it. They'd never been apart for more than a few hours. Losing her was like losing part of himself.

"Emira. Where *are* you?" he called out silently.

In the past he'd always been able to sense her presence,

near or far. Now he felt nothing.

"I'll find you, Emira," he whispered, in the vain hope that somehow she would be able to hear him. "No matter where you are, I'll come and find you."

An eternity passed. Finally there was the sound of horses' hooves and, moments later, Lemo appeared by the fire.

Sharat jumped to his feet, his heart beating as he ran up to his father. "What happened?" he demanded.

The ringmaster's face was grim. He dumped sacks of gold and jewels on to the ground. "They gave me all this treasure," he said bitterly. He handed Sharat a bag of gold. "This is for you."

Sharat dropped the bag and stared up at his father in disbelief. "I don't want gold," he said. "Where's Emira?"

"I don't know," admitted Lemo. He looked down at Sharat, his face crumpled with helpless regret. "I'm so sorry," he said. "I did my best. I spoke to the Emperor's secretary, but he just warned me not to cause trouble." He jerked his thumb towards a group of men on horseback that were waiting in the darkness. "They even sent soldiers to escort me back to camp."

"What for?" asked Hussein, his voice sharp.

Lemo glanced at his friend. "They want to make sure we leave town first thing tomorrow," he said. "Somebody doesn't want us asking any more questions."

"But we can't leave Emira here!" cried Sharat.

"We can't stand up to the Imperial Army either," said Lemo unhappily. "Do you know how many troops are

stationed in this city?"

Sharat felt sick.

Lara had just come back from tending to the horses. Her dark eyes were heavy with sorrow. "Oh, you poor boy," she said, stepping forward to embrace him, but he wriggled out of her grip. He was in no mood for sympathy.

The circus crew stood around helplessly. Silent tears wet Risa's face. Even Pias and Ram looked sorry as they hung back in the shadows. Sharat glared at them.

"You've got your gold now. Are you satisfied?" he demanded.

Pias looked as though he'd eaten something bad and Ram just bowed his head.

"All this is *your* fault!" Sharat told his father, bitter with grief. "You promised Uma you wouldn't come back to the City of Jewels. *Now* look what's happened."

A look of horror crossed Lemo's face.

"The *promise*!" he said.

"Oh, you remember it now, do you?" snapped Sharat.

Lemo passed a hand across his forehead. He looked confused. "Yes, of course I remember," he said. Then he shook his head. "It's just that Mohini wanted to come here so badly ... I ... I somehow forgot."

Sharat stared at his father. "Mohini?"

Lemo nodded miserably. "It was her idea to perform for the Emperor. She told me she knew someone at court. I thought it would solve all our problems with money."

Suddenly Sharat felt everything fall into place. Mohini

64

had arranged the show. Mohini had sometimes called herself the Mistress of Illusion. She'd even given him his new hoop and whip.

"Where *is* Mohini?" he demanded. "Did anyone see her come back?"

There was a stirring of movement around the fire, but Mohini was nowhere to be seen.

"I haven't seen her since the show," said Risa with regret.

"She didn't travel back with me," said Lara.

"Or me," added Bhim.

With a murmur, the rest of the crew shook their heads, their faces looking sombre by the light of the fire.

"I'll go and check your caravan!" said Ram. He ran off without looking Sharat in the eye.

"She was supposed to come back with Lemo," Hussein remembered, "but he stayed behind."

"I didn't see where she went," Lemo admitted. "I was too busy trying to find Emira."

Ram came running back.

"She's not anywhere in the campsite," he said. "I checked all the tents as well as the caravans."

A feeling of sick certainty passed through Sharat.

"*She's* the one that made Emira disappear and now she's disappeared as well," he said. "It must have been some kind of trick."

"I never did like that woman," muttered Lara.

Lemo was pale. "How could I have married someone who would do something like this?" he asked.

65

Fezzik the fire-eater shrugged. "She was very beautiful," he admitted.

Lara tossed her head in disgust. "I wouldn't call that beautiful!" she snapped.

Bhim puffed out his chest importantly. "As a fellow magician, I would say that she was some kind of *enchantress*!" he said. He waved his pudgy hands dramatically in the air. "She wove a web of illusion around us all."

"She didn't fool me," said Sharat bitterly. "I never liked her from the start."

Lemo let out a deep sigh, but he didn't look like he'd just lost a wife. Instead he looked as though a heavy weight was slowly lifting from his shoulders.

"I can't say I'm sorry she's gone," he admitted. "I never really felt like myself while I was with her." He frowned. "It's as though I've been under some kind of spell."

Hussein sighed. "Well, if she *did* steal Emira she won't be coming back," he said. "Perhaps we should all get some rest." He reached down to put a comforting hand on Sharat's shoulder. "Why don't you go back with Lemo to the caravan? You'll feel better after you've had some sleep."

Sharat pushed his hand away. "No!" he said. "I'm staying by Emira's cage. This is where she'll come if she escapes."

Lemo and Hussein exchanged worried looks.

"Maybe I could stay with him?" Risa volunteered. "We could put up a tent near the animal enclosure."

Lemo nodded. "Do whatever makes Sharat happy," he said. His voice was tired.

While the arrangements were made, Sharat sat brooding by the fire, trying to make sense of it all. For a moment he almost looked around for Emira to comfort him. His stomach wrenched when he remembered she wasn't there.

Just then Risa came over. "Come on, I've made your bed," she murmured. "Let's get some sleep."

Lemo put a hand on his shoulder. "Go on," he said.

Numbly, Sharat followed Risa to the tent and collapsed back on the sheepskins while she crawled in next to him.

"I know how you feel," she whispered once they had settled down. "I remember when my mother died."

Sharat bit his lip. "Emira's not *dead*," he said. "She's been stolen."

"Why would Mohini steal Emira?" wondered Risa.

Quietly, Sharat told Risa Uma's story.

"It could be that Emira's a jinni," he said.

He heard Risa gasp in the darkness. "Do you think this has anything to do with the creature in the rigging?" she asked.

"Perhaps," said Sharat. "It could have been a spy. I don't think Mohini was working alone. I saw a man hanging around Emira's cage last night. That same man was there tonight with the Emperor."

"Which man?"

Sharat described the man in black.

Risa drew in a sharp breath. "I saw him!" she exclaimed.

Sharat remembered the triumphant look on the man's face. "He was the only person who wasn't surprised when Emira disappeared," he said. "I'm sure *he's* got her."

"Watch out," Risa warned him. "That man must be important if he's at court. He could have you killed."

Sharat squeezed her hand. He was used to Risa bossing him about, but this time he had no intention of listening to her. He remembered the Emperor. Hussein had mentioned that he loved his animals, and Sharat felt sure that he would understand the bond he shared with Emira. All he had to do was find a way to speak to him, but first he had to wait until Risa fell asleep.

Staring out into the darkness, he waited impatiently. Luckily she was always exhausted after a show and soon her breathing became shallow and regular.

As quietly as he could, he peeled back his covers and crawled out of bed, but as he was lifting the door-flap Risa sighed. For a moment he froze, silent and wary, but she was just turning over, so he slipped out quickly and made his way to his own tent.

Only the waning moon lit his way. Sharat was glad. He knew the soldiers were waiting nearby and the darkness made it easier for him to move around unseen.

Packing a small bundle with a change of clothes, he slipped in the bag of gold that Lemo had given him. Then he tucked his new whip into his trousers and threw on a woollen shawl. Finally he retrieved his mother's amulet. He still had *that* at least. For a moment, as he held the

68

winged jewel in his hand, a different kind of yearning nudged at his heart. If only his mother was still alive. With a sigh he tied the leather cord around his neck. He knew there was no use in wishing, but perhaps it would bring him good luck.

Looking out over the city, he wondered which was the best way back to Shergarh. At first he considered following the river, but in most cities the homes of the wealthy faced on to the water and he didn't want to risk being caught by sentries or guard dogs. And after seeing the faces of the people earlier that day he didn't want to walk through the centre of town either.

Feeling a chill, although the night was still warm, he pulled the shawl tighter and decided to take the long way around, climbing the western ridge to put as much distance as possible between himself and the circus. Once the sun rose he could move in towards the fortress.

Silently, he crept past the soldiers who had tied up their horses and were playing cards by the dying light of the fire. Once he was out of range, he paused and looked back. The circus tent loomed in the night sky, but he could hardly see the caravans that were huddled behind it. With a shiver, he realised that if they were really driven out of town he might never see them again. He wondered whether they would miss him. Hussein and Lemo might, he thought. Pias would probably be glad he'd left. He set his mouth in determination as he turned away. None of that mattered anyway. All he cared about now was finding Emira.

The faint light of the moon guided him until it set. After that, there was only the glow of the stars. Several times he heard rustling in the scrub at his feet and, once, the shriek of some nearby animal, which almost made him jump out of his skin. He threw up his staff, but nothing came at him so he moved on with a hammering heart.

The noises of morning started before sunrise: cockerels, wild dogs and the call to prayer. Then, as the sun rose, Sharat found himself descending into the city.

This was the poor side of town. Behind the fortress were low buildings, spewing out black smoke that choked the morning air. The city was as famous for its foundries as it was for its jewels. Children wandered naked on the streets, flies buzzing around their eyes, while a group of angry-looking boys threw him dirty looks as they played dice on a corner. An old man with no fingers hobbled up to Sharat with his begging bowl held out. Sharat stepped away from the leper in horror.

"I have to go! I'm in a hurry!" he said, forgetting the gold in his bundle. The old man cursed and spat.

Sharat ran on, past a woman with a baby in her arms, mutely holding out her hands, past gaunt cows with dried-up udders and dogs who were too weak even to lift their heads. Keeping Shergarh in his sights, he ducked from alley to road until he stood on the banks of the moat. Up close the fortress walls looked even more formidable and the water at his feet was deep and murky with scum floating on the surface, but he followed it around until he reached a bridge that led to a gate in the thick walls.

It was a different gateway to the one that had frightened the elephants the previous day. This one was cast in the shape of a great bird, its beak open wide. There was a guard standing on either side.

Lifting his chin defiantly, Sharat crossed the bridge as if he had every right to be there. Immediately the bird's mechanical eyes swivelled to look at him, and the beak slammed shut with a raucous clang. Sharat barely had time to jump aside.

One of the guards sniggered. The other, a burly man with a boxer's face, stuck out his sword.

"Where do you think you're going?" he grunted.

"I need to speak to the Emperor," said Sharat.

"Did you hear that, Manu?" said the guard, turning to his friend. "This little scruff wants to see the Emperor!"

Manu was a young man with a closely trimmed beard. He might have had a kind face once, but now he just looked tired. He glanced down at the circus boy. "What business would *you* have at court?" he asked.

Sharat hesitated. "I've had something stolen," he said.

The guards exchanged a glance.

"Royal audience every other full moon, by appointment only," Manu told him in a bored voice. "The next one's in six weeks."

Sharat stared at him in dismay. "I can't wait six weeks!" he said.

"You're going to have to," snapped the older guard. "Now stop wasting our time." He used the flat of his sword to shove the boy back across the drawbridge.

Sharat felt annoyed, but he wasn't about to give up. There were four gates into Shergarh and he was determined to try them all. But it was no good. At the second gate he was almost squeezed in the coils of an iron snake, at the third, the teeth of a monstrous fish threatened to grind him to bits, and finally he was almost burnt to a crisp by the dragon that had allowed the circus to pass through the day before. It was as if the gates themselves knew that he didn't belong there.

"Get out of here!" snapped a guard at the last gate, as he drove Sharat back across the bridge into the street below.

Helplessly, he stood looking up at the fortress walls. So far his only plan had been to appeal to the Emperor for Emira's release, but now he was starting to see how hopeless his quest was. After all, he didn't even know if Emira was alive.

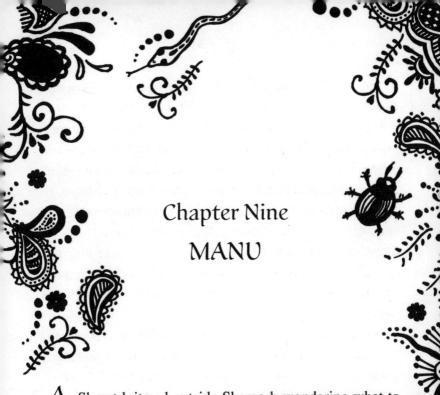

Chapter Nine

MANU

As Sharat loitered outside Shergarh wondering what to do next, a sweet smell wafted past him and he noticed that there were food stalls along the road. Suddenly he realised he was hungry. His mouth watering, he went to see what was being sold.

"What's that?" he asked, pointing at a slab of something white that lay glistening on the table.

"Food." The reply was curt.

It didn't look like any kind of food Sharat had seen before, but he took a slice and paid with a piece of his gold.

The coin had a greenish glow. The stall-keeper eyed Sharat suspiciously.

"This is palace gold," he said. "Where'd you get it?"

"I did some work for the Emperor," Sharat told him, keeping his voice down.

The merchant grunted in reply. "Who's got change for palace gold?" he called out to the other stallholders.

Sharat suddenly became the focus of curious looks. He got his change in local money, but the news of his gold had spread. As he hurried off, beggar children surrounded him.

"Money! Money! Money!" they chanted, scrabbling at him with emaciated hands. He handed out all his change, and tried to escape, but a scrawny girl with one blind eye wouldn't let him go. She tried to grab hold of his bundle.

"I don't want your stinking coppers. Give me some of that gold!" she hissed, glaring at him sharply through her good eye.

Sharat pulled back. There were too many of them. If he started handing out gold, soon there would be none left. "Go away!" he said, but it was no use, he was surrounded, and the girl with one eye was almost on top of him.

In a panic, he pushed her away and began to run, dropping the food as he fled. With whoops of glee his tormentors set off after him, armed with sticks and rocks.

Sharat felt a stone whistle past his head as he darted through an alleyway and jumped over a broken wall into the derelict gardens that lined the moat, but he was a good runner and one by one the children fell back until soon he was running alone. Quickly, he ducked through the door of a deserted summerhouse, panting for breath as he listened for signs of pursuit, but to his relief everything

was still. He'd lost them.

It was the hottest part of the day, but the summerhouse was shady and Sharat was exhausted after his terrible night. He lay on the floor, trying to cool off by pressing his skin on to the stone. He only meant to rest for a moment but before long he'd fallen asleep.

He woke with a start at the sound of a pebble being kicked nearby.

"What's that?" he said, jumping to his feet.

He heard stifled laughter, then silence.

Warily, he peered through the door, but whatever had disturbed him was gone. Then, as he looked up at the sky, he realised it was already sunset. He cursed. He'd wasted nearly a whole day.

With renewed determination he looked over the stagnant moat towards the fortress and sized up the sheer walls. They were there to keep out armies of grown men, but that didn't put him off. He was a circus boy. He'd climbed walls steeper than that just to steal an apple. Looking around to make sure the coast was clear, he bundled his possessions on to his head and slid into the water. To his disgust it was hot and stank of sewage, but he kept his mouth shut and began to swim.

He had only taken a few strokes when he saw a black shadow under the surface and something huge slid past him at breathtaking speed. Then, before he could catch his breath, there was a gobbling sound and the flash of yellow teeth as the creature turned back towards him. Suddenly a fear like Sharat had never felt before clutched

75

at his guts and he turned tail and swam as fast as he could back to shore.

Hauling himself on to the bank he stared helplessly down at the moat. For a moment the water churned. Then, whatever had been chasing him sank slowly beneath the surface. Frustrated, he picked up a rock and hurled it towards Shergarh. It hit the fortress wall with a crack, and bounced back into the water.

"Oi!" called out a voice nearby. "What do you think you're doing?"

Sharat barely had time to spin around, when someone caught his arm. He found himself looking up into the face of the young guard, Manu.

"Nothing!" he said quickly. "Washing."

The guard snorted. "*Nobody* washes in the moat," he said. "There are *things* in that water."

Sharat shivered as he glanced back down at the calm surface of the moat. "What *are* they?" he asked.

Manu's face was grim. "Behamot," he said. "Demon fish. Be glad they didn't get you. They can pull a man apart in seconds." He tightened his grip on Sharat's arm.

Sharat tried to shake him off. "I'm not going back in," he said. "Let me go!"

The guard shook his head. "I'm afraid it's more than my life's worth to let you go now," he said. Reaching down he took Sharat's whip. "You're under arrest."

"What, just for taking a wash?" asked Sharat in disbelief.

"You weren't just taking a wash," said Manu. "I

76

remember you. You were trying to get into Shergarh."

Sharat felt his guts twist. He had to convince the guard that he was innocent.

"I didn't mean any harm," he blurted out. "I was just trying to find my tiger."

An expression of surprise crossed the guard's face. "What?" he said. "You mean the *white* tiger?"

Sharat looked up at him eagerly. "Yes!" he said. "Have you seen her?"

"Only at the circus," Manu admitted. For a moment he forgot he was a soldier and he looked at Sharat with undisguised admiration. "That tiger was beautiful!" he said. "How do you keep her under control?"

Sharat bit his lip. "She's tame," he said. "I've had her since I was a baby."

Manu frowned. "What makes you think you'll find her inside Shergarh?" he asked.

"She disappeared last night, while we were performing for the Emperor," explained Sharat. "That's why I wanted to talk to him. I need his help. I think she's been stolen."

Manu gave a short laugh. "There's no use talking to the Emperor," he said. "He doesn't have any power. All he cares about is hunting."

Sharat felt a crash of disappointment.

"Surely there must be someone who can help me," he said.

Manu shook his head. "*Nothing* gets out of Shergarh alive," he said. "I've heard they do experiments on the animals they round up from the forest in there."

77

He shivered.

Terror clutched Sharat's heart. "What am I going to do?" he cried.

"I'm afraid you're going to have to come with me," said Manu firmly.

Sharat stared at him in dismay. "You're not still going to arrest me, are you?"

Manu glanced around. "I'm sorry," he said. "I can't let you go now. There are spies everywhere in this city."

"But I haven't done anything wrong!" Sharat protested.

Manu sighed. "Don't blame me," he said. "I never wanted to be a soldier. I wanted to be a farmer. When they first started clearing the forests I thought I might even get my own place, but since the trees were cut down it's stopped raining and now nothing grows. That's why I had to join the army. It's the only way to make a living."

Sharat felt a glimmer of hope. If the guard was unwilling, perhaps he could be bribed. He fumbled in his pack to find the treasure Lemo had given him. With a chink of metal, he lifted the bag.

"Here, take my gold," he said. "You could run away then. Stop being a soldier."

Manu hesitated. "Is that gold from Shergarh?" he asked.

Sharat nodded. "Yes," he said. "We were paid to perform for the Emperor."

The guard shook his head. "I don't want the Emperor's gold," he said. "It's too easy to trace." His eyes lingered on the jewel at Sharat's throat. "Give me the diamond

78

instead," he offered. "Then I'll let you go."

Sharat's heart sank. He put his free hand up to touch the amulet.

"Hurry up!" Manu told him. "The longer we wait, the more likely it is that we'll be seen."

"All right! All right!" said Sharat. "I've just got to get it off."

Playing for time, he reached back to fiddle with the cord at the back of his neck. After a moment he gave up.

"I can't get it undone," he said, exasperated.

Manu was getting impatient. "Hold still!" he said, letting go of Sharat's arm. "I'll do it."

With a frown he bent over to peer at the knot.

It was the chance Sharat was waiting for. Without hesitation, he elbowed the soldier in the gut and began to run.

"Hey!" Manu stumbled back in surprise as Sharat slipped out of his grip. For a moment he caught his breath. Then with a cry of fury, he set off in pursuit.

Without looking back, Sharat sped over the dried mud paths between the crumbling huts and ditches of this unknown neighbourhood. All along he was dimly aware of Manu right behind him. Soon he reached the main road. His heart pounding, he darted between horses and carts, past buffalo wagons and through groups of scrawny cows that were scavenging from the piles of rubbish that smouldered at each crossroads.

He had no idea where he was going. All he knew was that he had to get away. Gasping, he ducked through a tiny

gap into a twisting alleyway and threw himself behind a ruined hut to catch his breath.

His beating heart felt like it would split his ribs, and his lungs were burning, but there was no sign of pursuit. He'd lost the guard.

Catching his breath, the first thing he did was check the amulet. To his relief it was still there, but as he touched it the knot at the back of his neck came undone and it dropped into his hand. He folded it safely into the band of his trousers. Then, as he stepped carefully out of his hiding place his nose wrinkled in disgust. The air was foul with the stench of decay and sewage.

Breathing as lightly as he could, he peered into the twilight, but before he could get his bearings, something hit him between the shoulder blades and he collapsed, winded, on to the ground.

Chapter Ten

SULEIMAN

Emperor Suleiman tried to concentrate as he leaned over the campaign table, but it wasn't easy. Rookh had brought him here to discuss their latest offensive, but instead he couldn't stop thinking about the circus. How wonderful it must be to be free, like that boy with his beautiful white tiger! Unfortunately he knew that this could never be. He was the Emperor of the richest empire in the world. He had duties to perform, meetings to attend and armies to command.

With a sigh he looked down at the maps that lay spread out before him. War. He knew it was a necessary evil if he was going to keep his empire safe. Rookh had explained it to him many times.

"Yours is the richest empire in the world," he'd said.

"But it only got that way because your father stepped in to control the jinnis."

Suleiman had nodded. All his life he'd been hearing about these mysterious jinnis that threatened to bring him down if he so much as slept in the wrong position. Ugly, vicious creatures, everyone knew that their sole delight was to wreak havoc on the world of men. After all, it was the jinnis that had cast a curse on the Empire and brought famine to this once fertile land. Luckily, all the jinnis in the city had been enslaved, and now it was Suleiman's responsibility to expand on the good work that his father had begun. Or so Rookh always told him.

He was facing Rookh over the campaign table. On either side of him were two of his top generals, and in front of them all was a large map showing the frontiers of the Empire and positions of their troops. "So what do we need to do now?" he asked.

Rookh bent down over the table. With a sweep of his hand he pointed at a green area on the map that lay far to the south of the City of Jewels. "These forests here need to go," he said. "There are several towns in this area with jinnist sympathies." His face twisted in distaste. "They even harbour *witches*."

"Oh dear," said Suleiman. He knew all about witches. Old women who pretended to use plants to heal people, when in reality only proper doctors with a licence from the government could do that.

Rookh unrolled a scroll and placed it on top of the map. "If Your Imperial Majesty would just sign here, the

armies can be dispatched," he said.

Suleiman sighed as he reached for the quill. He understood the logic behind this never-ending war. Jinnis lurked wherever there were green places. Some said they came and went from their world to our own through the roots of the trees, but he dimly remembered the gardens he'd played in as a baby, and he couldn't help feeling curious about the forests that he'd only read about. Now as he looked down at that area of green on the map he felt slightly sick, and today, for the first time, he stopped before making his mark.

"Isn't there any other way?" he asked.

Rookh looked at him sharply. "Your Majesty, are you questioning the value of our campaign?" he demanded.

For a moment Suleiman glared back at Rookh. He was the Emperor after all, and Rookh was only his regent, but for some reason he couldn't find a way to object. He'd been under his control for so long.

As if sensing his reluctance, Rookh put his hand on the boy's arm. "I know it pains you to do this," he said. "But you must realise how important it is for the Empire to expand. The jinnis control the elements. It's thanks to them that the earth is barren, the air is dry, the sun is so merciless and the rain refuses to fall. Only when they are *all* under our power will we be able to reverse this famine and bring life back to the land. Besides, it's in everyone's interest to enslave the jinnis. Only they know how to find the jewels that lie buried deep below the earth, and without the jewels how would we pay for food?"

83

Rookh looked reproachfully at the Emperor. "Surely Your Majesty doesn't want his people to starve?"

Suleiman pressed his lips together. He knew all about the mines of course, but so far he'd been refused access. Only Doctor Rookh was allowed down there, along with a few select members of his inner circle.

"Isn't it time I was allowed to visit these mines?" he demanded. "How can I be expected to make decisions about *anything* if you won't let me know what's really going on?"

Rookh's voice was smooth. "My dear boy, allow me to point out that you are still very young," he said. "Trust me. The mines are very dangerous, and I have a duty towards you. I was your father's best friend and most valued advisor. When he died so tragically, he appointed me as regent, and I promised to keep you safe."

The generals exchanged glances. Rumour had it that Rookh had been instrumental in the old Emperor's death, but he was so powerful that nobody had been brave enough to challenge his version of events. Besides, there were numerous financial advantages in keeping close to the man who controlled the jinnis.

"Your Imperial Majesty, we are waiting for your command," said one of the generals, a stocky man with grey hair and a soft voice.

"Yes, yes. I know," said Suleiman. The weight of responsibility pressed on him. He wished he didn't have to make these kinds of decisions, he would far rather be feeding his elephants.

84

Feeling helpless, he leaned over to sign the scroll, but even as he did so he resolved that one day he would take matters into his own hands. Soon he would be thirteen – old enough to appoint his own advisors, and when that time came he was determined to inspect the mines, but most importantly of all, he wanted to have a full enquiry made into these mysterious jinnis.

Chapter Eleven

SEWER-GIRLS

"Gotcha!"

Sharat heard a high-pitched squeal of joy from somewhere in the darkness. It sounded nothing like the palace guard.

"Well done, Lalita!"

There was another squeal, followed by giggles. Then, before Sharat had time to get to his feet a sack was thrown over his head and his arms were bound to his sides. He struggled as he felt himself being held tightly by several pairs of hands.

"Don't move! We've got knives!" a high voice warned him. Cold metal was pressed against his throat.

By the size of their hands and the sound of their voices Sharat realised they must be children. They chattered

noisily as they pulled him along.

"We've been following you all day," bragged the one who was holding his arm.

"Who are you?" demanded Sharat, his voice muffled by the sacking. "What do you want?"

"Listen to him!" someone giggled. "He talks funny."

"I'm not from around here," said Sharat, struggling against his bond. "I'm from the circus. Let me go!"

"They're travellers in the circus," piped up a little voice off to the right. "They don't come from anywhere."

"That's a bit like you, then, isn't it, Lalita!" someone shrieked with a giggle.

"Shut up!" a sharper voice called out from behind. "No fraternising with the prisoner!"

"We're not fraternising!"

"Yes, you are! You're talking to him!" snapped the voice. "Now take him down without a word, or there'll be trouble."

There was a sober silence.

"All right, Nara," someone muttered.

Sharat's captors tugged the rope that bound his arms to his sides, and he stumbled down some steps.

Once they reached the bottom he was shoved unceremoniously to the ground. Then the cord around his neck was released, and the sack was lifted off his head.

"Let's have a look at you, circus boy!" crowed a high voice.

Sharat blinked. About fifteen scrawny children clustered around him. They were on a stone ledge that

jutted out into a narrow channel filled with slow-moving sludge. A fire burned behind them, lighting the space, and the nasty smell he'd caught a whiff of earlier was almost overpowering. Just then a pair of rats scampered past and plopped into the fetid waste below. With a shudder he realised that they were in the sewers.

He turned to face the children. Some of them were so tiny that they were almost babies. He examined their grimy faces in the firelight.

"You're all girls," he said in surprise. "What are you doing down *here*?"

"We live here," said a little girl with a cleft lip.

Sharat looked at her in disbelief. "But why?" he asked.

"We were dumped," hissed a voice from the back.

"Nobody wants girls like us," another voice cut in.

"We know you think it's disgusting, but it's better than putting up with some of the things that go on up there," said the dark girl defensively. "Cooler too, in the summer."

"Rajani, shut your mouth!" It was the girl with the sharp voice. She pushed angrily through the crowd, elbowing the other girls to one side. "I told you not to tell him anything!"

She stopped in front of Sharat with a nasty smile on her face.

"I got you in the end," she sneered.

Sharat felt the shock of recognition. It was the one-eyed beggar girl from the palace gates; the one who had tried to take his gold.

88

She grabbed his bundle and emptied his possessions on to the ground. With a hiss of triumph she picked up the bag of gold and felt its weight in her dirty hands.

"Here we are," she said. "At last!"

"Hey!" Sharat jerked forward. "That's mine! Give it back!" He felt the rope digging into his arms as the girls behind him tightened their grip.

Nara sneered. "You won't be needing gold where you're going," she said.

"Don't forget you're sharing that with us, Nara," said Rajani, stepping forward.

"You'll get your share, don't you worry," Nara told her. "Once we've disposed of the boy."

Sharat began to feel uneasy. He hadn't been scared of the other girls, but this one was vicious. He could feel the force of her hatred glaring out of her good eye.

"Let me go," he demanded. "I've got to find my tiger."

"Tiger?" A murmur of interest filled the space.

"She's a white tiger," Sharat explained. "She was stolen when we performed for the Emperor. That's where I got all that gold."

Rajani's eyes lit up. "I've heard stories about white tigers," she said. "Stories about jinnis."

"Shut up!" snapped Nara, shoving Rajani out of the way.

She turned to Sharat. "Never mind your tiger," she told him. "You're here with us now, and we're leaving you for the *ghuls*."

There was a stirring among the girls.

Sharat had never even heard the word before but it made his skin crawl. He glared at Nara. "What's a ghul?"

Nara was about to answer when one of the smaller girls took a step forward. A birthmark stained her pretty face.

"You can't leave him for the ghuls," she protested. "He hasn't done anything wrong."

Nara's face twisted with anger. "Shut up, Lalita. Do you want them to get *you* instead?" she hissed.

There was a murmur of fear among the others, but the little girl held her ground.

"The ghuls never took anyone when Aya was here," she said stubbornly.

"Forget about Aya," spat Nara. "She abandoned you, just like your mother did."

A shadow of pain crossed Lalita's face. She dropped her eyes.

Something nagged at the back of Sharat's mind. *Aya*. He'd heard that name before. All at once he remembered the little girl by the river, the one who had taken him to see Uma.

"I know Aya!" he exclaimed.

There was a buzz of chatter. Lalita's eyes lit up. "Where is she?"

"I saw her by the river," said Sharat, stepping forward eagerly.

"He's lying!" interrupted Nara. "I told you not to talk to him." She slapped Lalita's face. The little girl fell back and hit her head on the rock. Silently, she began to cry.

"You don't know Aya," said Nara, scowling at Sharat.

"She's dead."

"She's *not* dead," said Sharat.

"Yes, she is!"

With a swift move, the sewer-girl snatched his hair, pulled back his head and stuffed a rag into his mouth, roughly tying the ends. Then she took out a grimy bottle and tipped something on to the cloth. Sharat felt a rush of blood to his head.

"That'll shut you up, circus boy," she whispered nastily into his ear.

Sharat felt his heart pounding in his ears. Dizzy, he stumbled, but he kept his eyes open and tried to steady himself.

With quick, sure movements, Nara emptied his bag of gold. Then she handed a coin to each of the girls.

"Here's your reward," she said. "Don't ever say I don't look after you."

The girls snatched greedily at their treasure, Aya forgotten.

Nara stood over Sharat, glaring at him with her good eye. "You should have given it to me when I asked for it," she sneered.

Sharat couldn't answer. He could hardly see any more and his head was spinning. *What was in that bottle?* he thought fuzzily.

Nara turned to Rajani and slipped her a second coin. "You take him down," she said. "The rest of you, get ready for the ceremony."

The girls hurriedly withdrew to the dens they had made

at the back of the rocky ledge and hid the gold in their rags. Then, one by one, they returned to gather around the fire, carrying pots, pans, sticks and gourds.

Rajani grabbed the rope binding Sharat's arms, and held a knife to his throat. "Come with me," she ordered, "and don't struggle, or I'll kill you."

Sharat stumbled. His arms and legs didn't seem to belong to him any more. He desperately wanted to talk to Rajani, to beg for release, but the gag was firmly in place. Without speaking, the girl led him down some slippery steps to the level of the sludge before pulling him roughly towards the wall so that they were out of sight of the others.

"Have you really seen Aya?" she asked, her voice urgent.

Sharat's mind was a blur, but he managed to nod.

Rajani hesitated. Then she pressed her mouth to his ear.

"When the ghuls come for you, play dead!" she hissed. "They'll only take you if they think you're alive."

Sharat nodded again, but Rajani had already left him, clambering quickly back on to the ledge.

Just then the fire flared up and the lengthened shadows of the girls seemed to surround him. Dully, he saw that Nara was crouched over a big wooden drum. Then, with a cry, she began a slow, steady beat and, one by one, the others joined in, rattling and tapping their shakers and drums as they began to sing.

As the drumbeat echoed on the damp walls of the

sewers the sound of their voices seemed to reach deep into Sharat's guts. He struggled to free himself, but in his panic he inhaled more of the drug Nara had poured on to the gag and a wave of nausea passed through him.

Knowing only that he had to stay awake, he breathed as lightly as he could through his nose. The stench was almost unbearable, but he didn't have long to worry about that, for as the girls carried on singing a pale figure slowly appeared out of the darkness of the sewers. A ghul.

Tall and stooped, its skeletal body was dressed from head to foot in white robes, while its face was hidden by a hood. Only the glint of desperate eyes gleamed out from beneath the fabric's ghostly folds.

Sharat's first instinct was to scream, and to try and escape, but through the haze in his head he somehow remembered Rajani's advice.

Slowly, he sank to the ground. Then, lying as still as a corpse, he watched as the ghul came closer and closer, its glinting eyes turning to scan every nook and cranny in the sewer walls.

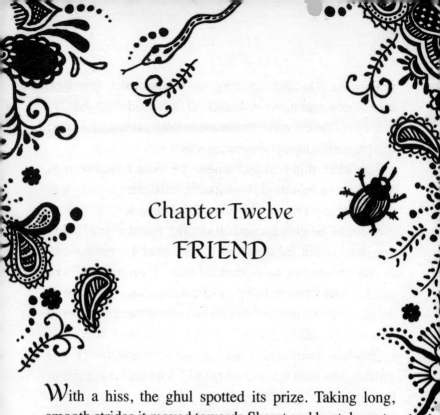

Chapter Twelve
FRIEND

With a hiss, the ghul spotted its prize. Taking long, smooth strides it moved towards Sharat and bent down to prod his body with its bony hands.

Using every ounce of his willpower, Sharat tried not to breathe as he lay still as a corpse and kept his eyes clenched shut. It was a terrible struggle, but just when it seemed he couldn't hold on any longer, the ghul finally straightened up and, with silent steps, retreated back into the darkness of the sewers.

In relief, Sharat sucked in a lungful of air, but as he did so he drew in more of Nara's drug and his mind began to spin again.

With a groan, he closed his eyes and allowed his head to slump back. Above him the sewer girls were still

drumming. On and on they went, the wild, hypnotic sound penetrating every cell of his body as he lay helplessly on the cold, stone ledge until, at last, with one final triumphant cry, they were still.

The next thing Sharat knew, he was being shaken awake and a mouth pressed itself to his ear.

"Don't say a word," hissed a familiar voice.

Sharat's head was pounding. He felt the gag being released and a cup of water was held to his mouth. Feeling nauseous, he gulped it down. Then, two pairs of hands pulled him up and guided him along the narrow tunnel without untying his wrists. Soon sunlight started penetrating the darkness through holes and cracks in the ceiling above and Sharat made out the shape of two girls. It was little Lalita and the girl who had tied him up, Rajani.

"Keep your mouth shut!" snapped Rajani when she saw him looking at her.

"This way," whispered Lalita, tugging the rope around his wrists.

The path was slimy underfoot. Sharat tried not to think about what he was walking on as he hurried to keep up.

"Where are we going?" he asked.

"You're taking us to Aya," replied Rajani, taking out her knife. "Unless you were lying."

"I wasn't lying!"

"Where is she, then?"

"She lives near the crematorium, close to the circus encampment," said Sharat, praying that he was right.

95

"We'll go as far as we can underground. Then we'll have to come out near the blue mosque and follow the river north," Rajani told Lalita.

"We need to be fast. We don't want Nara to catch us," Lalita pointed out.

"It's three against one," muttered Rajani.

"*He* doesn't count."

"Two against one, then."

"Unless she brings the others."

"Well, hurry up, then!"

They set off again, clambering out at last into a ruined hovel that hid the entrance to the sewers.

In the bright light of day, Sharat got a better look at the girls. Their greyish skin was covered in sores, their hair was matted, and they were painfully thin. They flinched in the sunlight.

"The crematorium is up here," said Lalita.

Rajani had her knife pressed into Sharat's side. She seemed ill at ease and her wild eyes darted nervously around, as if she were waiting for attack, but Lalita was looking at Sharat with curiosity.

"Do you really have a white tiger?" she asked.

Sharat felt a wave of nausea. "I used to," he said weakly.

"No talking!" snapped Rajani. "We still don't know if we can trust him."

Guiltily, Lalita pressed her mouth shut.

As they made their way along the river, Sharat caught sight of the travellers' inn that he'd passed on his first

96

morning in the city. With a pang, he saw that the camel traders were still there, playing chess in the shade of its tattered awnings.

In the distance he spotted the skeleton of the banyan tree.

"She should be around here somewhere," he said.

"No messing about!" Rajani warned him. "If you run away we'll get the other girls to hunt you down and give you back to the ghuls, and this time we won't be there to save you."

Sharat shuddered. "What *are* ghuls exactly?" he asked.

The girls exchanged a glance.

"Nobody knows for sure," Rajani admitted.

"I think they're ghosts," said Lalita.

Sharat frowned. The hands that had prodded him the night before hadn't seemed ghostly at all. "What do they want?" he asked.

"They want children," said Rajani. "They've started coming every night."

"What for?" asked Sharat. "Food?"

Rajani shook her head. "We don't think so. They only take people alive. That's why I told you to play dead."

"They never used to bother us while Aya was with us," said Lalita. "That's why we're looking for her. We want her to come back. She's the only one who could ever stand up to Nara."

"She lives near that tree, I'm sure of it," promised Sharat, pointing towards the banyan. "I saw her there yesterday."

"I'll go and have a look," said Lalita.

Rajani nodded, and the smaller girl ran off, disappearing down the slope to the riverbank. A moment later her head reappeared. "There's nobody here," she called, sounding disappointed.

Rajani pressed her knife into Sharat's side.

"Did you lie to me?" she hissed.

Sharat had finally loosened one of his hands. He sized up Rajani. She might have a knife, but she was no match for him. He was about to make a break for it when a liquid noise like the call of some fabulous bird hit his ears and he froze, mesmerised by the sound. It was coming from the river.

Rajani's face split open in a wide smile.

"Aya!" she called. She lowered her knife.

The singing stopped abruptly.

Lalita ran ahead. The other two hurried after her.

The little girl with curly hair was hidden behind a cluster of boulders on the riverbank. When she heard them coming, she jumped to her feet, her face shadowed with fear.

Rajani cut Sharat's bindings.

"You can go now," she said, her voice curt.

Sharat glanced over at Aya. A familiar face. He felt a spark of hope.

"I think I'll stay," he said.

Rajani shrugged. "Suit yourself."

Aya had caught sight of them now. Her expression turned from fear to surprise as she stepped forward.

98

"Rajani?" Her eyes darted over and took in the other two. "And Lalita!"

Lalita smiled shyly. "Hello, Aya."

Sharat stood awkwardly behind the girls. He lifted his hand in greeting. "I'm Sharat," he reminded her. "The boy with the white tiger?"

Aya looked at him coldly. "I know who you are," she said. Pointedly, she ignored him, and turned to the girls. "What are *you* doing here?" she demanded.

"We came to find you," said Rajani. "We want you to come back to the sewers."

Aya frowned. "Why?"

Rajani looked uncomfortable. "It's Nara and the ghuls," she said.

"What about them?"

"The ghuls have started taking children," Rajani told her.

Aya took a sharp breath. "What *for*?"

"We don't know," said Lalita, "but it's getting so bad that Nara's making us catch boys to use as a sacrifice, so that they'll leave us alone."

"That's horrible!" said Aya. She finally caught Sharat's eye. "Is that why you're with them?" she asked.

Sharat nodded. "Nara took me prisoner," he said.

Aya shook her head. "Oh, Nara..."

"I did try and stop her, but the others are all too frightened," said Lalita. She gestured at Sharat. "We only rescued this one because he said he knew you."

"Please come back, Aya," begged Rajani. "Nothing

like this happened when you were there."

"I'm never going back to those sewers," said Aya with a shudder. "It's disgusting down there."

She reached over and took Lalita's hand. "You don't have to stay with Nara," she said. "Come and live with me. There aren't any ghuls up here."

"I *can't*!" Lalita whimpered. "All this sky ... it gives me the creeps."

"We aren't like you, Aya," Rajani agreed. "We've never lived above ground. It doesn't feel safe."

"You'd get used to it," Aya encouraged them.

Lalita looked around nervously. "Even if we wanted to, we couldn't stay," she said. "Nara's sure to come looking for us if we go missing."

"You have to stand up to her," said Aya.

"I do stand up to her!" Rajani protested. "But you know what Nara's like."

Aya sighed. "Yes, I know," she admitted.

"We'll visit you again soon," promised Lalita, her eyes filling with tears.

Quickly, she turned away, and together the girls slunk off, huddled together against the immensity of the sky.

Aya watched them, her face worried. "Be careful!" she called.

They lifted their grimy hands and waved.

While the girls were saying their goodbyes, Sharat took the opportunity to dive into the river and wash away the filth of the sewers. When he was finished, he pulled himself back on to the bank and shook out his hair.

"What happened to you?" demanded Aya. "I went to the circus like you said, but there was no one there."

Sharat glanced in the direction of the circus encampment. So they really had gone. A desperate wave of loneliness swept through him. He swallowed.

"I'm sorry," he said. "It wasn't my fault. The circus was forced to leave town."

"Why aren't you with them?" asked Aya.

Sharat bent down to pick up a stone, avoiding her gaze. "I've run away."

"What about your tiger?" said Aya. "Where's *she*?"

With a quick movement, Sharat skimmed the stone across the river. "Emira's gone," he said, unable to hide the misery in his voice.

Aya frowned. "Wasn't she with that old lady I told you about?" she said. "Uma?"

"Oh, she was with Uma when I saw *you*," said Sharat, "but she disappeared again when we performed for the Emperor. Only this time it was for real."

"What do you mean, disappeared?" said Aya sharply.

Sharat took a deep breath. "She jumped through a hoop at the end of our show, and never landed," he said.

"Do you mean she disappeared by *magic*?" asked Aya, her eyes widening.

"Magic, or some kind of trick," said Sharat bitterly, thinking of Mohini. "Either way, she's been stolen."

A look of anxiety played across Aya's face. "Maybe she really *is* the tiger from the rhyme," she said, more to herself than to Sharat.

Sharat looked at her, puzzled. "What are you talking about?" he asked.

Aya hesitated. "It's a nursery rhyme my mother used to tell me," she said. "I remembered it when I first saw Emira."

"What nursery rhyme?"

"It goes like this," said Aya.

"Earthbound, breathled, firefound and watermet,
Brought to his fate by tiger white, and called by name
from death to life,
The Prince of Jinnis will come again,
To overthrow the rule of men,
And save our queen from slavery,
So all her creatures can be free."

Sharat felt his skin come out in goosebumps. "What does it mean?" he asked.

"It's a prophecy," Aya told him. "My mother said that when the jinnis were enslaved, there was one who escaped – the Prince of Jinnis. She said he was the most powerful jinni of them all, and that one day a white tiger would lead him back to the city to free the Queen of the Forest and overthrow the Empire."

Sharat stared at her. "Who is this Prince of Jinnis?" he demanded. "Uma never mentioned him to me."

"That's because he's a *secret*," said Aya. "He's hidden by magic – only his white tiger knows where he is."

His white tiger? Sharat felt a pang of jealousy. "We

don't know if Emira is the tiger from your mother's rhyme," he pointed out.

"Oh, I know," said Aya, "but wouldn't it be wonderful if she was?"

Sharat bit his lip. He didn't think it would be wonderful at all. Both Uma and Aya seemed to think that jinnis were a good thing, but he still wasn't convinced. Besides, Emira belonged to *him*, not to some long-lost prince.

He hesitated. Aya seemed so hopeful, he didn't know how to voice his fears. "Even if Emira is the tiger from your rhyme, she's still been stolen," he said. "All I want is to find her."

"Let's go and see Uma," suggested Aya. She lowered her voice. "She's a *witch*, you know."

Sharat nodded. Aya was right. If anyone could help him now it would be Uma. Magic had made Emira disappear, and he was beginning to think it would take magic to get her back, but he couldn't help feeling uneasy.

"When I was there looking for Emira, Uma made me run away," he said. "There was something coming from Shergarh. It was heading for her garden."

Aya took a sharp breath. "In that case we definitely have to go," she said. "She may need our help."

Quickly, she gathered her few possessions into a little bag. Then, slinging the bag over her shoulder, she turned to make her way towards the cremation grounds as Sharat hurried to follow her.

Although it was still only morning it was almost too hot to breathe. Mirages shimmered in the dusty plains all

around and the air was deathly still. Soon they arrived at the burning *ghats*. Today there were no grieving relatives sitting with their dead, but a few funeral pyres still burned here and there, guarded by the stray dogs that lay panting nearby.

The only people present were the *sadhus*, who sat together in a circle around the bones of a dead fire, their legs in the lotus position. They looked like statues as they meditated with their skin, long hair, and beards covered in ash, barely moving, except to pass their pipe. They didn't seem to notice the boy and girl that tiptoed past them.

Sharat looked towards the temple on the banks of the river. He wiped the sweat from his forehead and tried to get his bearings.

"This way," said Aya, leading him towards the narrow door hidden in the temple wall.

Sharat lifted his fist to knock, but at the pressure of his hand the door fell away and came crashing loudly to the ground. Too late, he saw that it had been ripped from its hinges. With a sense of foreboding, he ducked to go through the low doorway and entered the garden.

He stopped dead in his tracks.

"What is it?" asked Aya as she followed him through. Then she gasped.

In front of them was a terrible scene. Uma's hut had been reduced to a pile of rubble, while all her possessions lay jumbled in the dust. Most terrible of all was the state of the garden. Every one of her beautifully tended plants

had been chopped into a thousand wilting pieces that lay smouldering in the wreckage.

Aya's face crumpled in pain. "No!" she whispered.

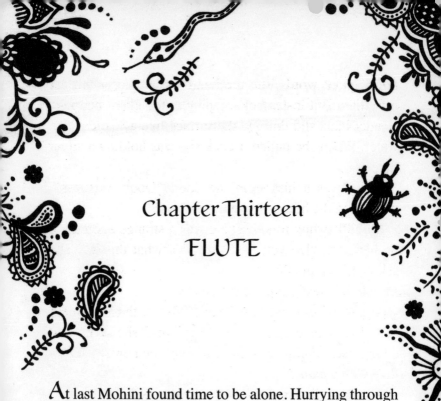

Chapter Thirteen

FLUTE

At last Mohini found time to be alone. Hurrying through the covered walkways of the *Zenana* she reached her chambers. A disembodied head with bulging eyes and pointed teeth grinned out from the door.

"Greetings, mistress," the house-marshal called as the door opened to let her in.

Mohini barely glanced at it. "Lock up!" she snapped.

With a creak of metal the door swung shut and the head swivelled to face into the room.

Moving quickly towards her dressing table, Mohini took a deep breath. So far so good. She'd convinced Rookh to let her catch the tiger, but she wasn't finished yet. For her plan to work, she needed one more ingredient.

Sitting at the table, she gazed into the mirror. Muttering

a few quick words, she reached over as if to touch her reflection. But instead of stopping at the glass, her pale, slender hand slid through the surface like a bird through water. When she pulled it back she was holding a silver flute.

There was a hiss from the door. "Oooh, mistress!" whispered the house-marshal. "Secrets!"

Mohini swung round. There was a strange expression on her face. "Do you have any idea what this is?" she asked, lifting the flute.

"No, mistress," replied the creature.

Mohini's lips twisted in disgust. "*This* is the instrument that brought on the downfall of the jinnis," she said. "And all because your queen – the Queen of the Forest – fell in love with a *man*."

A look of distaste crossed the creature's face. "Nasty!" he said.

Mohini's gaze grew distant. She remembered it as if it was yesterday. It had all started in the garden in the middle of the city. Human beings were scared to go there – they called it the Garden of the Jinnis. But there was a young musician who wasn't afraid. He used to come there every day to practise under the shade of the trees.

"His name was Krishna," she said. "At first he only had a wooden flute, but his playing was so beautiful that the Queen left him a magic flute that had the power to open a passageway into the land of the jinnis."

The creature let out a slow hiss. "Dangerous!" he said.

"Exactly!" said Mohini. Her hands tightened around

the instrument. She'd been furious. For thousands of years Aruanda had been safely hidden from the world of men, and rightly so. Men were a blight on the world. Unnatural. An aberration. Parasites. Vandals. She'd warned the Queen that giving Krishna the flute would only bring danger to them all.

Casmerim hadn't agreed. Blinded by love, she'd insisted that Krishna was different from other men. The only condition she'd placed on him was that he had to leave at sunset, for after dark, the jinnis disappeared and Aruanda was overrun by hungry ghosts – disincarnate spirits who were tied to earth by their anger and greed and who would be lying in wait to possess any man who might be foolish enough to spend the night there.

"What happened next?" asked the house-marshal eagerly.

Mohini glanced over at him. "For a while, everything went to plan," she said. "Every morning Krishna came back to the garden to entertain the Queen, and every evening he went home." Her lips tightened. "Then of course the inevitable happened. A second man followed him into Aruanda."

The house-marshal took a sharp breath. "Rookh!"

"Yes," said Mohini. "Rookh." She clenched her fists as she remembered that fateful day. Rookh was Krishna's brother, but they'd been as different from each other as night and day. Where Krishna was good, kind and beautiful, Rookh was cruel, jealous and ambitious. As soon as he'd set eyes on Casmerim, he'd decided he

had to have her for himself. Hiding in the shadows, he'd waited until Krishna left, hoping to surprise the Queen, but as darkness fell, the jinnis disappeared and he was surrounded by hungry ghosts.

Mohini could only imagine what happened next. All she knew was that Rookh and the hungry ghosts had entered into some kind of diabolical partnership. The next morning, fed by the power of a thousand hungry souls, Rookh had knocked down his brother and kidnapped the Queen. Then, once they were in the land of men, the hungry ghosts flew out of his eyes and possessed the crows that were said to guard the garden. Turning into demons, they swept through the city, hacking down the trees. This trapped the jinnis underground, where they would soon be put to work mining for jewels. Only two jinnis had escaped that fate. Foolishly believing that he could win her heart, Rookh had brought the Queen to the surface with Mohini as her handmaid.

Mohini could hardly remember anything about that day, but Casmerim hadn't lost her wits. Somehow she'd managed to find Krishna's flute. Afterwards she'd given it to her handmaid for safekeeping.

"Hide it!" she'd said. "One day a white tiger will lead the Prince of Jinnis back to the city to free us all, and when he plays this instrument it will dissolve the veil between the worlds, so that jinnis and humans can live in peace and harmony again."

Mohini shook her head. Casmerim's dream was her

worst nightmare. Live in harmony with human beings? Never!

A look of determination came over her face as she stepped towards the house-marshal.

When he saw her expression, the little monster tried unsuccessfully to draw back. "What are you doing?" he squeaked.

Mohini didn't reply. She had no real power of her own any more, unless she did Rookh's bidding, but with any luck there was enough magic left in the house-marshal for her to complete her task.

With lightning speed she reached out and grabbed him by the throat. "All I need is a kiss," she said.

The house-marshal shrieked as he tried to twist his head away, but it was too late. Mohini's lips were already clamped on his, sucking away his life force, until soon, all that was left of the unfortunate creature was an empty husk dangling helplessly from the door, his eyes wide with shock.

As she stepped away, Mohini felt slightly nauseous, but she had no regrets. She would do whatever it took to escape the City of Jewels.

Quickly, she lifted the flute, and her hands began to dance around the gleaming metal.

A muttered incantation left her lips, a bead of sweat appeared on her brow and her skin began to burn with supernatural heat. For a moment nothing happened. Then, slowly but surely, the silver flute began to change its shape.

110

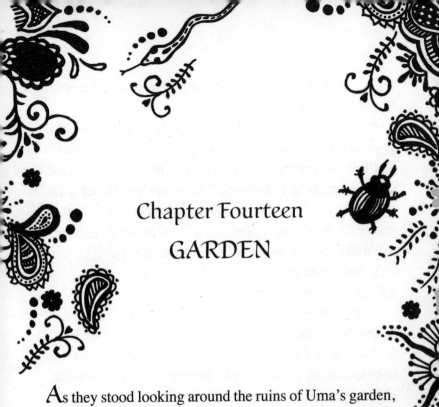

Chapter Fourteen

GARDEN

As they stood looking around the ruins of Uma's garden, a trail of silent tears rolled down Aya's face. With shaking hands she reached out and touched the shredded remains.

Sharat felt sick. "Who would do something like this?" he asked in horror.

Aya turned to him, her eyes torn with helpless fury. "They're called lickers, short for similickers," she said. "They come from Shergarh."

Sharat remembered the jewelled golden beetle with the razor-like legs and a chill passed through him.

"I wonder what happened to Uma?" he asked. "Do you think they caught her, too?"

Aya's face was tight. "I hope not," she said.

With a grimace, Sharat turned back to face the door.

"Well, there's no point in hanging around," he said. "Let's get out of here."

Aya put out a hand to stop him. "Wait!" she said. She was scanning the garden with a practical eye. "Don't go yet. Let's see what we can salvage first."

Sharat glanced back through the doorway. He could see Shergarh downriver. It felt like the fortress was watching them.

"What are you looking for?" he asked.

"Food," said Aya.

Suddenly Sharat realised how hungry he was.

"That's not a bad idea," he admitted.

"Get the fire going and I'll see what I can find," Aya told him.

Sharat nodded. "All right," he said.

While Sharat stoked the flames, Aya rummaged through the wreckage of the hut. Soon she gave a cry of triumph as she unearthed a couple of clay pots. "Found it!" she called. "All I had to do was dig."

Sharat lifted his head. "What do you mean?"

"Uma always kept her food buried," Aya explained. "Just in case the demons ever found her garden."

Sharat stiffened as he remembered the creature in the rigging. "What *are* demons exactly?" he asked.

A dark expression crossed Aya's face. "During the day they look like horrible little men with thin legs and hooked noses," she said. "But at night-time they turn into crows and gobble up all the seeds that have fallen to the ground, to make sure nothing grows."

"I knew it!" said Sharat. "There was one in the big top the first night we were here. It almost caused an accident."

"I'm not surprised," said Aya. "They *feed* on evil. That's how they get their power."

Sharat shivered. The more he learned about the City of Jewels, the less he liked it, but he knew that if he was going to find his tiger he was going to need his strength. He picked up a dented copper pot. "I'll fetch some water," he said. "The sooner we eat, the sooner we can get out of here."

Leaving Aya sorting through the lentils, he went down to the river, past the *sadhus*, who were still sitting in meditation. This time two or three of them looked up as he went past, so he hurried back to Uma's garden with his head bowed.

Putting the water next to Aya, he carefully propped up the doorway so that they couldn't be seen. "I'll see if I can find any vegetables," he offered, rummaging through the greenery.

Aya lifted her head and gave him a quick smile.

As they prepared their food, Sharat noticed that there was something refined about her movements and the way she spoke.

"What are you doing living out here all on your own?" he asked. "Where's your mother?"

For a moment Aya didn't reply. When she lifted her eyes, they were heavy with pain.

"I don't have a mother," she said. "She's dead."

"Oh." Sharat felt a pang of pity. "I'm sorry."

113

He paused, not sure what to say next. "How did you end up with the sewer-girls?" he asked.

A shadow crossed Aya's face. "I met them when I escaped from the *Zenana*," she said.

Sharat stared at her in surprise. "What?" he said. "The *Zenana* inside Shergarh?"

Aya nodded.

Sharat remembered the screened ladies' quarters inside the palace. His eyes widened. "Are you a *princess*?" he asked.

"No," said Aya firmly. "My mother was a princess. *I* ran away."

Sharat frowned. "But I thought the *Zenana* was guarded. How did you get out?"

Aya lifted her chin defiantly. "I got out through the latrine," she said.

It took a moment for Sharat to understand what she was saying. "Do you mean you jumped into the *sewers*?" he said in disgust.

Aya's face tightened. "I didn't have any choice," she said. "My mother was being murdered. If I'd stayed I probably would have been murdered, too."

Sharat was shocked. He wasn't sure what to say. "I'm sorry," he ventured.

"Don't be," muttered Aya. "At least I'm still alive." She turned to stir the pot that was bubbling over the fire. "Nara was the one that rescued me," she added after a moment's silence.

Sharat gave a short laugh. "I'm surprised she didn't

114

kill you."

"Poor Nara," said Aya. "She can't help how she is. Terrible things happened to her above ground. She wasn't dumped in the sewers like the other girls. She ran away."

Sharat grimaced as he thought of the sewer-girl's vicious, one-eyed face.

"The sewer-girls aren't so bad once you get to know them," Aya told him. "I learned a lot more from them then I ever did in the *Zenana*. They taught me how to survive in the city."

"If you say so," said Sharat.

He was unconvinced, but Aya's story had given him an idea.

"Do you think it would be possible to get *into* Shergarh through the sewers?" he asked.

Aya shook her head as she ladled their food on to banana leaves. "The sewer-girls had the same idea," she told him. "Nara even had a crazy plan to break in and raid the treasury, but the holes into the latrine are too far up."

Sharat sighed. All he wanted was to find Emira and get her back, and yet it seemed as though every doorway was being closed to him. However, he was also beginning to see that his wasn't the only tragedy to occur in the City of Jewels. He glanced over at Aya again.

"What was it like in the *Zenana*?" he asked.

She managed a smile. "I was happy living with my mother," she said. "We even had a little garden ... until it was destroyed by the lickers."

Sharat paused in sympathy, but he couldn't help being

115

curious. "What about the other princesses?" he said. "Were they very beautiful?"

Aya wrinkled her nose in distaste. "I hardly ever saw them," she said. "Most of the children were older than me. The only person who used to play with me was my mother's lady-in-waiting."

"Oh." Sharat felt a little disappointed. He'd had a much more romantic view of the *Zenana*. For a moment he fell into a thoughtful silence while they ate.

"I never knew my mother," he said after a while.

"Why not?" asked Aya, glancing at him.

"She died when I was born," Sharat told her. "My father looked after me. He's the circus ringmaster." As he thought about Lemo, a wave of loneliness passed through him. For a moment he wondered what they were doing at the circus now. He swallowed his food with difficulty.

Aya gave him a curious look. "How come the circus left town?" she asked. "Emira must be very valuable. Doesn't your father want to get her back?"

Sharat shook his head. "They were driven out by the Emperor's soldiers," he told her. "That's why I had to run away."

"How did you end up performing in Shergarh?"

Sharat scowled as he thought of Mohini. "It was my father's new wife," he said. "*She* arranged for us to perform for the Emperor, but when I tried to find her after Emira disappeared she'd gone."

"Do you think she had something to do with it?" asked Aya.

116

Sharat nodded. "I'm sure of it. She gave me a new hoop and a new collar for Emira just before the show." His heart tightened. "Emira disappeared when she jumped through the hoop."

A look of determination crossed Aya's face. "We've got to find her!" she said. "What if she's the tiger from the prophecy?"

"I don't care about any old prophecy," said Sharat miserably. "I just want to get Emira back."

"Don't you know anyone else in the city?" Aya asked him. "Anyone who can help?"

Sharat hesitated. "Uma told me my mother came from the city," he said. "But she's dead."

Aya looked thoughtful. "What was her name?" she said. "Perhaps you have family here that you could track down."

Sharat felt a pang of regret. "I wish I knew," he said, "but my father never wanted to talk about her." Carefully he unfolded the golden bee from his waistband. The blue stone at the centre glittered in the sunlight. "All I have is this."

Aya's eyes lit up. "Oh!" she said. "It's so pretty!"

Sharat nodded. "Uma gave it to me," he said. "It belonged to my mother."

Aya reached out to take the amulet and weighed it in her hand. She looked impressed. "This is old gold," she said as she glanced up at him. "Your mother must have come from a very rich family."

"That's not much help," said Sharat. "We can hardly

go knocking on the door of every grand house in the city to see if anyone recognises it."

There was a thoughtful look on Aya's face. "I'm not saying we should do that," she said, "but there are other ways of finding out who it belonged to."

"Like what?" asked Sharat.

"There's a woman called Fonke who lives in the old town," said Aya. "I used to hear the sewer-girls talking about her. She used to pay the girls for stuff they found in the dump. They always got extra for things made out of old gold."

"I'm not selling this!" said Sharat.

Aya shook her head impatiently. "I'm not saying you should sell it," she said, "but this amulet looks quite rare. Perhaps Fonke can help us in some way. She might be able to tell us where it comes from." Her eyes lit up. "Maybe it even has magical powers!"

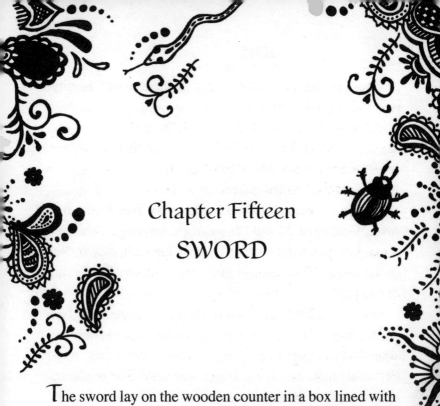

Chapter Fifteen
SWORD

The sword lay on the wooden counter in a box lined with purple velvet. Fonke bent her turbanned head over the shining metal and her bracelets jangled as she reached down to pick up the weapon, taking care not to touch the blade. Slim, straight and perfectly balanced, it shimmered like magic in a shaft of sunlight from the windows above, silvery-white against the dark skin of her hand.

The woman next to her stood waiting quietly, with the patience of the poor. Her head was covered in a scarf and her face was pale and uninteresting.

"Is this the sort of thing you were looking for?" she asked.

For a moment Fonke didn't reply. Only yesterday Rookh had been in her shop.

"I need you to find me a sword," he'd told her. "A sword that kills jinnis. Use every contact you've got. Once you find it let me know. I'll be back to pick it up personally."

As soon as he'd left, Fonke had sent out her agents to spread the word. She was looking for objects, antiques, anything made of jinni metal. She knew which channels to approach, of course. Pawnshops, criminal networks, guttersnipes, and those that lived outside the law. She prided herself on being able to provide whatever her customers ordered, no matter how obscure, but even she hadn't expected results so quickly. Now, as she raised her head to look down at the woman who stood before her, she tried to veil the excitement in her eyes.

"What did you say the sword was called?" she asked.

"It's called the Sword of Shiva," the woman told her.

Fonke felt a flutter in her stomach, but her face remained impassive. She was almost certain that the woman was telling the truth, but it wouldn't do to believe her too soon. "Are you sure?" she snapped.

The woman nodded. "It's been in my family for generations," she promised. She lowered her voice. "I've got jinni blood..."

Fonke looked up at her sharply. That wasn't an admission that came easily to most. Dropping her head, she pursed her lips as she examined the finely honed silver blade once more. If this really was the Sword of Shiva she might never have to work again.

"Tell me again what it does," she demanded.

"It's a sword that kills jinnis," the woman said. "But only a jinni can use it. It's very dangerous for human beings. In the hands of a man, any injury he inflicts will be directed straight back at him."

Fonke felt a thrill of triumph, but she still didn't look impressed. "What good is that?" she asked. "There are no more free jinnis left. Who's going to want to buy a sword nobody can use?"

The woman shrugged. "I wouldn't know," she said. "I just heard you were looking for old weapons, and I need the money."

Fonke's eyes were hard. She looked down at the sword. Then she looked back at the woman. "Two gold crescents," she said, her voice sharp. "That's all I'm prepared to pay."

The woman's face was a picture of disappointment. "Surely the metal itself must be worth more than that," she begged. She lowered her voice. "It comes from *Aruanda*."

Fonke paused to think about it. "All right, then, two and a half crescents," she said at last. "That's my final offer."

There was a moment of silence. Then, mutely, the woman held out her slim, pale hand. "I'll take it," she whispered.

Fonke felt the thrill of success as she took out a well-used purse and handed over the money. "Such a pleasure to do business with you," she said.

To her surprise, a faint smile crossed the woman's

121

lips. For the first time Fonke noticed that she had eyes like a cat.

"The pleasure is all mine," she replied.

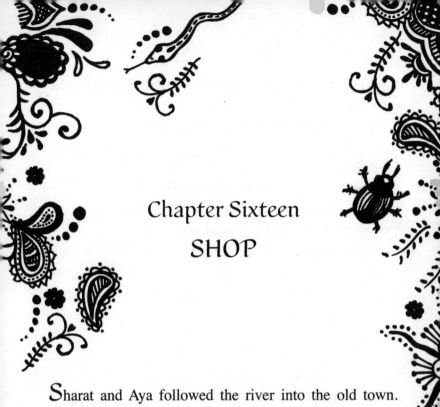

Chapter Sixteen

SHOP

Sharat and Aya followed the river into the old town. Above them, Shergarh loomed, its sheer walls as forbidding as ever. But this time they weren't heading for the fortress.

Before long they reached an arched gate festooned with banners advertising clothing, perfumes, medicines, skin lighteners, eye brighteners, incense, unguents, and credit to pay for it all. Outside the gate were scores of buskers and beggars, snake charmers, ear-cleaners, gamblers and shoe repairmen, all hustling for business.

"This is the market," said Aya. "Come on."

They dodged past the hawkers and in through the gate.

Cucumbers, carrots, rich green leaves, aubergines as black as night, mangoes, bananas, papayas and coconuts

were piled high on the stalls, each one as perfect as the next. Sharat couldn't help staring.

"Where does it all come from?" he wondered.

"This is the food that's imported for the rich," Aya told him. "It comes from the lands the Empire conquers."

Sharat frowned. "What about the poor?" he asked.

Aya's mouth twisted in disgust. "They *make* food for the poor," she said. "But I wouldn't eat it."

Sharat remembered the white stodge he'd bought the day before, but before he could ask more a haughty servant wearing royal livery almost knocked him over. Aya grabbed his hand.

"This way!" she hissed.

They hurried through lanes lined with fruits and vegetables. Then they turned a corner and found themselves in the meat market.

Carcasses hung above every stall, all of them sweating slightly in the heat of the sun, and buzzing with flies. There was a rank smell in the air.

Aya grimaced, quickly leading Sharat through a space between buildings into a quieter alleyway lined with mounds of powdered pigments, mala beads, prayer flags and holy parchments. Here the air was sweet with sacred oils and resins.

A small painting caught Sharat's eye. A woman in a green cloak stood under a tree. Above her head hovered a tiny bird. The colours of the painting were like jewels, and the figure looked almost real. The storekeeper, a woman in a veil, saw him looking and

snatched at his arm.

"It's the Queen of the Forest," she hissed in his ear. "Do you like it? I can give you a good price."

For some reason, Sharat found it difficult to tear his eyes away from the painting, but just then Aya's voice broke into his thoughts.

"Down here!" she called, dodging to the left.

Quickly, Sharat muttered his apologies and hurried to follow Aya through an alleyway lined with stalls selling bundles of silk and velvet. Soon they arrived at a square where bored horsemen were watching the coaches and palanquins of the rich.

Aya pointed towards an avenue of proper shops made of marble and guarded by slaves. "That's the jewellery market," she said.

Sharat glanced at the glittering wares.

"We'd better hurry," he said, conscious of his shabby clothes. "People will be wondering what we're doing here."

"Keep an eye out for a picture of the goddess Kali," Aya told him. "Fonke lives nearby."

They kept their eyes lowered, trying not to catch anyone's attention. Finally they reached a side alley, where someone had painted the face of a black goddess with a long, purple tongue, wild hair and terrible eyes.

Sharat stopped. "Here's Kali," he said.

They faced a dead end between two tall buildings. At the end of the alley was an arched wooden door covered with metal studs. As they approached, a mangy dog got

up and limped out of their way.

There was a head set into the door in the shape of a monster with bulging eyes and sharp fangs.

Sharat lifted his hand to knock, but before his fist reached the door, the monster's mouth flew open.

"What do you want?" it demanded in a high, thin voice.

Sharat jumped back in alarm.

Aya laughed. "It's all right," she said. "It's only a house-marshal."

"What's that?" said Sharat, eyeing the little monster with suspicion.

"It's a kind of jinni," Aya told him. "But don't worry, it doesn't have any power. It's trapped in the door. It can't hurt you."

"Yes, I can," protested the monster angrily, gnashing its fangs.

Aya stepped forward impatiently. "We've come to see your mistress," she said. "Let us in."

"Are you sure? Are you sure?" teased the monster. Then, before either of them could answer, the door swung silently open. Sharat glanced at Aya.

"Does that mean we're supposed to go in?" he asked.

Aya nodded.

As they stepped across the threshold the door swung shut behind them, and the house-marshal's head swivelled to look in at them. Sharat glanced back at it nervously, but it had fallen still.

They found themselves in a room with high ceilings. Dim light filtered in through cracks in a double doorway

126

at the back of the room.

"Hello?" called Sharat.

The only reply was the sound of rustling and whispering, like dry leaves shaking in the breeze, so they stepped forward and stood blinking for a moment to allow their eyes to get accustomed to the gloom. One wall of the shop was lined with shelves, on which were arranged a selection of statues, scrolls, daggers and other miscellaneous objects. In front of it stood a polished rosewood worktop, and there were also a couple of display cabinets. The first was filled with a collection of odd little dolls and the other contained charms, vases, oil lamps and bottles. Among these fairly innocuous objects there was also a more macabre collection, including what looked like a mummified baby, a pair of shrunken heads, a skeleton with four arms and several stuffed animals. Worst of all, a desiccated ghul stood propped up against the wall, its long white robes grey with dust, and its bony, twig-like hands poking out from the sleeves.

Sharat stifled a gasp, but the ghul didn't move.

"It's dead," Aya whispered.

Letting out a breath of relief, Sharat stepped into the room.

Sitting on the worktop was a long thin box. Whatever was inside was glowing faintly and Sharat found himself drawn towards it. Curious, he flipped open the box, and his eyes widened as he looked down at a beautiful silver sword, but before he could examine it more closely, Aya let out a gasp.

Sharat turned to look.

She was standing in front of a pedestal. On top of the pedestal was a small wooden drum, and on the drum's surface were mounted two delicate silver hands that glowed with the same light as the sword.

"What's that?" asked Sharat.

In the dim light Aya's face seemed transformed with joy. "It's a musical instrument," she said in wonder.

Sharat frowned. "That's not a musical instrument," he said.

"Yes, it is," insisted Aya. "Listen."

She placed the drum between the heels of her hands, lined her fingers up with the silver fingers, and as she plucked their metal tips a sweetly chaotic sound filled the dusty air. "See?" she said with a grin.

Sharat's scalp began to prickle. "Don't!" he said. "Someone will hear you!"

It was too late. All at once the skeleton had begun to move, its joints creaking. With a crack it detached itself from its stand and stood quivering unsteadily as it turned its empty sockets in search of the source of the music. Just then, a gust of stale air spread the smell of decay as the mummified baby woke up and a gurgling phantom floated above its cradle. The eyes of the shrunken heads snapped open. With a cackle of delight they began to rise up into the air, their tiny mouths glittering with pointed teeth. The ghul stirred, a stuffed wolf let out a howl and they heard the flapping of invisible wings. Then ghostly creatures started popping out at them from every nook

and cranny, some big, some small, some sleepy, some alert. Glowing faintly in the darkness, they advanced on Aya, reaching towards her with half-seen hands.

Aya let out a cry as she ran for the door to shove it open. It didn't budge. The house-marshal opened its mouth and began to cackle with glee.

The phantoms surged forward.

Aya knocked into one of the display cabinets, dispersing the dolls with a clatter as she backed into a corner.

"Do something!" she cried.

Sharat's eyes flicked towards the countertop. Without thinking he snatched the sword and as he touched the metal he felt a rush of power shooting up his arm. With one swift move he swung the shining blade towards Aya's phantom attackers.

"GET OFF!" he shouted.

As the sword sliced through the ghostly forms it made a sizzling sound like flesh being branded with a hot-iron. The apparitions disappeared in a puff of steam and the skeleton came crashing to the ground.

Aya was still clutching the instrument.

"Let's get out of here!" she gasped.

Sharat dropped the sword back on to the countertop and ran over to the door.

"Let us out!" he snapped, but instead of letting them out, the house-marshal began to shriek:

"Thieves! Thieves! Thieves!"

Moments later, the double doors at the back of the shop were thrown open, and the room was flooded with light.

Silhouetted at the centre of the doorway stood a tall, imposing figure.

Her skin glowed like oiled ebony against a sweeping turquoise dress that made the most of her voluptuous curves, and a turban was perched on top of her extravagantly curled hair. Enormous earrings dangled from her ears and her arms clattered with bracelets.

Sharat and Aya glanced at each other in dismay. This could only be Fonke.

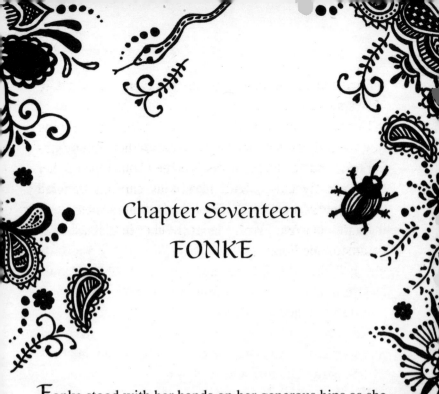

Chapter Seventeen
FONKE

Fonke stood with her hands on her generous hips as she surveyed the mess in her shop. Then, before Sharat and Aya could say anything, she marched over and seized their ears.

"What's going on here?" she demanded, glaring down at them.

"It's my fault, madam," said Aya quickly. "I'm sorry."

Fonke let go of their ears and looked down at Aya with distaste. "What have you done?"

Looking guilty, Aya held up the instrument that she was still clutching in her hands. "I accidentally played this, and all these *ghosts* started attacking us," she said.

Fonke snatched the instrument away from her.

"What do you mean you *accidentally* played it?"

131

she snapped.

Aya's eyes were round and innocent. "I just knocked the fingers and it made a noise," she said. "I didn't know it was a musical instrument. It doesn't *look* like one."

Fonke eyed her with suspicion. Then she shook her head. "You shouldn't play with things you don't understand," she said. "Even *I* don't know exactly how these things work." With a jangle of her bracelets, she put the instrument back on its pedestal. "Be glad it was only ghosts," she added. "You never know what you could have brought creeping up from the underworld. What if you'd summoned a *demon*?"

"Yes, madam," said Aya. "I'm sorry. I didn't mean it." She sounded sincere, but she couldn't help glancing back at the instrument with a look of longing.

Fonke scanned the rest of the room and caught sight of the sword lying carelessly on the countertop. With a gasp she strode over and seized it. "Who's been playing with *this*?" she demanded.

This time it was Sharat's turn to look guilty.

"That was me," he admitted. "I used it to frighten away the ghosts."

Fonke glared at him. "Do you have any idea what this *is*?" she said.

Sharat shook his head, mute.

"This is a very special sword," Fonke told him. "Only a jinni can use it safely. It's not a weapon for human beings. Any injury it causes is directed straight back to the one who uses it. You could have killed yourself." She

placed it carefully back into its box, and closed the lid with a snap.

"I'm sorry," said Sharat. "The house-marshal let us in but nobody was here so we decided to look around. After all, it *is* a shop."

The monster in the door let out a chuckle.

Fonke threw it a look of disgust. "Call yourself security?" she snapped. "I'll have your fangs removed if you're not careful. Or perhaps you'd like a job in Shergarh?"

The house-marshal clamped its mouth shut and swivelled so that only the back of its head could be seen from the inside of the room.

Impatiently, Fonke marched over and propped up the skeleton. Then, with a few swift moves she tidied up the rest of the pieces that had fallen to the floor. When she was finished she turned to glare at Sharat and Aya. "Now are you going to tell me what you're doing here, or shall I have you arrested?" she demanded.

"No! Please don't," said Sharat. "We've come to ask for your help."

Fonke eyed him with distaste. "What do you want?" she said. "You must be selling something. You don't look like customers."

Quickly, Sharat pulled out the golden bee. "I'm trying to find out what this is," he said.

Fonke looked bored as she held out her hand, but her eyes flashed with interest when she saw the diamond.

"Where did you get this?" she asked.

Sharat hesitated. "It's a family heirloom."

"We were wondering if you could tell us something about it," said Aya. "We might want to sell it."

Fonke took the amulet to look at it more closely. "Well, all right," she said, her voice sounding reluctant, "but I'd better warn you there's not much of a market for this kind of thing." With a rustle of silk she turned and took the piece over to the countertop.

Sharat and Aya stood watching nervously as Fonke cleaned the jewel with a soft cloth. Then she set it on a block of wood and subjected the stone to a variety of tests: tapping it gently with a small pointed hammer, rubbing it against various materials, dunking it into a series of liquids and finally looking at it through a magnifying glass.

"I hope she doesn't break it," whispered Sharat.

Aya was watching Fonke carefully. "Don't worry," she whispered back. "She knows what she's doing."

A moment later Fonke raised her head. This time she couldn't hide her excitement.

"Do you have any idea what this is?" she demanded.

Sharat shook his head.

"Come here," Fonke told him.

Both Sharat and Aya hurried over.

Fonke lifted the amulet into a beam of sunlight.

"Look into the stone," she said.

They peered down. For a moment all they could see was the dazzling surface, but as Fonke twisted the stone they caught sight of a fleck of gold deep in the centre of

the diamond, trapped like a fly in amber.

Aya gasped.

"What is it?" asked Sharat.

Fonke's eyes widened dramatically.

"This, young man, is the stuff that dreams are made of," she told him. "There's a jinni in this amulet."

Sharat's heart jumped. "A jinni?" he asked, his mouth hanging open in surprise.

There was a look of triumph on Aya's face.

"I knew it!" she said.

Sharat tried to keep his voice calm. "Do you mean a jinni that can grant *wishes*?" he asked.

Fonke inclined her head. "That's exactly what I mean."

Sharat caught Aya's eye. She looked as excited as he felt.

"A jinni that can grant wishes!" she said. "That's very rare!"

"Very rare," agreed Fonke. "Of course, we have no guarantee how *powerful* the jinni is," she added quickly. "I'd be happy to take it off your hands if you'd care to sell it."

Sharat's heart was pounding. With a jinni to grant him wishes he could rescue Emira! He shook his head.

"No. I'm not selling it," he said. "All I need is to know how to use it."

A fleeting look of disappointment crossed Fonke's face, but she nodded. "I can help you with that, too," she admitted, "but before I can do anything we need to discuss a price."

"A price for what?" asked Sharat, looking at her blankly.

"A price to summon the jinni, of course!" replied Fonke. "You didn't think I would do it for free, did you?"

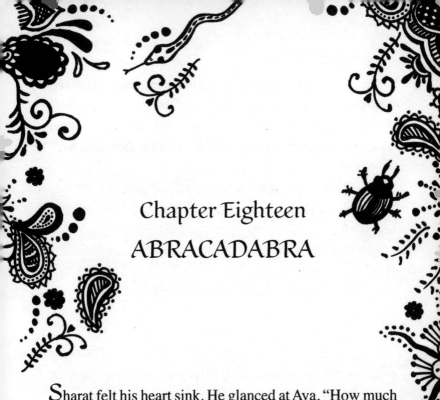

Chapter Eighteen
ABRACADABRA

Sharat felt his heart sink. He glanced at Aya. "How much does it usually cost to summon a jinni?" he asked.

Fonke pursed her lips. "That depends on a number of factors," she said. "Some jinnis are bound to serve only one master. They are very difficult to summon. Also, it depends on the strength of the jinni. Unfortunately there's no way of telling how strong a jinni is before he's been summoned, so you'll have to leave *that* to my discretion. Finally, it depends on the customer. For wealthy customers my prices are considerably higher." She glanced at Sharat. "You don't look very wealthy at all, if I'm not mistaken."

"No," said Sharat quickly. "I'm not."

"In that case, I'll keep the price very reasonable,"

Fonke told him. "Let's say, ten gold crescents."

Sharat stared at her in disbelief. "Ten gold crescents?" He thought with regret of the gold the sewer-girls had taken. "Couldn't you let me work off the debt instead?" he asked.

"Work off ten crescents of gold?" Fonke shook her head. "With the kind of work you can do, it would take years!"

Aya looked thoughtful. "How many wishes will Sharat get?" she asked.

Fonke eyed her. "Three wishes," she said. "After that the jinni's free."

"Can't he use one of the wishes to get the gold?"

"It's never as easy as that," said Fonke. "As I've said, until we do the summoning there's no way of knowing how powerful the jinni will be. There are very few who can produce gold out of thin air. Most of them need to transform something else into gold, but the trouble with that is that once the jinni is free it has no incentive to maintain the spell, and the gold disappears or turns into dust or leaves, or whatever it was made of in the first place. The only way most jinnis can produce real gold is by stealing," she said, looking sternly at Aya. "I love gold, but I don't approve of stealing. It's extremely bad karma."

"What's the use of having a jinni if he can't bring you gold?" Aya muttered.

Sharat wasn't interested in gold. All he wanted was to find Emira and get her back to the circus. That shouldn't

138

take more than two wishes. He hesitated, then looked up at Fonke.

"Could you show me how to call the jinni in exchange for one of the wishes?" he asked.

Fonke looked pleasantly surprised. "A wish in exchange for the secret?" she mused. "Now that's an intriguing idea."

Sharat felt a surge of hope.

"Will you do it?" he demanded.

There was a glint in Fonke's eye. "You know, a little jinni magic could come in very handy," she said. "But we'll have to hurry. I'm expecting the gentleman who ordered the sword any minute now, and I don't want him to find *you* here."

With a decisive swish of her dress she strode over to the pedestal where the musical instrument was displayed.

"Come here!" she ordered.

Sharat hurried over.

"The jinni will only obey the person who does the summoning," Fonke told him. "So once it's here you'll have to tell it to grant my wish."

"Yes, of course," said Sharat. He cleared his throat. "How much time will I have to make my own wishes?" he asked. He had heard all sorts of stories about jinnis and about wishes going wrong for one reason or another. He was determined not to make any mistakes.

"Once you've summoned the jinni, you can take as much time as you like," said Fonke. "Just call him. He'll be bound to serve you until all three wishes

139

have been granted."

Sharat nodded. "What do I have to do?"

"To summon a powerful jinni, you need to know its name," Fonke told him, "but since this is just a minor jinni you're going to use a magic word, and the magic word is Abracadabra!"

"Abracadabra?" Sharat looked at her in disbelief. "Surely if it was that simple people would be calling jinnis all the time?"

Fonke's eyes flashed. "Magic words are useless unless you know how to use them," she said. "Be quiet and let me explain."

"Sorry," said Sharat.

"The secret to using a magic word is that you don't say it," Fonke told him. "You sing it."

Sharat's heart sank. "I have to sing?"

"Yes," said Fonke. "It's the vibration of the notes that activates the spell. That's where this instrument comes in."

Fonke picked up the amulet and touched the jewel against the wooden drum. Instantly, the silver fingers began to twitch.

Aya gasped.

"That's it," said Fonke. She gave Sharat the bee, then lifted a small wooden hammer. "Now listen," she said.

Using the hammer, she carefully played five crystalline notes on the quivering fingers: *ting, ting, ting, ting, ting*. Then she looked at Sharat. "Did you get that?" she asked.

Feeling miserable, Sharat nodded. "I *heard* it, yes."

"Good," said Fonke. "Now sing the tune without using the magic word first. Just sing la, la, la, la, la."

Sharat practised humming the notes a few times, but when he went on to sing la, la, la, la, la, something more like a donkey's bray came out instead.

Aya and Fonke looked at him in shock.

"What on earth was that?" demanded Fonke.

Sharat was getting irritated. "It's not my fault," he muttered. "I never said I could sing."

"Relax your throat," Aya told him. "Like this." She opened her mouth. "La, la, la, la, la!" she sang. "See? It's easy."

Sharat saw, and he heard, but although he tried and tried again, he only seemed to get worse. Finally he snapped. "I can't do it," he said, dropping his hand in frustration. "There must be another way."

"I'm afraid there isn't," said Fonke. "If you want to wake up this jinni, you're going to have to find your singing voice."

"But I can't sing. I've never been able to sing," said Sharat angrily. Then he glanced over at Aya. Suddenly he remembered the magical sound he'd heard by the river. He swallowed. Aya could sing, but could he trust her?

Aya seemed to read his mind. "Do you want me to do it for you?" she asked.

Sharat hesitated, uncertain.

"Make up your mind," said Fonke impatiently. "I don't have all day."

"I promise I'll wish for what you want," said Aya.

141

Sharat knew he didn't have a choice. "All right," he said. "You do it."

Aya looked both nervous and excited as he handed her the amulet. She looked over at Fonke.

"What's the tune again?" she asked.

Again, Fonke played the silver fingers. Once she'd finished, Aya raised the amulet in front of her.

"A-bra-ca-da-bra!" she sang, clear and true.

At first nothing happened. Then, just when they were beginning to think that it wasn't going to work, the bee began to flicker at the edges, a bit like a piece of paper catching fire, and then it started to vibrate as tiny wisps of smoke started curling up from the tips of the wings. Aya looked scared and glanced over at Fonke.

"Don't drop it!" Fonke warned her.

With a nod, Aya kept her hand steady as the amulet began to buzz and the wisps of smoke turned into plumes. Then all of a sudden there was a great whooshing noise, and something shot out of the stone, expanding as it flew wildly around the room.

"That's it!" said Fonke.

The jinni's trajectory was becoming less erratic now. It circled Aya three times in a blur of blue and gold before landing smartly on the countertop.

It was a slim blue boy, about the size of a monkey but with translucent golden wings. His face was pointed, a pair of antennae quivered on his head, and his slanted eyes were not altogether friendly.

"Who are you?" he demanded.

142

Aya stepped forward. She cleared her throat. "My name is Aya," she said. "I er … I just summoned you."

The jinni eyed her with hostility. "I never agreed to serve human beings," he informed her.

"What nonsense!" snapped Fonke. "You'll serve whoever summoned you. You know the rules. Three wishes and you're free."

"Three wishes?" exclaimed the jinni. "That will use up all my magic!"

"You should have thought of that before you allowed yourself to be bound," Fonke told him. "Now kindly introduce yourself and prepare to serve."

With a sigh, the jinni eyed Aya, then bowed. "Alcherisma at your service," he said, in a surly voice. "What do you want?"

Aya glanced nervously up at Fonke. "What am I supposed to do?" she asked.

"First of all, you need to tell the jinni to accompany me and to grant my wish as we arranged," Fonke replied.

Aya nodded and turned to Alcherisma.

"Er … jinni," she said. "Please go with this lady and grant her one wish."

"If I must," muttered the jinni. He took off with a buzz of his wings.

Her dress swirling, Fonke led Alcherisma out through the back of the shop and closed the double doors behind her.

Aya and Sharat looked at each with a mixture of excitement and worry.

143

"He doesn't seem too keen to grant my wishes," said Aya.

"It's *my* wishes he'll be granting," Sharat reminded her.

"Yes of course," said Aya, but she seemed strangely distracted. With a frown she bent over to take another look at the instrument she'd used to wake Alcherisma. "Where did Fonke *get* this?" she said, more to herself than to Sharat.

"Don't play it again!" he warned her.

Just then the doors into the courtyard opened up and Fonke came back into the shop with Alcherisma flying around her head. Aya spun round, her face flushed.

Fonke was beaming, her irritation forgotten.

"Thank you, my dears," she said graciously. "This is, as I expected, a minor jinni, but he was still able to fulfill my modest requirements."

Sharat stared at Fonke. There was something different about her face. He frowned, trying to work out what it was, but Aya was in a hurry to go. She glanced up at the jinni, who had landed on top of one of the cabinets and was looking down at them in scorn.

"What shall I do with him now?" she asked.

"Just ask him to conceal himself," Fonke told her. "Then, when you're ready to summon him again, all you need to do is touch the amulet and call his name."

Quickly, Aya held the amulet up in front of her. "Conceal yourself, please," she told Alcherisma.

"Gladly!" said the jinni.

Glowing with a golden light, his wings began to buzz

as he shrank to the size of a speck of dust and disappeared back into the sparkling blue stone.

"Now you really must be going," said Fonke. "My gentleman caller will be here any minute." She ushered them towards the door. "Let them out!" she snapped at the house-marshal.

Aya didn't need asking twice. As the door swung open she hurried out, but Sharat didn't want to leave just yet. He was still strangely captivated by Fonke. He sidled a bit closer.

"You look … um … very nice, Madam Fonke," he said. For some reason he realised that he was blushing. He felt deeply uncomfortable, but he couldn't stop staring.

Fonke looked down at him and a smirk crossed her lips. "Irresistible is the word you're looking for, I think," she said, patting her hair smugly.

"Oh, is that what it is?" said Sharat, wondering why it had taken him so long to notice what luminous eyes Fonke had.

Fonke pushed him impatiently out of the shop. She hadn't used up a wish for the likes of Sharat.

"Run along now!" she said.

Sharat tripped back into the alleyway, as Fonke closed the door in his face. For a moment he just stood there with his mouth open. Then, wondering what had come over him, he quickly pulled himself together. He had to make his wishes and get Emira back to the circus.

"Aya?" he called.

Turning to go, he ran to the end of the alleyway, but

as he looked left and right he felt his heart sink. The only people he could see along the main road were men drinking coffee and women haggling over jewels. It was just as he'd feared. Aya had disappeared, and she had taken Alcherisma with her.

Chapter Nineteen

MAZARIA

Aya ran a short way down the road and ducked behind some baskets to hide. Then, squatting down to make sure that she couldn't be seen, she carefully opened her bag. Her heart felt as though it might burst with excitement.

"The Mazaria!" she whispered as she reached in to touch the magical instrument that she'd stolen right from under Fonke's nose. She caught her breath as she hugged it possessively to her chest. She could hardly believe it. Her mother had been playing this instrument in their garden on the day she'd died.

Aya's heart wrenched. It had all happened so quickly. One minute she had been playing peacefully in their little garden, and the next minute her mother had pulled her into the privy.

"Rookh's coming!" she'd said in a panic. "You've got to get away."

Thrusting the instrument into Aya's hand, she'd pointed at the hole that led to the sewers below. "You'll have to jump in here," she'd said. "Find a witch called Uma. She'll help you."

Aya had stood there, shell-shocked, barely able to understand what it was that her mother wanted her to do. Then, before she could gather her wits, the door had flown open and *he'd* lunged in, spitting words of fury in his harsh, foreign voice.

"I'll kill you!" he'd hissed as he seized her mother by the throat. "You'll never escape me then!"

For a moment Aya had stood there, frozen in fear.

"Jump!" her mother had gasped as she struggled for breath. "Otherwise he'll kill you too!"

Aya shuddered. All she could remember after that was being washed clean in the river by Nara, having her head shaved by Rajani, and being offered scented oils to take away the smell – a one-off treat for new girls. The Mazaria had disappeared.

"Where is it?" she'd asked, sobbing in front of them all.

"You dropped it when you fell," Nara told her impatiently. "Let it go. You'll never get it back."

At the time, of course, she'd been innocent enough to believe it, but now Aya knew exactly what had happened. The Mazaria hadn't fallen in the sewers at all. Nara had stolen it and sold it to Fonke. That's just the sort of thing

she would do. And yet here it was, back in her hands again.

For a moment the triumph in Aya's heart mingled with pain. If only her mother could have taught her to play. But there was no use dwelling on the past. Swallowing down her regrets, she slipped the little instrument back into her bag. Then, keeping a tight grip on the Mazaria, she suddenly remembered the amulet in her other hand and a thrill passed through her. So far she'd been powerless against the man who had killed her mother but now, perhaps, she had the tools for revenge.

Chapter Twenty
ALCHERISMA

As Sharat stood under the sign of Kali, desperately trying to think of what to do next, he heard the clatter of hooves and an ebony coach pulled up, blocking his way. Moments later, a pair of tiny hunchbacked footmen dressed in matching black trousers and turbans festooned with inky feathers hopped down and opened the carriage door, bowing deeply.

Sharat stared at the midgets in horrified recognition. Demons! Quickly, he tried to dodge past them, but one of them pushed him roughly into the dust.

"Out of the way!" he sneered.

Sharat was about to leap to his feet in protest when his insides turned over in shock. Stepping down from the carriage with a swish of his robes was the man in black;

the man he thought had stolen Emira.

He ducked his head and pressed himself against the wall, but to his relief, the man just brushed straight past him, and strode up the alleyway. Then, as the door opened, Sharat heard Fonke's warm greetings.

The man in black was her gentleman caller.

Sharat's first instinct was to storm back into the shop and demand to know where his tiger was, but he knew it would be far too dangerous to confront a nobleman. Somehow he had to find Aya and Alcherisma.

Squeezing past the coach, he ran into the road. His eyes darted left and right.

"Sharat! Sharat!"

The top of Aya's face peeped out from behind a pile of baskets.

Sharat felt a rush of relief. "What are you doing?" he demanded. "I thought you'd taken the amulet and gone."

Aya frowned. "Of course not!" she said. "I promised I'd make those wishes for you." She cast her eyes nervously back in the direction of Fonke's alley. "But first we need to get out of here."

"Let's go back to the square," suggested Sharat.

They raced each other through the market. Sharat reached the fountain first. He turned to face Aya. "If you weren't stealing the jinni, why were you hiding?" he demanded.

Aya caught her breath. "I'll tell you once we're out of the market," she said. "We need to find somewhere where I can make your wishes."

Sharat was thinking fast. "Yesterday I found an old summerhouse on the banks of the moat," he said. "We can hide there."

"Do you think you can find it again?"

"I think so," said Sharat. "It was close to the dragon gate."

They hurried through the maze of alleyways and out through a gap in the wall. Soon they could see Shergarh looming up ahead.

Getting his bearings, Sharat led Aya along the river and over crumbling walls to the ruined gardens. To his relief, he soon found the old stone building covered in dead vines. They ducked inside and stood facing each other in the dim light. There was a look of excitement on Sharat's face.

"I've been thinking about my wishes," he said. "I don't want to make any mistakes. First I'll ask the jinni to bring me Emira, and then I'll ask him to take us back to the circus." He felt a thrill. "I can't wait to see my family!"

Aya looked wistful. "I've never had a family," she said.

"Come with us!" said Sharat. "You could become part of my family. Risa can teach you how to fly on the trapeze."

For a moment Aya's eyes were filled with yearning. Then a stubborn look crossed her face, and she shook her head. "What if you're not supposed to take Emira back to the circus?" she said. "What if she's come here for a reason?"

Sharat felt uncomfortable. "Are you talking about your

152

mother's nursery rhyme?" he asked.

"Yes," said Aya. "What if Emira really *is* supposed to help the Prince of Jinnis overthrow the Empire?"

Again Sharat felt a pang of jealousy. He didn't like the sound of this Prince of Jinnis, but he didn't want to argue with Aya, either. After all, she was the one making the wishes.

"Let's get Emira back first," he suggested. "Then we can think about what to do next."

This seemed to satisfy Aya. "Shall I call Alcherisma?" she asked.

"Yes," said Sharat.

As instructed, Aya held the amulet in her hand.

"Alcherisma!" she called.

For a second they wondered whether anything was going to happen. Then, just as before, the jewel began to shiver and a speck of gold shot out of the stone, rapidly expanding as it flew around the room, until the jinni landed on the dusty window sill of the summerhouse. With a sullen look on his face, he folded his wings neatly and eyed them with suspicion.

"What do you want this time?" he demanded.

"This time I need you to grant Sharat's wish," said Aya.

Alcherisma glanced at Sharat with a look of disgust. "Do I have to?"

Aya pressed her lips together. "The sooner you're finished, the sooner you'll be free," she reminded him.

Alcherisma gave a long-suffering sigh. "Free, and drained of all magical power," he muttered.

He glared at Sharat. "What do you want, then?" he asked.

Sharat was concentrating. He didn't want to make a mistake. "My wish is that you will find Emira, my white tiger, and bring her back to me alive," he said.

A look of surprise crossed Alcherisma's face. "*Your* white tiger?" he said in disbelief. "Why would *you* have a white tiger?"

Sharat's hackles rose. "None of your business," he snapped. "All you have to do is find her. She's been stolen. I think she's somewhere inside Shergarh."

"Shergarh?" The jinni looked worried. "That's not good," he said. "Not good at all."

"I know. That's why I need your help," said Sharat impatiently. "Can you do it or not?"

Alcherisma drew himself up indignantly. "Give me a chance!" he said. "Magic doesn't just happen, you know." His wings started vibrating. Then, with a buzz, he took off and flew around the summerhouse a few times, becoming smaller and smaller with each turn until finally he disappeared, leaving only flecks of golden dust floating in the air around them.

Once he was gone, Sharat turned back to Aya. "I thought jinnis were supposed to *obey* you," he complained.

"It can't be much fun having to grant wishes," said Aya. "I wonder how he ended up in that amulet?"

"I don't care," muttered Sharat. "I just hope he brings Emira back."

For a moment they waited in silence. There was a

154

thoughtful look on Aya's face. "I wonder if Emira really *is* the tiger from the prophecy," she said.

Sharat bit his lip. He wished Aya would just let it drop. "How *can* she be?" he said. "She grew up at the circus. She doesn't know anything about jinnis."

But Aya wasn't going to be put off. "How do you know?" she insisted. "I bet you didn't even know that Emira came from the City of Jewels. For all you know you might be the Prince of Jinnis yourself!"

Sharat gave a short laugh. "I wish I was!" he said. "But in case you hadn't noticed I don't have any magical powers."

Before Aya could answer him, they were interrupted by a flash of light, and they ducked in alarm as a golden missile appeared out of nowhere, expanding as it flew wildly over their heads.

Moments later, Alcherisma landed on the floor. There was no sign of Emira.

"Where is she?" demanded Sharat.

Alcherisma looked very flustered and the rebellious look in his eyes had been overshadowed by fear.

"I've found your tiger," he said, "but I can't get her back."

Sharat's heart sank. "Why not?"

The jinni shuddered. "They're keeping her in the mines."

"What difference does that make?"

Alcherisma gave Sharat a look of contempt. "Doctor *Rookh* is in charge of the mines," he said.

Aya took a sharp breath.

Sharat glanced at her. "Who's Doctor Rookh?"

Aya's face was grim. "Doctor Rookh is the man who killed my mother," she said.

"He's also the man that enslaved all the jinnis in the City of Jewels," said Alcherisma.

A feeling of certainty was spreading through Sharat.

"Does he have very white skin and wear long, black robes?" he asked.

Aya nodded. "That's him."

"I knew it!" said Sharat. "I saw him at the circus – and he was Fonke's next customer. He arrived just after we left."

Aya's face dropped. "If he'd caught me there..." She shook her head.

Sharat took a sharp breath. "Do you realise what this means?"

"What?" asked Aya.

"Fonke told us that the sword on her countertop was for her next customer," said Sharat. "It's a sword that kills *jinnis*."

Aya's eyes widened in understanding. "Do you think Rookh wants to use it to kill Emira?"

There was a grim look on Sharat's face. "I'm sure of it."

"We've got to stop him!" cried Aya.

"What do you think I'm trying to do?" asked Sharat. He threw Alcherisma a dirty look. "It would help if I had a jinni who could actually grant wishes."

156

"Why don't you go and get her yourself if you think it's so easy?" snapped the jinni.

"I would if I could get into Shergarh," said Sharat.

"That can certainly be arranged," sniffed Alcherisma.

Aya grabbed Sharat's arm. "Wait!" she cried. "You can't go in there on your own!"

"What else am I supposed to do?" said Sharat. "I can't let Doctor Rookh kill Emira."

Aya's eyes lit up. "Why don't we ask Alcherisma to find the Prince of Jinnis?" she said. "He's *sure* to be powerful enough to rescue Emira. Then he can overthrow the Empire, like the prophecy said."

"Good wish!" said Alcherisma, glancing at Aya with increased respect.

Sharat glared at them. "I don't *want* to find the Prince of Jinnis," he said. "All I want is to rescue Emira and get back to the circus."

Aya stared at him in disbelief. "But if you take Emira back to the circus, the Prince of Jinnis might never find his way to the City of Jewels."

"I don't care," snapped Sharat. "It's *my* amulet and I'll wish for whatever I like."

"You can't do it unless I help you," retorted Aya. "I'm the one that summoned Alcherisma."

The jinni tossed his head in irritation. "By rights I shouldn't be taking orders from either of you," he said. "My *true* mistress is the Queen of the Forest!"

Aya gasped. "The Queen of the Forest?" Her eyes lit up in hope. "Oh, I wish we could find her!"

Sharat stepped forward in alarm.

"No! Stop!" he shouted. "You made a wish! Take it back!"

It was too late. Alcherisma's wings were vibrating furiously. There was a triumphant look on his face as he bowed to Aya.

"Mistress," he said. "Your wish is my command."

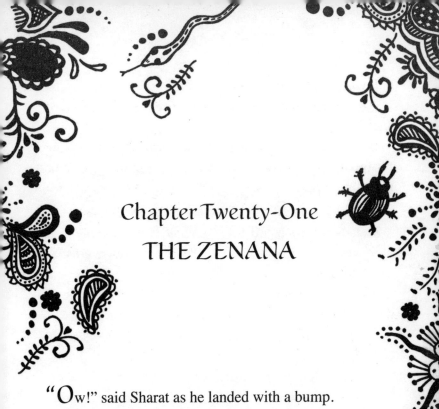

Chapter Twenty-One
THE ZENANA

"Ow!" said Sharat as he landed with a bump.

"Ooof!" Aya's voice echoed next to him.

For a moment they just lay there, feeling dazed. Then, as their heads cleared, they sat up and looked around.

They were in the middle of a paved courtyard that was surrounded by arched alcoves leading off in to shady passageways. Dazzling mosaics decorated the walls and fountains bubbled nearby.

Once he'd got his bearings, Sharat struggled to stand up, and almost tripped over. To his surprise he saw that his feet were encased in a pair of jewelled shoes with pointed toes. Worse still, yellow silk billowed around his legs and earrings jangled at his neck.

Aya stared at him. "What are you wearing?" she asked

in surprise.

"Speak for yourself," snapped Sharat. Aya looked down. She too was robed in silk, but her outfit was green.

"We're dressed as princesses!" she exclaimed.

They heard buzzing, and Alcherisma landed nearby.

"We're in the *Zenana*," he explained. "I thought I'd better put you in disguise."

Just then they heard the sound of laughter, followed by a waft of perfume, and a group of women crossed the courtyard, dazzling in their coloured gowns. Sharat tripped over his pointed toes as they dodged into one of the alcoves for cover. He turned to Alcherisma in fury.

"Are you crazy?" he hissed. "I'm a *boy*. If I get caught here they'll torture me to death."

"What a shame," muttered Alcherisma.

Aya's face was deathly pale. "Why have we come to the *Zenana*?" she asked him.

There was a smug look on Alcherisma's face. "You wanted to find the Queen of the Forest," he said. "Well, this is where she is."

Sharat turned to Aya. "Now look what you've done," he said. "We've wasted a whole wish."

Aya looked sick. "I'm sorry," she said. "It was a mistake. I would never have come back here on purpose."

"I personally think it was a very good wish," said Alcherisma. "If anyone can help you, it's the Queen of the Forest."

Sharat took a deep breath as he tried to calm down. At least they were inside Shergarh. He glanced at the jinni.

"Where is she, then?" he demanded.

Alcherisma flew towards one of the shady corridors that led off the courtyard. "This way," he said. "But hurry, I don't want to get caught."

Sharat grunted, but he didn't reply. He was having trouble with his slippers.

Despite the gravity of the situation Aya stifled a giggle. "Don't shuffle so much," she told him. "And try and move a little more gracefully."

"It's these stupid shoes," Sharat complained.

"If anyone stops us, just stand still and look pretty," Aya told him.

Sharat gave her a dirty look.

As they hurried down the corridor, they did pass one or two servant girls, but nobody gave them a second glance.

"Everyone important will be asleep now," whispered Aya. "It's the hottest part of the day."

Flitting ahead, Alcherisma led them past several grand archways until they reached a smaller wooden doorway.

"This way," he told them.

Sharat pushed the door open. They stepped into an airy chamber with a cool marble floor. The room was bare of furniture, but an arched doorway led outside.

With a gasp, Aya ran to look. Once there must have been a garden there, but now it was bare. She clung to the doorway.

"What is it?" asked Sharat.

Aya's eyes were shadowed with pain. "These were my *mother's* rooms," she whispered. She turned to

Alcherisma, her face a picture of confusion. "Why have you brought us here?"

"Because the Queen of the Forest is downstairs," said Alcherisma.

"Where?" Aya asked him. "In the cool room?"

"Exactly," said Alcherisma.

"What are you talking about?" said Sharat.

"There's another level under the palace where the court can go to get away from the heat in the summer," Aya explained. She lowered her voice. "There are all kinds of secret passageways down there. It's where the princesses go to meet their *lovers*."

Sharat didn't care about court gossip. All he wanted was to find Emira and get out of here. "Where is it?" he asked.

Aya walked over to an arched door in one of the inner walls. "Through here," she said.

She reached out to turn the handle and pushed. The door creaked open to reveal a stone staircase that led down into the darkness below. A dusty oil lamp stood on the top step.

Sharat glanced at Alcherisma.

"What's the Queen of the Forest doing down there?" he asked.

"She's in an enchanted sleep," the jinni told him.

Aya frowned. "But why did you bring us through here?" she asked. "Why not take us straight to her?"

Alcherisma shook his head. "It's too dangerous," he said. "The Queen is Rookh's prisoner. It's better if one of

162

you goes down on foot and tries to wake her up while the other one stands guard."

Aya caught Sharat's eye. "What do you want to do?" she asked.

His face was set in determination. "I'll go down," he said. "You stay here with Alcherisma. If anyone comes you can wish yourself to safety."

Aya nodded. "All right," she said, "but take the amulet for luck."

Sharat waited as she hung it around his neck. Then he picked up the lamp, but before he could light it, the flame sprung to life of its own accord.

"More magic," he muttered.

He kicked off his pointed shoes.

The stone of the staircase was cold on his bare feet. Carefully, he began to walk down the stairs, ready to snuff out the flame at the first sign of noise, but nothing flew out at him or grabbed him from behind and soon he had reached the bottom.

Slowly, he lifted the lamp.

He was in a large, square room with a tiled floor and a vaulted ceiling. A huge stone urn stood in a niche in one of the walls. Sharat drew closer. Out of the darkness a white face stared up at him. He stifled a scream and jumped back, his heart pounding. Then, when the man didn't move, he braved a step forward and almost laughed in relief. A marble sarcophagus was lying against the wall. On its lid was a life-sized statue of a man.

There was no sign of the Queen of the Forest, but there

163

was a picture above the urn similar to the picture he'd seen in the market of a woman below a tree. Curious, he moved closer, but before he could look at it properly he heard a muffled roar.

His heart leapt. Emira! The sound was coming from a door in the wall behind him. He was just about to hurry towards it when he heard the slap of bare feet running down the stairs and Aya shot into the room with Alcherisma hot on her tail.

"What are you doing down here?" hissed Sharat.

Aya's eyes were wide with terror. "Someone's coming," she gasped. "I think it's Doctor Rookh!"

Sharat felt his guts twist in shock. "What's *Rookh* doing in the *Zenana*?" he demanded.

Alcherisma flew around their heads in a panic. "Who cares?" he yelped. "Wish us all to safety!"

Sharat didn't want to give up. He'd heard Emira roaring. If he wished them out now he might never get another chance to find her.

"I can't go yet," he told Aya. "Emira's down here somewhere. You use the wish. I'm going through here."

He spun around to face the door in the wall.

Aya hesitated.

"Quick!" cried the jinni.

Sharat lunged forward, but before he could reach the door, the handle started turning and he heard voices.

"Too late!" moaned Alcherisma. "Hide!"

With a buzz he disappeared.

As the door began to open, Aya threw herself behind

164

the marble coffin while Sharat snuffed out the oil lamp, pulled off the lid of the urn and leapt inside, frantically tugging the lid shut after him.

Moments later he heard voices and footsteps. Holding his breath, he clenched his fists, sure that he would be discovered, but nothing happened. They didn't know he was here.

Slowly, he started breathing again. The air inside the urn was sweet and spicy and he seemed to have landed on something lumpy, like a bundle of cloth. Grateful that it hadn't been full of oil or wine he wriggled to make a bit more space. But just then, whatever was beneath him let out a sigh.

Sharat froze. In horror, he realised that what he'd taken for a bundle of cloth was in fact a *body*.

Outside he could hear a harsh voice ordering someone around, but, before he could think of what to do next, there was a flurry of movement, and a pair of bony hands reached up to wrap themselves around his waist.

Chapter Twenty-Two

QUEEN

Sharat's pounding heart seemed loud enough to wake the dead, but whatever had reached up to grab him didn't move again. Instead, the arms around his waist slowly relaxed and he heard the sound of gentle breathing.

The creature underneath him was asleep.

With trembling hands he felt behind him and his fingers encountered the smooth skin of an emaciated arm, the crispness of silk, and a tangle of hair. He breathed a sigh of relief. This was no monster. It was just a sleeping woman. But women did not usually sleep in urns. All at once his heart leapt. Could *this* be the Queen of the Forest?

He felt a growing sense of excitement, but just then he heard a sharp voice outside and was thrown to one side as

the urn was heaved off the ground. His body tensed, and the hands around his waist gripped tighter.

Catching his breath, he expected the lid to be pulled off at any moment, but instead the urn landed with a jolt and moments later they began trundling forward.

Trapped in the dark, Sharat wondered what to do next. He thought about the woman underneath him. He felt certain that she must be the Queen of the Forest, but if she was going to help him find Emira he'd have to wake her up. Nervously, he turned to give her a shake.

"Hello? Hello?" he whispered as loudly as he dared.

For a moment she stirred. The movement of her body dredged up more of the spicy smell that filled the urn, but she didn't wake.

Sharat sighed. He should have known that it wouldn't be that easy. After all, she was in an enchanted sleep. In frustration he slumped against the side of the urn.

"I just wish you could help me find Emira!" he said.

There was a moment of silence as the urn rocked gently from side to side. Then, very quietly, the woman began to sing.

Sharat froze, wondering if he'd woken her after all. But then he realised she was singing in her sleep and that the song was in a language that he didn't understand.

Since there was no way to escape, he tried to make himself comfortable. At first he felt awkward, very aware of the woman lying underneath him. Then, to his surprise, she shifted to give him more room, so he curled up next to her and let the sound of her singing wash over him.

Despite his feeling of helplessness, Sharat felt strangely relaxed as the urn trundled slowly forward, but he kept his eyes open, waiting for an opportunity. Then, as he stared up into the darkness, he noticed tiny points of light appearing in front of his eyes. He blinked, wondering if he was imagining things, but soon they began to branch out, like cracks in the shell of an egg, splitting the walls of the urn into a luminous mosaic that flickered in time to the woman's voice.

Curious, he put out his hand to see where the patterns were coming from, but as his fingers touched the inside of the urn, the stone seemed to explode into a thousand pieces and he was bathed in a glow of blue, green and gold. Just then, a fresh breeze hit his face, carrying the smell of flowers and earth.

Rubbing his eyes, he looked around. The urn and the woman beneath him had disappeared. Instead he was lying against the roots of a tree, its branches arching overhead as sun glimmered through the leaves above.

He sat up to take a better look. As he did so, he saw that he was no longer wearing Alcherisma's disguise. Instead he was dressed in a simple white tunic belted at the waist and crowned with a garland of leaves. He was just reaching up to touch his crown when he heard a trilling sound and saw a flash of colour. He blinked. Hovering in front of him was a tiny bird with a silver beak and iridescent blue feathers. For a moment it flitted to and fro, its wings moving so fast that he could hardly see them. Then, once it had his attention, it let out a burst of song.

Sharat could feel magic in the air. Quickly, he jumped to his feet.

"What do you want?" he asked.

The bird trilled again as it flew into a clearing. There it waited in a sunbeam, its body shimmering against the vivid green of the forest.

Certain that he was meant to follow, Sharat hurried to catch up. As he did so he thought he could hear snatches of music carried on the breeze. It sounded like the tune the woman in the urn had been singing, but if he tried to concentrate on it, it slipped away and disguised itself as wind in the leaves or the sound of running water.

The tiny bird led him along a stream towards a grove of trees. Here, the stream formed a loop, almost encircling the space as it babbled past. In the middle of this grove stood a magnificent tree, its canopy of leaves glowing copper-gold as the sun shone through them, and fading to blackish green in the shade. Around its broad trunk grew a vine, bursting with scarlet flowers, and its spreading branches were laden with succulent orange fruits.

With a gasp Sharat started forwards, his mouth watering, but before he could reach the tree, the tiny bird let out a staccato warning and he stopped abruptly, almost falling over himself.

There, half hidden in dappled shadows at his feet, was the body of a woman.

Sharat put out his hand and steadied himself on a branch. For a moment he held his breath, hoping that his blundering approach hadn't disturbed her. Then, when

169

she didn't move or make any sign that she'd heard him, he squatted down to take a better look.

The woman lay on her side, cushioned by moss. Tall, shapely, and very wild looking, her soft, green dress blended with the colours of the forest, and her dark hair tumbled over her face.

Carefully, Sharat reached over and brushed away a strand of her hair, uncovering high cheekbones and a curved nose under strong, dark brows. Her eyes were closed peacefully, as if in sleep. Feeling brave, Sharat put his hand on her shoulder and gave her a shake.

"Wake up!" he whispered.

She didn't move.

Sharat got a sinking feeling at the pit of his stomach. He took her hand, but no matter how hard he tried he couldn't find a pulse. It was as if she had been living only a moment before and he'd arrived just a moment too late. All at once his heart was filled with a sense of inconsolable loss.

Sharat never cried, but here, alone, he couldn't help it. A single tear ran down his cheek and fell on to the woman's lips.

He rubbed his eyes, annoyed with himself. He hadn't cried for Emira, why should he cry for this strange woman? Getting to his feet, he started to walk away, but he had only taken a few steps when suddenly he heard a gasp behind him.

Startled, he turned to look. The woman under the tree had woken up.

For a moment she just yawned and stretched, leaves falling from her hair, but as she caught sight of Sharat, her face broke into a smile.

"Krishna!" she called.

With one graceful move, she was on her feet, hurrying towards him.

Sharat looked quickly behind him. There was no one there.

"I'm not Krishna," he said. "I'm Sharat." He touched his tunic. "I don't know how I ended up in these clothes," he added apologetically.

"Oh!" The woman stopped short. She paused, her eyes lingering on his face. "I'm sorry," she said. "I see now … I thought you were someone else, but of course you can't be." A look of sadness crossed her face. "Krishna is dead."

Sharat didn't know how to reply. Instead he looked at the trees around them and at the magical forests beyond. For the first time it occurred to him how strange it was that he had found himself here. "Where are we?" he asked.

"Don't you know?" said the woman. "This is my home, Aruanda." Just then the tiny bird appeared, its feathers shimmering as it flitted around her head. She lifted her hand and it landed on her finger.

Sharat's heart leapt as he remembered the picture in the market. "Are *you* the Queen of the Forest?" he said.

The woman smiled. "That's what they call me," she said softly. "I have many names."

Sharat felt a thrill of excitement, but he wasn't sure

he understood.

"If you're the Queen of the Forest, then what are you doing here?" he asked. "I thought you were Doctor Rookh's prisoner."

The Queen sighed. "Yes, I'm afraid that's true," she said. "Unfortunately all this is only a dream."

With one part of his mind Sharat knew he must be asleep, but the smells of the forest were unmistakeable. He reached over to touch a branch. The bark was rough under his fingers and the leaves caressed his arm. "It doesn't *feel* like a dream," he said.

"That's because it's not your dream," the Queen told him. "It's mine."

At last Sharat understood. "So you *are* the woman in the urn!" he exclaimed.

"Is that where he's keeping me?" murmured the Queen.

"Yes," said Sharat. "That's how I found you. I climbed into your urn to hide from Doctor Rookh." He frowned. "But what am I doing in your dream?" Suddenly he felt a thrill of hope. "Are you going to grant my wish?"

The Queen hesitated. "That depends," she said. "What did you wish for?"

Sharat swallowed, trying to contain his excitement. "I wished you would help me find my tiger," he said.

All of a sudden the Queen's eyes widened. "Tiger?" she said. "What tiger?"

"She's a white tiger," Sharat explained. "We worked together at the circus, but ... but now Rookh's got her." As he spoke he could feel tears welling up inside him.

172

Angrily he bit his lip, but the Queen had already seen his expression. A look of shock crossed her face.

"Oh!" she cried. "My poor child!"

Stepping forward, she took him into her arms. It was too much for Sharat. Something in her touch brought his tears springing to the surface, and at last he allowed himself to cry while the Queen murmured words of comfort. Afterwards she let him go.

"Tell me exactly what happened," she said as she wiped away his tears.

Feeling calmer, Sharat explained how the circus had come to town, and how Emira had disappeared while they were performing for the Emperor. As he was speaking, the Queen frowned.

"Did you say *Mohini* brought the circus to the city?" she demanded.

"Yes," said Sharat. "Do you know her?"

"Of course I know her," said the Queen. "She was my best friend." For a moment she looked confused. "But why would she betray me to Rookh?"

Sharat shook his head. "I don't know," he said miserably. "All I want is to get my tiger back."

The Queen's eyes flashed. "And so you will," she said. "The question is *how*?"

Sharat felt confused. "Can't you help me with magic?" he asked.

The Queen let out a sigh of frustration. "I wish I could," she said. "But while I'm Rookh's prisoner, my powers don't extend beyond the world of dreams."

Sharat's heart sank. "What am I going to do?" he cried. "If I don't rescue Emira, Rookh's sure to kill her."

The Queen lifted her hand. "Wait!" she said. "*I* may not be able to help, but there could still be a way for you to rescue your tiger."

"How?" said Sharat.

There was a thoughtful look on the Queen's face. "There is still one free jinni in the City of Jewels," she said. "If you can find him you might stand a chance."

"Who is he?" asked Sharat.

The Queen's eyes were dark with mystery. "He's called the Prince of Jinnis," she said.

Sharat bit his lip. So Aya had been right. He felt a moment of regret when he thought of the wasted wish.

"I've heard of the Prince of Jinnis," he admitted. "Someone told me that a white tiger is supposed to lead him back to the city."

The Queen stiffened. "Who told you that?" she asked.

"A girl called Aya," said Sharat. "She's helping me find Emira."

"Aya?" said the Queen sharply. "Where is *she*?"

Sharat felt a pang of guilt. "She's hiding from Doctor Rookh," he said. "Just like me."

The Queen took a deep breath. "Make sure you find her again," she said. "You'll need her help."

Sharat nodded. He knew he needed Aya. After all, they still had one more wish, and she was the only friend he had in this city, but he was still thinking about the Prince of Jinnis. "So is it true?" he asked. "Is Emira the tiger

174

from the prophecy?"

The Queen nodded. "Yes, that is true," she said, "but the time for the prophecy to be fulfilled is yet to come. All you need to do now is find the Prince of Jinnis. He's the only one who's strong enough to rescue your tiger."

Sharat's heart was torn. "But what's his connection to Emira?" he asked, unable to hide his anxiety. "Does ... does Emira belong to him?"

The Queen's eyes softened in understanding. "No," she said. "Emira only belongs to you."

Gently, she reached out to take his hand. "Don't worry," she reassured him. "You don't need to be afraid of the Prince of Jinnis. Together you'll rescue Emira, and who knows, perhaps one day you'll even help him rescue *me*."

Her words and touch were like a balm. Sharat felt his resistance melt.

"But where is this Prince of Jinnis?" he asked.

The Queen shook her head. "I'm afraid I can't say exactly where he is," she said. "He's protected by a spell that even I can't break. All I can tell you is that there's a sanctuary deep below the city, a place of magic. You'll find him there."

Sharat swallowed. More magic. But now he felt a sense of excitement.

"How will I find this sanctuary?" he said.

"If you're with me you're almost there," said the Queen. "Don't be afraid. Keep to the left, stay off the beaten track and use your senses." She reached up into the branches of the tree above and plucked one of the

fruits that were hanging there.

"Here," she said, pressing it into his hand. "Eat this, it will help you find your way."

Sharat's mouth watered as the fragrant smell of the fruit filled his nostrils, but he didn't take a bite. "What am I supposed to do when I find this sanctuary?" he said.

"You don't need to do anything," the Queen told him. "Once you reach the sanctuary, Vasuki will do the rest."

As she spoke, the earth seemed to tremble underfoot and the leaves shivered in the trees above. Sharat felt his hair standing on end. "Vasuki?" he said. "Who's *he*?"

"Not he," said the Queen. "It."

There was a mysterious look on her face as she opened her mouth to explain, but before she could say a single word, they heard the sound of a caw and a dark shadow flew overhead. Taking a sharp breath, she seized Sharat's hand and pulled him under the tree.

"What is it?" asked Sharat.

"It's Rookh!" said the Queen. "He must have heard us speaking."

Again, they heard the sound of a caw. This time the Queen let out a cry of pain as her hands flew to her neck.

"What's happening?" asked Sharat in alarm.

The Queen looked like she was being choked. "He's trying to silence me!" she gasped. "He must have opened the urn."

Sharat had almost forgotten that this was all a dream. His heart skipped a beat.

"What are we going to do?" he cried.

The Queen was struggling to breathe. She clutched his arm. "You have to get away!" she said, her voice strained. "Find the Prince of Jinnis. It's our only hope!"

Sharat stared at her in dismay. Suddenly he didn't want to leave the Queen and her beautiful garden. "But what about you?" he asked. "I can't just leave you behind."

"Don't worry about me," whispered the Queen. "Just remember, keep left … off the beaten track, and … and…" She began to sway.

Sharat put out a hand to steady her. "And what?" he asked.

The Queen's face was white. "When you find the Prince ask… Ai!" she gasped. She fell to her knees.

Sharat's heart was pounding. "Ask what?" he said urgently.

"Ask… Ai!" she gasped again as she reached up to clutch his hand.

Sharat could see that her mouth was moving. Desperately he bent his head to hear what she was trying to say. But before another word could pass her lips, she gave one final convulsion and the only sound to escape her mouth was a final "Ahhh…" as she collapsed, lifeless at his feet.

Moments later her world began to disintegrate as leaves began to wither and fall, exposing the bare skeleton of the tree above.

"Wait!" cried Sharat, seizing the Queen's shoulders in desperation.

But it was no use. She was as still and lifeless as she'd

been when he'd first found her.

"Please ... don't go!" he whispered.

As he spoke, scorching winds blasted through the landscape, and with a rumble of thunder, a crack of lightning split the mighty tree at the centre of the clearing in two. Suddenly the whole dream was plunged into black and white. Only the fruit in Sharat's hand stood out, shining orange in a single beam of sunlight that penetrated the black clouds above.

Spotting its prize, the monstrous crow let out a shriek of triumph. Then it dived, bringing with it the stench of decay.

"No!" gasped Sharat.

In fury, he stuffed the fruit in his mouth, almost choking on the seed as he swallowed it whole. Suddenly he was back in the urn. Then, before he had time to think, a pair of hands reached in to grab him, and he was thrown roughly to the ground.

Chapter Twenty-Three

GHULS

Feeling dazed, Sharat was hauled to his feet by two hooded creatures with glinting eyes and long, white robes. Ghuls.

They were in a tunnel lit by flares. Most of the tunnel was filled by the cart that was carrying the urn. Next to it was Doctor Rookh. With a sharp movement he slammed down the lid. Then, robes swirling, he swung around to face Sharat. His skin looked pallid by the light of the flickering flames, and his face was icy calm as he stepped forward.

"So," he said. "What do we have here?"

For the first time Sharat felt grateful for Alcherisma's disguise. He lowered his eyes, praying that Rookh wouldn't guess who he was, but Rookh seized his chin.

179

"Look at me, girl!" he snapped as he forced Sharat's head up.

Sharat flinched. Rookh's pale, inhuman gaze sent shivers running up and down his spine. He felt like a mouse trapped by a snake.

Rookh's mouth twitched. "Trying to escape, were you?" he said. "Haven't you heard? Nobody escapes from the *Zenana*."

Sharat bit his lip. Just then, Rookh froze as he spotted the amulet. Roughly, he seized the jewel.

"Where did you get this?" he demanded.

Sharat's mind was racing, but he kept his eyes lowered.

"It … it was in the urn," he whispered. "There was a *woman*." He swallowed. "I … I found it around her neck."

A look of disgust crossed Rookh's face. "So," he said. "You're a thief as well as a runaway." With a sharp movement he snapped the cord and dangled the amulet in front of Sharat. "Do you realise I could have you killed for taking this?"

There was a moan from the front of the cart. It was the sound of despair.

"Please don't kill me, sir," Sharat begged.

Rookh stuffed the jewel into the folds of his robe.

"Don't worry," he said. "You're much more useful to me alive than dead."

He motioned to the ghuls. "Tie her up!"

Silently, the ghuls stepped forward and lifted Sharat off the ground.

His flesh shrank from their touch as they wrenched back his arms, but he didn't lose his head. As they tied his wrists behind his back he twisted his hands and tightened his fists.

"Let me go!" he said.

His voiceless captors seemed not to hear him. Still holding his arms, they carried him past the urn. The cart was laden with treasures from the cool room. With a start he recognised Aya's hiding place, the marble coffin, but before he could think about his friend he heard another moan. Bound together at the front of the cart were three wretched children – two boys and a girl.

The ghuls hauled Sharat on to the cart and tied him up with the others.

"Don't make any more mistakes," Rookh warned them.

The ghuls stared at him emotionlessly as he lifted his staff. Then, with a swirl of his robes he was gone.

At a signal from the ghuls, the cart started moving. Pulling it was a strange mechanical creature with bowed iron legs and the mournful face of a donkey. Sharat glanced at his fellow prisoners. The boys had their heads bowed listlessly and hardly noticed him, but the girl was glaring at him.

It was Nara, the sewer-girl.

Sharat looked away quickly, but it was too late. Nara had already seen him. Her face broke into a nasty smile.

"Hey! You!" she said. "Tiger boy!"

Sharat didn't answer.

With a sneer, Nara looked him up and down. "You're

very pretty," she said. "Where did you get the fancy clothes? At the circus?"

Sharat kept his head bowed and his mouth shut, praying that no one had heard her.

Nara wasn't going to be put off. She leaned in closer. "You know it's your fault I'm down here," she said, her voice heavy with threat. "When you got away, the ghuls came for *me* instead."

Sharat glanced at their captors, but the ghuls were paying no attention to the conversation.

"They got me, too," he said, keeping his voice low. "That's why I'm here. I was trying to run away."

"You're lying!" said Nara. "I bet you got caught looking for that white tiger of yours." The look she gave him was challenging and triumphant.

Sharat felt his blood run cold. He was sure Nara would find a way to use her knowledge against him. For a moment he panicked. How was he going to find Emira *now*? He glanced at the tunnel all around him.

"Where are we going?" he asked.

Nara shrugged. "We're being taken to the mines," she said. She lowered her voice. "They say Rookh has thousands of slaves working for him down there. It's like an underground kingdom." Her eyes glinted.

"You sound like you're looking forward to it," muttered Sharat.

"Oh, I won't be a slave for long," Nara told him. "I know how to make myself useful. Rookh will want people like me who know how to take charge."

182

Sharat shivered at the ruthless determination in her voice. His eyes darted about, looking for a way out, but it was impossible to know how far this warren of tunnels might extend. All he knew was that he had to get away.

His fingers had been fiddling with the rope behind his back ever since being tied up. Now he relaxed his arms completely, taking care not to touch any of the other prisoners. With a twist, he pulled one of his hands out of the loop. Then he freed the other hand. Despite his dire situation he smiled to himself in satisfaction. Bhim the magician had taught him that trick years ago. He'd never thought he would need it.

Don't ever try tying up a circus brat, he thought as he kept his hands hidden behind his back.

"If we're going to be working in the mines I'm going to get some sleep," he told Nara, feigning a yawn.

Nara shrugged. "Do what you like," she said, but she kept her eyes on him, suspicious.

Sharat rested his head on his knees and tried to keep his breathing steady, but he was watching for any opportunity to escape. In front of him lay the marble sarcophagus. The sculpture on the lid stared up at him lifelessly, but there was a smaller figure hidden under the man's cloak that Sharat hadn't noticed before. As his eyes rested on the statue he saw a flicker of movement.

Before he could react, a little face peered out from behind the cloak.

Sharat stifled a cry. It was Aya.

Aya's eyes widened and she pressed a finger urgently

183

to her lips. As she moved, colour shimmered back to her skin, fading away as she became still. Sharat blinked to indicate that he'd seen her. Then he carefully pulled out the hand furthest from Nara to show her that he was free.

Nara spun round and caught him at it.

"What are you doing?" she snapped.

Sharat had no choice. He had to get away. Now.

He flicked the rope from his wrists into Nara's face and threw himself over to grab Aya's hand. As he touched her she sprang fully back to life and together they jumped off the moving cart to the ground.

"Escape! Prisoner escape!" called Nara, her voice harsh.

The ghuls lifted their flares, eyes glinting beneath their hoods, but Sharat wasn't about to let them catch him.

"Don't look back," he gasped at Aya. "Run!"

Then, keeping a tight grip on her hand, he took off into the darkness as fast as his feet could carry him.

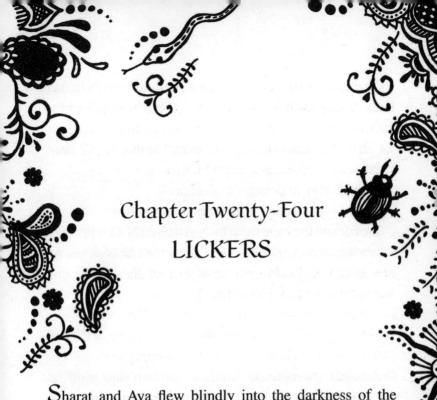

Chapter Twenty-Four
LICKERS

Sharat and Aya flew blindly into the darkness of the tunnel ahead. Behind them a glimmer of light showed them that the ghuls were in hot pursuit.

"They're catching up!" cried Aya as she stumbled forward.

Just then the shadow of one of the ghuls shot down the corridor towards them. Aya stifled a scream, but Sharat pulled her close with a quick movement.

"Get on my back!" he hissed.

She clung to his shoulders as he threw himself towards one of the walls, desperately feeling for cracks as he pulled himself up. He just managed to lift his knees to his chest, when their pursuers sped past.

His trembling fingers felt like they would snap, and

his arms were burning, but he hung on until the light had faded away down the tunnels. Finally he dropped to the floor and Aya tumbled off his back.

"Quickly," he said, his voice barely audible. "We need to get away before they come back."

"Which way?" gasped Aya.

Sharat's head was spinning. His meeting with the Queen of the Forest was already starting to fade, just like any other dream. All he could remember was that they had to stay to the left. He took hold of Aya's hand and felt for the wall. To his relief the passageway branched into two.

"This way," he said, pulling her down the left-hand path.

Running through the darkness, he kept his hand on the wall as a guide. At every corner he kept expecting the ghuls to leap out and catch them, but the tunnel was empty. Soon he could feel Aya struggling to keep up, so he slowed down to a walk.

He caught his breath. "I think we've lost them," he whispered.

Aya clutched his arm as she stumbled along beside him. She was breathing heavily. "I'm so glad I found you!" she said. "I didn't know what I was going to do when they started moving the urn."

"How did you get inside that statue?" asked Sharat.

"As soon as I jumped behind it to hide, the man on the lid came to life and pulled me in," Aya told him.

"Another jinni!" said Sharat.

186

"Maybe," said Aya, but she didn't sound too certain.

"What about you?" she asked. "Did Rookh catch you?"

Sharat couldn't wait to tell Aya all about the Queen of the Forest, but just as he was about to speak, he felt a gap opening up in the wall to his left. He stopped, dropping Aya's hand.

"Just a minute!" he said. "What's this?"

Feeling around, he felt the earth crumble under his fingers. The gap widened, but the way through was blocked by rubble. His heart leapt. "I think it's a passageway!" he said.

Aya was already checking for herself. "That's not a passageway," she said. "It's just a hole in the wall." Impatiently, she moved away.

"Wait!" said Sharat. But before he could explain, he heard her stifle a gasp.

"What is it?" he asked.

"I can see light!" she hissed. "Look!"

Leaving the gap in the wall, Sharat hurried to catch up. As he peered up ahead, he could just make out a faint glow in the darkness.

"Maybe it's a way out," whispered Aya.

Sharat hesitated. He knew that to rescue Emira he had to find the Prince of Jinnis, but he could feel himself being drawn towards the light.

"Let's have a look, then," he said.

As they moved closer, they began to make out each other's faces and the rough walls of the corridor. At the same time, a strange scuttling sound reached their ears.

187

"What's that?" breathed Aya.

Just then they turned a corner and were blinded by a beam of sunlight that shone down from a circular hole in the roof. As their eyes came into focus, they saw that the walls were swarming with hundreds of creatures that were crawling up out of a well in the floor, all glittering in the golden light as they flew for the surface. A streak of ruby fire shot in front of their faces and there was an angry clicking sound.

Aya's breath caught in her throat. "Lickers!" she gasped as a cluster of glowing eyes turned in their direction. "Run!"

In a panic they spun around and sprinted back the way they'd come, but the lickers were already bearing down on them.

"This way!" yelled Sharat, desperately feeling for the gap.

Flashes of red light shot straight at them as they scrabbled at the rubble blocking the way. Just in time, the earth gave way and they tumbled through the wall as the ceiling collapsed behind them.

Sharat caught his breath as he lay on his back, but they weren't out of danger yet. Three of the missiles had made it into the crumbling passageway with them. He could see them hovering above, their eyes shining as they scanned the floor.

"Stay still!" gasped Aya, gripping the first part of Sharat she could find, which happened to be his foot.

"Wait!" breathed Sharat. "I'm going to try and

188

catch them."

With tiny movements, he unravelled the chiffon scarf from around his neck and hooked his earrings to the corners. One of the missiles zoomed in and Aya dug her fingers angrily into his big toe. Sharat froze and waited until the lickers hovered above him again, three pairs of eyes watching from the darkness. He jumped to his feet.

"Over here!" he yelled.

The three dived as one, but Sharat was ready for them. He threw up the weighted scarf, tangling the insects in its flimsy cloth. Then, before they could react, he caught both ends and smashed it to the ground again and again until the whirring stopped.

"Got you!" he said.

Keeping a tight grip, he examined his catch. He had caught three mechanical beetles. Two were still and the fire in their eyes had died, but the third lay there twitching, its eyes still blazing. He snatched up a rock to finish it off.

Aya put out her hand. "Don't!" she cried. "We can use the light to find our way."

Sharat glanced at Aya. "Good idea!" he said.

Dropping the rock, he bound the beetle's legs to its body. Then he lifted the bundle and the creature's eyes burned with fury, exposing the stone walls that surrounded them.

Aya crawled over to check the way they had come in. When she turned back to Sharat her face was frightened.

"The ceiling's collapsed," she said.

"Good," said Sharat. "That means no more of Rookh's bugs can get us."

189

Aya stared at him in horror. Her face was pale.

"But we're trapped," she said. "This isn't even a proper passageway, it's more like a *cave*."

"That's what we're looking for," said Sharat. "We've got to get off the beaten track."

At last he told her about his meeting with the Queen of the Forest.

As he spoke, a look of triumph crossed Aya's face.

"So we *do* have to find the Prince of Jinnis," she said.

"Yes, you were right all along," admitted Sharat. "He's the only one who can help us rescue Emira."

"Let's call Alcherisma!" said Aya. "I bet he'll be able to help."

With a sinking heart, Sharat put a hand to his throat. "It's no good," he said. "Rookh's got the amulet. He took it when he caught me."

He heard Aya take a sharp breath.

"What are we going to do?" she said.

Sharat frowned as he tried to recall the Queen's instructions. "All I know is that we have to stay to the left," he said. "We're looking for some kind of sanctuary."

Aya looked thoughtful. "One of the legends about the Prince says he's sleeping deep beneath the city," she remembered.

"In that case we must be on the right track," said Sharat, "but before we go any further let me take this stupid costume off. I don't want to meet the Prince of Jinnis dressed as a *princess*."

Aya managed a nervous giggle, and Sharat smiled

190

weakly back. But as he wedged the licker under a stone and stripped down to his loincloth, he still couldn't help feeling a little nervous about meeting the Prince of Jinnis. Swallowing down his fears, he picked up the licker again. He had to be strong. After all, only the Prince could help him stand up to Rookh. And besides, the Queen had said Emira was *his*.

"Which way?" asked Aya.

"The Queen told me to use my senses," said Sharat.

Aya had already moved away and was doing some exploring with her hands. "I think there's a way down here," she said, crouching to get a better look.

Quickly, Sharat hurried over. For a moment he caught a glimpse of a hole leading down into the darkness beyond. But no sooner had the light of the licker's ruby eyes touched the rock, than the earth began to tremble. Then, before either of them could do anything, the ground jerked beneath them and they lost their footing as a crack appeared at their feet.

Aya screamed.

Next to her, Sharat felt himself tumbling out of control. He threw out his hands.

"Hold on!" he gasped as the crack widened.

But there was nothing to hold on to.

Arms flailing, Sharat fell blindly into the darkness, stones falling around him like rain. Down, down and down he spun. For a terrible moment it felt as though the fall would never end. Then, finally, he landed with a thump and everything was still.

191

Chapter Twenty-Five

LOST

Sharat lifted his head, but when he tried to move he discovered that his arms were stuck. The landslide had almost buried him alive.

Struggling to loosen the blanket of rubble that pinned him down, he managed to pull himself free.

"Aya?" he called out weakly.

There was no reply.

Gasping for breath, Sharat was wracked by a fit of coughing. He rubbed his eyes. It was completely dark. The licker was nowhere to be seen.

"Aya?" he called out, loudly this time. "Where are you?"

Still there was no reply.

Stumbling on the uneven surface underfoot, Sharat felt around. On all sides his hands met stone. He really was in

a cave now, there was no mistaking it. But where was Aya?

With a feeling of panic, he threw himself into digging through the rubble until he came to a layer where the boulders were wedged tight. Finally, after almost breaking his fingers he fell back against the wall. He was all alone.

"Aya! Please give me a sign that you're alive!" he cried again in desperation.

Nothing happened.

Sharat had never felt so lost. First Emira and now Aya. It seemed as though everything was against him. In despair he slid down the wall. Silent tears wet his cheeks, but he no longer cared. Putting his head in his hands he curled up in a little ball and let them flow.

Just then he became aware of a gust of wind blowing insistently against his face.

At first it hardly registered. But as the wind blew a little harder, his mind began to clear.

All at once he sat up with a gasp.

If there was air blowing into the cave it could only mean one thing. There must be a way out. And if there was a way out, perhaps there was still a chance of finding Emira!

Taking a deep breath, he wiped his eyes and pulled himself to his feet. He was rewarded by another gust of wind. Raising his arms he realised it was coming from overhead so, feeling a growing sense of determination, he reached up and began to climb. To his relief he found a gap in the rock.

For a moment he stopped, turning back to the cave.

"Aya! I'm going to find the Prince of Jinnis, but I promise I'll come back and get you," he called.

Again there was no reply, but praying that he would find a way to make his promise come true, Sharat pushed aside his grief and began to feel his way along.

It was difficult going. The space between the rocks was narrow and jagged. Several times he almost got stuck, and then he fell, hurting himself quite badly.

Cursing, he sat up and clutched his injured knee, but this time, instead of despairing, he found himself getting angry with the Queen of the Forest.

"Why did you send me this way?" he gasped. "Why?"

Glaring out into empty space, he clenched his fists, but then his anger turned to excitement as he noticed a dim red glow opening up a crack in the darkness up ahead.

Pain forgotten, Sharat got to his feet and clambered towards the light. As he eased himself through a crack in the rock, he found himself clinging to the walls of a great cavern. He couldn't see the ground, but as he gazed up in wonder he saw that the dome overhead was lined with a web of branching cords that glowed like the embers of a dying fire. Carefully, he pulled himself on to a ledge and reached up to touch one of the branches. Whatever it was felt flexible and strong, almost like leather. With a start he realised that he was looking up at the roots of some ancient tree. But before he could investigate further, the silence was split by a burst of rippling music and the walls of the cavern lit up with a flash of colour.

Freezing, Sharat looked around, seeking the source of

194

this dancing light. With a thrill he noticed that the rocks themselves were lighting up in time to the music, but these weren't just any rocks; they were jewels, and with every note that pierced the darkness more and more of the cavern was illuminated by massive crystal formations that hung from the ceiling and encrusted the walls.

Just then he heard an inhuman shriek and saw a flash of gold come shooting towards him.

The licker! Still alive.

As the mechanical insect made a beeline for his eyes, Sharat lost his balance. Arms flailing, he thought he was sure to fall when one of the glowing cords detached itself from the dome above and dropped into the palm of his hand.

Without thinking, his fingers closed around the root, and he swung away from the wall while the licker smashed into the rock behind him and tumbled into the abyss.

Swinging wildly, Sharat held on tight, his head spinning while the music echoed around him. Then all of a sudden the music stopped, and he heard a voice calling up from below.

"Sharat!" it cried. "Is that you?"

Chapter Twenty-Six
CRYSTAL CAVE

Sharat could hardly believe his ears.

Peering down at the cavern floor, he caught sight of the most spectacular outcrop of all. An enormous geode had split open like an oyster-shell to form a pool lined with sparkling diamonds. Next to the pool stood a small figure with a mop of curly hair.

Sharat felt his heart leap. "Aya!" he called out. "You're alive!"

With a final swing, he let go of the root and dropped into the water with a splash.

As he bobbed to the surface, Aya was waiting for him at the edge of the pool. Her clothes were wet, but she was grinning broadly.

"I thought you were dead!" said Sharat as he swam

over. "How did you get down here?"

Aya laughed. Her hair hung in curling tendrils around her face, her eyes were bright and her cheeks were flushed. "The earth cracked open and I fell straight into this pool," she said.

Sharat pulled himself up to sit next to her. "You're shining," he said.

"It's the water," Aya told him. "Try some!"

Sharat bent down to drink his fill. The water tasted pure and clean, and as he drank a sense of wild hope rose up inside him.

He looked around. The fiery roots that traced the cavern's dome were pulsating gently as they meandered between the twinkling rocks. It felt as though they had landed inside the heart of some living being.

"This must be the sanctuary the Queen mentioned," he said.

Aya's eyes shone. "That's what I thought, too."

"What was that music?" asked Sharat. "It sounded like the rocks were singing."

A secretive look came across Aya's face. She shook her head. "It wasn't the rocks," she said, clutching her bag to her chest.

Sharat eyed her suspiciously. "What have you got in there?" he demanded. Playfully, he reached over to grab it.

"Careful!" cried Aya. She tried to snatch it back, but Sharat was too quick for her. He held the bag out of her reach. Then, before she could protest, he opened it up and

pulled out an oval drum. On the surface two silver hands were folded demurely together.

Sharat took a sharp breath. "Fonke's instrument!" he said, looking at Aya in shock.

Aya's lips tightened. "It's not Fonke's," she said. "It's *mine*. My mother gave it to me when I escaped from the *Zenana*. Nara must have stolen it when she rescued me from the sewers."

"*That's* why you were hiding in the market," said Sharat.

Just then the silver hands began to unfold cautiously. One of the fingers reached out to touch him, then pulled away quickly.

He almost dropped the instrument in shock. "It's alive!"

"It started moving as soon as I got out of the pool," said Aya. "It was telling me what to play."

Sharat's eyes widened. "You must have brought the jewels to life!"

"I know," said Aya. "It woke them up, just like it woke up the ghosts in Fonke's shop."

Sharat glanced around the cavern. "I wonder if we could use it to wake the Prince of Jinnis?" he said.

"We have to find him first," said Aya. She jumped to her feet. "Come on! Let's explore!"

Sharat hesitated. "I'm not sure we can find him on our own," he said. "I think we're supposed to have help."

"What kind of help?" asked Aya.

Sharat frowned as he tried to remember the dream. "The Queen didn't have time to explain," he said. "All

198

she mentioned was a name. I think it was *Vasuki*."

"Vasuki?" said Aya. "Who's *that?*"

As she spoke, they felt a rumble in the earth and bubbles began to rise up out of the pool at their feet.

"What's happening?" said Aya, staring down into the crystal depths of the pool.

The water was starting to churn now, as if stirred by an invisible spoon. With a hiss something sleek and black broke the surface.

With a cry of recognition, Sharat grabbed Aya and pulled her back.

"Watch out!" he said. "It's a snake!"

The head of a mighty serpent shot out of the pool, black on one side and white on the other. Its face was stretched in a hungry gape, but just when it seemed that the mouth could open no wider, the head split in half, until there were not one, but two serpents rising up out of the swirling water.

Aya's eyes took on a look of terror. "Two snakes!" she cried. "Run!"

Turning, she tried to find a way through the wall of crystals that rose up steeply around the pool. "Ow!" she cried as she almost cut herself on the jewels.

Sharat's heart was pounding in fear. "This way," he gasped, grabbing her hand as he desperately tried to find a gap in the rocks. But no matter which way he turned, he was blocked by the glittering gems.

"There's no way out!" cried Aya, clutching Sharat's arm.

For a moment they stared at each other in horror. Then, realising that they had no choice, they spun around to face the monster in the pool.

Chapter Twenty-Seven
VASUKI

Rearing up out of the water, the serpent's heavy coils glistened in the light of the crystal cave. One side of the serpent was black, the other was white, and a scarlet tongue flicked from each of its mouths. With a ripple of pure muscle it half slithered out of the water, the bottom half of its coils still intertwined, while its upper halves swung around to face Sharat and Aya, glaring down at them with unblinking green eyes.

"We are Vasuki, Primordial Naga, holder of ssspace and time, and creator and destroyer of life," the snakes hissed in unison. "Who dares to call us here from the depths of the earth?"

Sharat and Aya pressed themselves against the wall of gems that trapped them at the edge of the pool as the

two serpents fixed them in their sights. Sharat's heart was pounding, but he knew he was going to have to say something.

"It was me," he said, trying not to let his voice shake.

The snakes narrowed their eyes, their tongues flicking as they turned to inspect him. "Human beings?" they whispered. "What are *you* doing in this sssanctuary?"

Sharat took a deep breath. "The Queen of the Forest sent me," he said.

The snakes eyed Sharat and Aya with increased interest. "How ssssweet of her," hissed the pale serpent, his voice deep and masculine. A drip of saliva dropped from his mouth as it widened in a grin. He turned towards his dark twin. "Look, sssister," he said. "One each!"

Sharat felt a pang of alarm. "No, no! It's nothing like that," he said quickly. "The Queen told me you'd help me."

There was a glimmer of disappointment in the pale serpent's eyes. "I sssee," he said. "What a shhhame." He swung his head around to examine Aya. "What about this one?" he whispered.

Aya shrank back in horror.

Sharat put out a protective hand. "She's with me," he said sharply.

Both heads turned towards Sharat again. He tried not to draw back as their delicate tongues tickled the skin of his face.

"Sssweet little things," whispered the dark snake, her voice softer and more gentle than that of her brother.

"Look at them, they're only children." She peered down at them. "But why would the Queen of the Forest sssend you to us?"

Sharat felt dizzy as he looked up into the serpent's glittering eyes. "I'm looking for the Prince of Jinnis," he said.

"Why would *you* be ssseeking the Prince of Jinnis?" hissed the snakes.

Sharat swallowed. "My tiger's been stolen," he said. "She's a prisoner of Doctor Rookh."

The pale head let out a hiss of disgust. "We know this *human*," he said. "Even now his ssslaves are looking for this cave."

"Then help me find the Prince of Jinnis!" said Sharat. "He's the only one who's strong enough to defeat him."

The serpents hesitated as they considered this. Then the dark side spoke. "It is possible that we may help you find the Prince of Jinnis," she said. "But first you must answer our riddle."

Sharat cleared his throat. "The Queen never said anything about a riddle," he said. "What if I get the answer wrong?"

As he spoke the pale serpent's mouth opened a little wider and its eyes gleamed hungrily. "If you fail to guess the answer, then you must offer yourself, and your sssweet, sssucculent little sssister as a sssacrifice," he hissed.

Sharat felt his heart contract. He glanced anxiously over at Aya. Her face was pinched with fear as she stared

at the writing serpents.

"I've got to *try*," he said. "It's my only way of saving Emira."

Aya tore her gaze away and caught his eye. "I'm … I'm sure the Queen wouldn't have sent you here if she thought you would fail," she said, trying to sound convincing.

Swallowing, Sharat turned back to Vasuki. "All right, then," he said. "I'll answer your riddle."

The twin serpents reared into the air, writhing. "Are you sssure?" they asked.

Sharat nodded. "Yes, I'm sure," he said.

Vasuki's eyes glowed and the heads began to sway. "Very well," they said. "Riddle us this and riddle us that."

And then they began to speak, each one of them alternating lines in their soft, sibilant voices.

> *"I'm a riddle for time, a riddle for space,*
> *A riddle that reveals a hidden place.*
> *My riddle's a doorway, my riddle bears fruit,*
> *My riddle will root out the lies from the truth.*
> *My lower seeks earth, my upper seeks light,*
> *I dance in the wind and breathe at night,*
> *I drink with the moon and feed on the sun,*
> *Within me heaven and earth become one."*

As they spoke, Vasuki's voice became hypnotic, and the serpents began to slither out of the pool, wrapping themselves around Sharat's body, overlapping each other until they were holding him tightly in their embrace.

Sharat held his breath. Soon the snakes' heads swung just centimetres from his face.

"Ssso … what am I?" they hissed into his ears.

Sharat tried to ignore the coils that were surrounding him as he squeezed his eyes shut to think.

A riddle for time, a riddle for space, a riddle that reveals a hidden place.

Something someone had told him was edging at his memory. What was it?

My riddle's a doorway, my riddle bears fruit, my riddle will root out the lies from the truth.

Sharat opened his eyes. Vasuki's twin heads were still staring hungrily at him.

My lower seeks earth, my upper seeks light, I dance in the wind and breathe at night.

He cast his eyes up and caught sight of the luminous roots that still glowed in the domed ceiling of the cavern above.

I drink with the moon and feed on the sun, within me heaven and earth become one.

Just then Sharat remembered the Queen in her garden, shadowed by leaves, and suddenly he knew the answer to Vasuki's riddle.

He looked over at Aya. Her face was tense, waiting for his answer.

"It a tree!" he said, his voice shaking. "It *must* be. Trees have their roots in the earth and their branches reach for the light."

"Yes!" said Aya, her voice light with relief. "That's

exactly what I thought. Also, Uma told me she waters her trees at night. It stops them drying up."

Vasuki slowly loosened its coils from around Sharat's body. For a moment of terror Sharat felt sure they were going to eat him. Then, all of a sudden there was a shiver of magic as the snakes disappeared and in their place stood a man and woman.

Tall and well formed, the couple had a sinuous grace. Neither of them had any hair but they were covered in fine scale-like markings that traced their skin and continued down the tight sheaths that encased their bodies. They would have been a matching pair, but the man was as pale as the moon and the woman was darkest ebony.

The woman turned her emerald gaze to Sharat.

"A tree is the correct answer," she said.

Sharat felt his shoulders drop and he threw Aya a quick smile, but he knew it wasn't over yet.

"How do I find the Prince of Jinnis?" he said, glancing at the man and woman on either side.

Now that they were in human form they weren't quite as frightening, but Sharat still shrank back as they seized his hands. Their grasp was cool and muscular.

"Gaze into the pool and tell it your desire," the dark woman whispered in his ear. "Only then will you find what you seek."

"I knew it was a magic pool!" exclaimed Aya.

Sharat looked down. The water in the crystal pool was perfectly clear and still. Light shimmered up from the stones below and he could see Aya's reflection behind

him. As he caught her eye she gave him a quick smile of encouragement and he took a deep breath.

"I'm looking for the Prince of Jinnis," he said. "Where is he?"

Just then, the water began to shiver, breaking up the surface into tiny ripples. Then, slowly, all the reflections died down and the pool became still and black, and Sharat peered into the depths. With a thrill of excitement he saw the figure of a boy appear out of the darkness and begin walking towards him.

"There's someone coming!" he said, glancing up.

"Keep watching!" hissed the pale man.

The figure in the pool strode forward. Then he lifted his head.

Aya gasped.

Sharat stared down at the vision in front of him. He was surprised to see that it was just a boy, perhaps only a year or so older than himself, crowned with leaves and robed in white. He leaned closer.

"Are you the Prince of Jinnis?" he asked.

As he spoke he could see the boy's mouth moving.

"What are you doing?" said Sharat urgently. "Come here! I need your help."

Again the boy seemed to be mouthing something.

Sharat shifted and the boy in the pool shifted, too. It was as if he was playing. Sharat felt himself getting irritated.

"Why won't you answer back?" he asked. Impatiently, he reached down towards the pool, but as his fingers

touched the water the image shivered and disappeared, and the surface returned to normal.

He stepped back, frustrated.

"It didn't work," he said. "He's gone!"

"Are you sure?" asked the dark woman.

As Sharat gazed down into the water, the surface shimmered briefly back to life. For a moment the older boy looked back up at him through glowing eyes. Then, as he watched, his own features appeared over the top like a ghostly image, until the two faces were as one.

Frowning, he looked from the woman to the man, and back again.

"What's that supposed to mean?" he demanded.

The dark woman shook her head. "It is not for us to interpret what the pool is showing you," she said. "You must draw your own conclusions."

Sharat stared at her. Then he glanced back down at the water again. The pool was showing him his face, there was no doubt about that, but there was something magical about the image. For a moment a wild thought occurred to him, but no sooner had the thought arisen than his logical mind clamped down in disbelief.

"It can't mean *I'm* the Prince of Jinnis," he blurted. "I come from the circus."

The pale man lifted an eyebrow. "Are you sure?" he asked.

"Of course I'm sure," said Sharat. "My father is the circus ringmaster. I've lived there all my life."

Aya took a sharp breath. "What about your mother?"

208

she said, looking up at him, her eyes wide with excitement.

Sharat felt his stomach twist. His mother. The mother he had never known. "Can jinnis and humans *have* children together?" he asked.

"That depends on what shape the jinni choses," said the dark woman. "It is not unknown for a jinni to take human form and marry into the world of men."

Sharat remembered Uma's story about his mysterious mother, her connection to Emira and the fact that she'd sent them both out of the city to protect them from the Empire. His heart skipped a beat.

"I suppose she *could* have been a jinni," he said doubtfully.

"Trussst the crystal pool," hissed the pale man. "It never lies."

Slowly his body began to narrow and he began to sway.

The dark woman smiled. "Have faith," she whispered.

As she spoke, a long tongue flickered between her lips.

"They're turning back into snakes!" gasped Aya.

Sure enough, the two figures before them were beginning to change, their arms shrinking as their shoulders disappeared and they slid gracefully into the crystal pool. Moments later, the twin heads of Vasuki emerged, dripping with water.

Sharat shivered as he watched the metamorphosis, but he no longer felt afraid. All he could think of now was the vision in the pool. Could it really be true? Was *he* the Prince of Jinnis?

Chapter Twenty-Eight
BLESSINGS

As Vasuki swayed before him, Sharat's mind was in turmoil. What if he *was* the Prince of Jinnis? Was this why Lemo had always been so secretive about his mother? Maybe it even explained why Pias hated him so much. And of course there was Emira. All the clues were there. But still he wasn't sure.

"I just wish I could find some kind of proof," he said.

Aya looked thoughtful. "What about my mother's rhyme," she said. "*Earthbound, breathled, firefound and watermet, brought to his fate by tiger white...* You wouldn't be here if it wasn't for Emira."

Sharat felt his heart wrench. Emira. It was true, he wouldn't be here if it wasn't for her. And the Queen had been quite clear. Emira was *his*.

"But what about the rest of the rhyme?" he said.

Aya looked thoughtful. "Well, we got stuck underground," she said. "That sounds a bit like earthbound. And then you fell into the pool, which could mean watermet…"

With a dawning realisation, Sharat remembered the rest of his journey. It was a breath of air that had led him towards this cavern. And he supposed that the light of the roots could count as fire.

"It does all fit…" he said slowly. "But if I'm the Prince of Jinnis, why didn't the Queen of the Forest just *tell* me? Surely she must have known."

Vasuki's heads swayed. "Some magical sssecrets cannot be revealed in words," said the pale serpent. "In order to awaken your powers, it was necessary for you to journey into this world of magic and discover for yourself."

"But I don't *have* any powers," said Sharat.

The pale head swayed as it let out a long, drawn-out hiss.

"Patience!" he hissed. "If you are half human, your jinni ssside will not emerge until you come of age."

Sharat frowned. "What do you mean?"

"To use your powers, you must first grow to be a man," Vasuki told him. "The pool was showing you your future."

"My future?" said Sharat in dismay. "But I need to get Emira back now!"

The serpent's tongues flickered. Then the dark head

211

swayed forward.

"It's not usually our job to offer advice," she hissed. "However, allow us to remind you that time is cyclical, and ssspace, like sssound and matter, is only a question of vibration."

"What are you talking about?" asked Sharat.

"She means that, given the right circumstances, any magical being can be sssummoned back from the future and forward from the past," the pale serpent replied.

Aya interrupted. "Are you saying Sharat can wake his jinni side early?" she said.

"Exactly," hissed both heads together.

"But how?" asked Sharat.

"In the sssame way that you would sssummon any powerful being," the pale head told him. "With his name."

Aya took a sharp breath. "That's in my mother's rhyme as well!" she said. "*Called by name from death to life.*"

Sharat frowned. "But people have been calling my name all my life," he said. "It's never woken any powers before."

"That's only your human name," said the pale serpent. "What we're talking about is your *jinni* name."

"What's that?" asked Sharat.

"Every jinni has his true name, given to him by his mother," explained the snake. "It is this that you must discover if you wish to be able to use your powers."

Sharat felt his heart sink. "But my mother is dead," he pointed out.

"Then you must ssseek another jinni who knows what

it is," Vasuki told him.

"But all the jinnis are in the mines," said Aya.

Vasuki's heads swung to look at her. Their eyes glittered. "So it would ssseeem!" they hissed.

All the excitement Sharat had been feeling was draining out of him. All he wanted to do was find Emira, but it seemed his quest would never end. He looked around. The cavern was gradually darkening. "But how are we going to get to the mines?" he asked.

"My sssister and I can take you and your friend wherever you want to go," offered the pale head. "If you prefer, we can even take you back to the circus."

At the mention of the circus, Sharat felt a terrible pang of homesickness. He knew he couldn't give up now, but perhaps he should give Aya a chance. He glanced over at her. "You don't have to come with me if you don't want to," he said.

Aya had a stubborn look on her face. "I'm not leaving you *now*," she said. "I want to make sure you finish off Doctor Rookh."

Taking a deep breath, Sharat turned back to Vasuki.

"All right, then," he said. "Take us to the mines."

With grins of delight the serpents reared up, growing to monstrous size.

"With pleasure!" they hissed.

As Sharat and Aya watched in horror, the snakes' mouths began to open wider and wider... And then they struck.

In the blink of an eye, Sharat saw the pale head

swallow Aya alive, but before he could make a sound, the dark serpent shot towards him and everything went black. Round and round he spun in a dizzying spiral, until finally he was rudely ejected out the other end and Aya was deposited next to him.

Breathlessly he crawled to his knees as the serpents disappeared through a crack in the rock.

Mohini was sitting at her dressing table as she watched the scene in the crystal cavern unfold in the mirror before her. With a wave of her hand the image disappeared, but her heart still fluttered with excitement. So, the *circus brat* was the Prince of Jinnis.

As she sat back in her chair it all came back to her. The old witch smuggling the child out of the city. And yet Mohini had forgotten that he'd ever been born...

She couldn't help feeling admiration. The Queen's magic was strong. But now the Queen's spell was broken and he'd found his way here, just as she'd hoped he would.

A smile of amusement twisted her lips.

"Brought to his fate by tiger white," she whispered.

Pushing back the chair she stood up and threw on her cloak. Everything was going to plan, but there was no time to waste. Quickly she strode towards the door. The Prince of Jinnis would be here soon, and when he arrived she needed to be ready for him.

Chapter Twenty-Nine
MOHINI

Feeling breathless, Sharat and Aya staggered to their feet.

Still underground, they were trapped on a narrow stone ledge at the edge of a huge cavern that utterly dwarfed Vasuki's crystal cave. Lapping at their feet was a murky lake that flickered with flames as bubbles of gas broke the surface. At the centre of the lake was an island of dark rock that rose almost vertically out of the water to tower far above them. Spindly bridges connected the top of the island to the cavern walls.

Sharat noticed that the walls were pocketed with holes and criss-crossed with pulleys and ladders.

"Those must be the mines," he breathed.

Aya stared out across the water. A bubble of gas broke

the surface and burnt out with a flare. An acrid smell hung heavy in the air.

"Never mind the mines," she whispered. "Someone's coming."

Trapped on the ledge, they watched helplessly as a golden canoe with a reptilian prow detached itself from the base of the island and cut through the fiery surface of the water towards them. At the helm stood a lady in red, her long black hair hanging down her back. As she brought the canoe to a standstill, the crocodile's head turned to look at them with winking, ruby eyes.

Aya gasped, but Sharat didn't notice. He was staring at the woman, his face fierce with recognition.

"Mohini!" he said.

Mohini bowed her head.

"Sharat," she replied. Her eyes glittered with triumph. "At last!"

Then, to Sharat's surprise, she turned to look at Aya. "Well, well, well," she said. "Look who else the cat dragged in."

Sharat flashed a startled look at Aya. "Do you know her?" he asked.

"Of course I know her," said Aya, her face rigid. "She lived with us in the *Zenana*."

"I didn't just live with you," said the woman reproachfully. "I used to look after you."

Aya's eyes showed a mixture of anger and pain. "You betrayed my mother," she said. "If it wasn't for you she'd still be alive."

216

Mohini reached out to caress the girl's face. "Dear little Aya," she murmured. "How can you say that? Your mother was like a sister to me. I did *everything* I could to help her, but she just wouldn't listen."

Aya pulled away in disgust and turned to Sharat.

"How do *you* know her?" she asked.

There was a scowl on his face. "This is the enchantress I told you about," he said. "The one that lured the circus to the city and helped steal Emira."

Angrily, he turned to Mohini. "Where is she?" he demanded. "What have you done with her?"

To his surprise Mohini's eyes filled with tears. "Please, don't be angry with me, Sharat," she said. "I *had* to steal Emira. It was my only way of finding *you*."

Sharat was taken aback. "What are you talking about?" he said. "I was with you at the circus."

"Yes," said Mohini, "but I didn't know who you *were* at the circus."

Sharat began to feel uneasy. "What do you mean, who I am?"

Mohini smiled. "Surely you must know by now," she said. "If you've made it to the shores of this lake there's only one person you can be." She leaned forward. "*Earthbound, breathled, firefound and watermet...* You're the Prince of Jinnis."

As he caught a waft of her perfume, Sharat's heart skipped a beat. Mohini *knew*!

Just then, Aya broke in.

"Why would *you* be looking for the Prince of Jinnis?"

217

she demanded, eyeing Mohini with suspicion.

A look of triumph crossed Mohini's face. "That's easy," she said. "The Prince of Jinnis is my *son*."

Sharat took a sharp breath. "Your *son*?" he gasped. He was so shocked that he forgot to keep his secret. "But how can I be your son?" he said, staring up at Mohini in disbelief.

Mohini's eyes glittered as she leaned down towards him. "Haven't you guessed yet?" she said. "I'm a jinni too."

Sharat's head spun as her scent enveloped him. He stepped back. "But I thought my mother was dead," he said.

Mohini shook her head. "That's just what I wanted you to think," she said. "When I made Uma smuggle you and Emira out of the city, I had to make sure that nobody knew who you were, so that Rookh wouldn't find you, but I always knew that one day your tiger would lead you home to free us all."

As Mohini spoke Sharat felt a strange mixture of emotions. Smuggled out of the city ... that was exactly what Uma had told him had happened. Then something occurred to him. "But if you're my mother, why didn't Lemo tell me?" he said.

A smug look crossed Mohini's face. "Lemo didn't know," she said. "They don't call me the mistress of illusion for nothing."

Feeling dizzy, Sharat stared at the enchantress. Everything made sense, but was it really true? Could she

really be his *mother*? As he took in another breath of her perfume he felt a shiver of excitement, but Aya wasn't convinced.

"If you're Sharat's mother then what's his jinni name?" she snapped.

Mohini glanced at her. "I'm afraid I can't say," she said. "If I wake Sharat's jinni side too soon, Rookh will be able to enslave him, just like he enslaved me. Then none of us will ever escape." She leaned closer. "I'm sure you wouldn't want that, would you?" she breathed, with a hint of threat in her voice.

Aya pressed her lips together, unable to reply.

Sharat was looking at Mohini in a daze. The more he thought about her story, the more he wanted to believe it, but there was still something bothering him.

"How am I going to free Emira, if I don't have any magical powers?" he asked.

Mohini shook her head. "Don't worry," she told him. "I'll take you to Emira. Then, once you've been reunited, I'll wake your jinni side and we can all escape to Aruanda together."

Aruanda! Sharat's heart leapt as he remembered the magical forest of his dream. "Will we be freeing the Queen of the Forest as well?" he asked.

There was a moment's hesitation, then a brilliant smile lit Mohini's face. "Of course we're going to free the Queen of the Forest," she said. "We'll free all the jinnis and *you'll* be their prince." She squeezed his hand. "Won't that be wonderful?" she whispered as

she drew him close.

This time Sharat felt a thrill as he inhaled her perfume. Gazing up at her in wonder, he nodded. Everything was starting to make sense. Of *course* Mohini was his mother. How else would she know so much about him?

"What do we have to do?" he asked.

"Emira is Rookh's prisoner," Mohini told him. "To get her back you're going to have to come with me to his workshop."

Despite his foggy head Sharat felt alarmed. "Can't you bring her to us with magic?" he asked.

Mohini shook her head. "You don't seem to understand," she said. "I'm Rookh's *slave*. I can't use my magic unless he gives me permission. All I can do is trick him." Eyes shining, she leaned forward. "We can trick him *together*," she whispered, "but you're going to have to be very brave."

Suddenly, all Sharat wanted to do was to prove himself to her, but before he could reply Aya interrupted again.

"Don't trust her, Sharat!" she said.

For some reason Sharat found himself getting annoyed. "Why not?" he asked.

"This is *Mohini*," Aya reminded him. "What if she's working for Doctor Rookh?"

Mohini looked down at her in scorn. "Why would I ally myself with Rookh?" she said. "I'm a *jinni*. I hate him as much as you do."

Aya shivered. She didn't know what to think. All she knew was that something didn't fit.

220

Sharat was hardly listening. All he cared about now was finding Emira. Still, he was nagged by a sense of guilt. He glanced back up at Mohini. "Can't we let Aya go?" he asked. "After all, this has nothing to do with her."

Mohini shook her head. "I'm sorry," she said, "but the only way back to the surface is through the mines." She indicated the canoe with a graceful hand. "I'm afraid you're *both* going to have to come with me."

The reptile at the prow watched them through half-closed eyes. With a lazy movement it stretched out a scaly forearm for them to climb on board.

Sharat and Aya's eyes met. Sharat saw resistance.

"Come on," he said. "It will be all right, you'll see." He tried to smile. "It's what we both wanted," he reminded her. "We'll get Emira back *and* we'll free the jinnis."

For a moment Aya held his gaze, then she glanced up at Mohini. "I hope you're right," she said tightly.

Refusing his outstretched hand, she stepped on to the boat while Sharat followed her in silence.

Mohini stood waiting at the prow. Once they were both seated she lifted her hand and the canoe moved smoothly away from the shore.

As they crossed the lake, Sharat's heart felt like it would burst with impatience. At *last* he was going to rescue Emira! He couldn't wait to see her again. And then there was the prospect of being a jinni. For a moment he felt butterflies in his stomach as he wondered what it would feel like to have magical powers. He was just imagining how he would take revenge on Pias and Ram

when his thoughts were interrupted by a gentle bump. They had reached the island, and now that they were up close he could see that a steep staircase had been carved in a dizzying spiral around its towering sides.

With graceful movements, Mohini led them ashore as the canoe slowly sank below the surface of the water, leaving only a trail of bubbles in its wake.

"Follow me," she said, climbing the black steps, her blood-red cloak trailing behind her.

The climb seemed endless. Echoing nearby, they heard a chip, chip, chipping noise, like pickaxes hitting rock, while silent figures swarmed in and out of crevices in the cavern walls. As they reached the top, they saw that the surface of the island was as flat and smooth as glass. At the centre burned a roaring fire manned by demons with pitchforks.

Just then, a procession of white-robed figures crossed one of the spindly bridges that joined the island to the walls of the cavern.

Sharat took a sharp breath. "Ghuls!" he said.

"Don't worry about them," said Mohini. "They won't hurt you if you're with me."

Sure enough, the ghuls didn't even glance up as they shuffled past. All they did was open their skeletal hands to drop the jewels they had gathered on to an ever-growing pile of treasure.

"That's what will happen to you if you're not careful," Mohini warned them in a low voice.

"What do you mean?" asked Sharat.

"The ghuls were all jinnis once," she said. "Before they were enslaved by Doctor Rookh."

Sharat looked at her in surprise. "Ghuls are *jinnis*?"

"That's right," said Mohini.

"Why aren't you a ghul, then?" demanded Aya.

"I'm not a ghul because I'm not trapped in the mines," said Mohini. "Jinnis only turn into ghuls if they're kept out of the sun. *I* live in the *Zenana*."

Just then one of the ghuls staggered and fell to the ground. As it did so, a pair of cackling demons hurried over with their pitchforks and tossed its still-moving body into the fire. As it was engulfed by the flames, its mouth opened in a silent scream.

Aya took a sharp breath, but before she could protest, Mohini was already striding ahead.

"Come on!" she told them. "We're almost there."

They hurried around the edge of the ebony island on to one of the bridges, and crossed over into a corridor in the cavern wall. A house-marshal with a wide, toad-like mouth glared out from the centre of a heavy wooden door. As they approached, it bared its fangs threateningly.

"Whaddya want?" it snarled.

"Let us in!" snapped Mohini. "I'm on the master's business."

The house-marshal clamped its flabby jaws shut and the door swung open to reveal a dark, womb-like room lined in red.

"Quickly!" said Mohini, putting her hand on Sharat's back. "Your tiger is through here."

223

Heart pounding, Sharat hurried in, closely followed by Aya.

For a moment they looked around in confusion. There was another door at the back of the room, but apart from that it seemed to be empty. Just then, Sharat got a prickling feeling in the back of his neck as if something wasn't quite right.

"Where's Emira?" he asked, turning to Mohini with a frown.

"All will be revealed," she replied, but there was a strange look on her face.

"Sharat, let's get out of here!" said Aya sharply.

But it was too late. As the door swung shut behind them, Mohini's hand swept through the air.

In an instant Sharat and Aya realised that the room wasn't empty at all. Horrified, they watched as Doctor Rookh materialised in front of them, flanked by two of his demons.

They started back, desperate to escape, but before they could turn, Mohini's hands landed on their shoulders like claws.

Her eyes were shining with triumph as she looked up at Doctor Rookh.

"Here he is, master," she said. "The Prince of Jinnis, just as I promised."

Sharat spun around to stare at her in confusion. "How could you?" he gasped in disbelief. "You're my *mother*."

Then his heart sank as he saw the look on her face. All at once he realised how she had played him for a fool. He

224

caught Aya's eye.

"I'm so sorry," he breathed.

Aya barely nodded. Her face was set in a mask of fear.

As Rookh stepped forward his eyes flicked contemptuously across Aya and landed on Sharat.

"Surely you know better than to believe a *jinni*," he said. "How could Mohini be your mother? You're the Prince of Jinnis. Your mother is the Queen of the Forest."

Sharat stared at him. "The Queen of the Forest?" he asked.

"But of course," said Rookh. His lips twisted in disdain. "She thought that by hiding you she could escape me, but now she'll never get away, and neither will you." With a gesture he pointed, and they saw the Queen's urn standing right behind them.

Sharat didn't know whether to laugh or cry. *The Queen of the Forest* was his mother! With a feeling of regret he remembered her warmth and her kindness. How was it he'd never guessed? He looked back at Rookh.

"What are you going to do to us?" he asked, trying to keep his voice steady.

"That depends entirely on you," Rookh replied.

"What do you mean?"

Gesturing for them to follow, Rookh turned to face the doors at the back of the room.

"Come this way!" he ordered as the second door swung open.

With long strides, he led them into a domed chamber with the proportions of some grand temple or mosque.

At the centre of the dome there was a hole that allowed a beam of light to shine down from the outside world, but this time the light was thin and cold, like that at dawn or dusk. Sounds of despair came from cages that were stacked along the walls, and the miserable faces of a thousand wretched creatures peered out from behind the bars. Worse still, the room stank of fear and excrement.

Sharat felt sick. Was Emira down here? Before he could look around, a thousand ruby eyes lit up and turned to catch him in their glare. Too late, he saw that the dome above them was crawling with life.

With a cry, he shrank back. Similickers!

A cold smile crossed Rookh's face. "I see you are already acquainted with my little friends," he said as he lifted his arm. Moments later there was a clicking sound and he brought down his hand. On one of his fingers was perched a tiny golden sparrow, encrusted with jewels.

The bird let out a burst of mechanical song.

"Don't worry. They won't hurt you while you're with me," Rookh told them.

A lanky man came hurrying forward. He wore a pair of green spectacles on his large nose, and his chinless face was spotty and unhealthily pale.

"Ah, Neek," said Doctor Rookh.

"Have you brought me more subjects, master?" asked Neek, his eyes flat and emotionless behind the thick lenses.

"Perhaps," said Rookh. "But first I wish to demonstrate

the power of our toys." He held up the sparrow. "Can you choose a suitable victim for this little fellow?"

"Of course, sir," said Neek. He leaned over to unlock one of the cages.

There was the sound of hissing. An eagle emerged angrily from the cage, lifting its wings to fly towards the sun. Neek hurried out of the way as Doctor Rookh released the golden sparrow. It flew straight for the eagle, and the two birds clashed in mid-air.

In nature there would have been no contest. Eagles were predators, sparrows were prey, but now there was a flurry of feathers and the eagle dropped heavily to the floor. The little bird perched on the fallen body, its needle-sharp beak stained with blood. It let out a triumphant burst of song.

"The similickers do whatever I want," Rookh remarked. "They are far superior to natural animals."

He glanced over at Sharat. "At first I could only use the technique on insects, and small birds," he said, "but then we found a way to convert reptiles, and recently Neek has been experimenting on larger mammals."

Neek bowed his head modestly.

Sharat felt a moment of panic. "Where's Emira?" he said, scanning the cages around the room.

"Show him, Neek," snapped Rookh.

Neek stepped towards an iron box at the edge of the room. Just then, something clanked urgently behind the door and there was a desperate roar.

"Emira!" cried Sharat. He started forward, but Mohini

227

put a cold hand on his shoulder.

"Wait!" she hissed.

Neek pulled out a jangling set of keys and unlocked the door to expose a golden cage. Behind the bars, Emira stared blindly out at them. It was the first time she'd seen light since being stolen. She looked gaunt and ill. As she caught sight of Rookh she bared her teeth in a violent snarl.

Sharat thought his heart would break. "Emira!" he called. "What have they done to you?"

Emira turned her head, and her snarl changed to a cry of longing. She pressed her head to the bars and roared more gently.

"Silence!" spat Doctor Rookh. "We're not here for some kind of emotional reunion."

Sharat couldn't hide his anger. "Why *are* we here, then?" he demanded.

Rookh's eyes burned into him. "You are the Prince of Jinnis," he said. "By rights I should just enslave you, like I enslaved your mother. However, I admire your spirit, so instead I would like to make you an extremely generous offer."

Sharat glared at him. "What sort of offer?"

"For years I've been looking for a suitable heir," Rookh told him. "Everything you see around you could be yours. All I require is a small gesture of loyalty."

A feeling of sick anticipation rose up through Sharat's guts. "What do you mean?" he asked.

Rookh stepped towards the workbench and opened a

thin wooden box. Lying inside it was a silver sword.

"Simple," he said. "Just pick up this sword, and kill the tiger."

Chapter Thirty

DUNGEONS

Sharat stared down at the sword. He'd recognised it at once. It was the sword from Fonke's shop. The sword that killed jinnis.

He glanced around the room. Rookh's face was icy calm, but Mohini's fists were clenched, and her fingernails were so deeply embedded in the palms of her hands that they were drawing blood. Suddenly he caught a whiff of her perfume as it mingled with the scent of decay that wafted up from the animal's cages. A wave of nausea swept through him. To think he'd believed she was his mother!

Feeling dizzy, he looked back at Emira. He *had* to get her out of here, but how?

Once more his eyes rested on the sword in front of him.

As he looked at it the silver seemed to glow slightly. It was almost as if it was calling to him. Taking a deep breath, he reached out and seized the handle. Immediately he felt its power running like electricity up his arm.

Aya gasped. "Sharat! No!" she cried, but Sharat had no intention of killing Emira. Instead he spun around, blade flashing, and lunged at Doctor Rookh.

"Aya, run!" he shouted.

The demons were ready for him. With a thump, they knocked him to the ground. Out of the corner of his eye he saw Aya struggling in Mohini's cruel grasp. Then they were both hauled to their feet. Rookh's mouth twitched as he looked down at Sharat.

"You'll regret this," he said.

Sharat stared up at him, wordlessly.

Rookh glanced at the demons. "Take them to the dungeons!" he ordered.

One of the demons cackled. "With pleasure, sir!" it said.

A terrible roar split the air as the tiger hurled herself against the bars of her cage.

"Emira!" said Sharat, twisting his head in desperation. For a moment the tiger's eyes blazed out at him in pain and fury. Then one of the demons jabbed him viciously in the solar plexus. Choking, all he could do was stumble forward.

Sniggering, the demons dragged them out of Rookh's workshop into a tunnel lit by flickering torches. As they descended, the air became stale, and the chip, chip,

chipping sound of the mines grew louder. Soon they reached a metal door. This time there was no house-marshal there to greet them. Instead the demons used an iron key that grated in the lock.

As the door swung open, a mouldy stench hit their nostrils. The room was barely lit, and the walls were hung with whips, goads and other cruel devices. To their horror they saw that two ghuls were hanging cruelly by their wrists from chains in the wall, but most terrible of all was the iron maiden – an open coffin in the shape of a woman standing in the corner, her insides lined with cruel metal spikes. As the demons dragged them past, her bloodshot eyes revolved to follow them.

"Fresh meat, fresh meat," she muttered, grinding her rusty teeth.

The demons shoved them on to a bench hacked out of stone and shackled them by their ankles.

"Enjoy your stay," one of them sneered before the door slammed behind him.

Sharat caught Aya's eye. Her face looked ashen in the flickering light. Once more he felt overwhelmed by guilt and shame. "I'm so sorry," he said. "Mohini … I can't believe I thought she was my *mother*."

Aya shook her head. "She enchanted you," she said, her voice bitter. "That's what she does, only her magic doesn't work on *me*."

"Now I know how she got my father to break his promise and come to the city," said Sharat miserably.

"And you know who your mother is," said Aya.

232

Sharat tugged at his shackles. "I just wish she'd told me my *name*," he said in frustration.

Aya's eyes scanned his face. "Are you sure she didn't?" she said.

Sharat hesitated. "She did try and tell me something right at the end," he said. "But she couldn't finish." He grimaced. "Rookh was trying to kill her."

Aya shook her head. "If only we still had the amulet!" she said. "I bet Alcherisma could help us."

Sharat glanced around the dungeon. "Even if we did, I doubt he'd come down here," he said.

"Poor Alcherisma," said Aya. "I hope Rookh didn't catch him."

"Never mind Alcherisma," said Sharat. "What about Emira?" He felt like his heart would break as he remembered the sight of her desperate eyes. "How am I going to rescue her now?"

All of a sudden, Aya clutched his arm. "Wait a minute!" she said. "Ghuls are jinnis."

"So what?" said Sharat miserably.

Aya's eyes were bright with excitement as she pointed at the ghostly forms that dangled in front of them.

"Maybe one of *them* knows your jinni name?" she said.

With a shiver, Sharat lifted his head to look up at their fellow prisoners. As they hung from the wall, their hoods had fallen back to reveal pitiful faces, barely more than skin and bone. Their hollowed eyes were closed in pain.

"They're half dead," he said dismissively. "I don't think they can even talk."

There was a steely look in Aya's eye. "So what?" she said. "I woke things up from the *dead* in Fonke's shop."

Sharat's heart skipped a beat. "The Mazaria!" he said.

Aya was already reaching into her bag. Quickly, she pulled out the little instrument. As she did so the silver fingers wiggled invitingly.

Sharat took a sharp breath. "It's showing you what to play!" he said.

Aya nodded. Trembling with excitement she cupped it in her hands. Then, as she began to pluck the silver fingers, the clear, pure sound of the Mazaria broke the silence of the dungeon. The ghuls' eyelids began to flutter.

Sharat felt a thrill. "Keep going!" he said. "It's working!"

But before Aya could play another note, the iron maiden's mouth flew open and she let out a series of blood-curdling screams.

"Aiiiii! Aiiiiiii! Aiiiiiiiiii!"

As she screamed, Aya froze. Moments later, there was a blast of searing wind, and before either of them could react, Doctor Rookh materialised before them, flanked by two of his demons.

"Silence!" he called out harshly.

Raising his staff, he took aim, and the ghuls disappeared in a flash of lightning as their robes crumpled, empty, to the floor. Then, with a sharp move, he flicked the Mazaria out of Aya's hands and brought a boot-clad foot down on to the delicate wooden drum, shattering it with a single stomp. As he kicked it out of the way, the

mangled silver fingers shrank into a fist and were still.

"No!" cried Aya.

Doctor Rookh looked down at her in disgust. "I'll kill you, too, if you're not careful," he vowed.

Aya's face crumpled in despair and she began to cry, hot tears spilling down her face.

Sharat felt sick with shock. Burning with helpless rage, all he could do was wrap his arms around his friend and hold her tight.

"Leave her alone!" he spat, no longer caring what Rookh might do.

Rookh's eyes were cold. "You're in no position to make demands," he said.

For a moment Sharat felt utterly helpless. Then suddenly he realised he did have one final bargaining point. Rookh wanted Emira dead, and if Fonke had been telling the truth, only *he* could use the silver sword. He shivered as he remembered the power of that weapon. If only it could find the right target.

Swallowing, he looked up at Rookh.

"Take me back to Emira!" he said. "I'll kill her, but please, please … just let Aya go!"

A look of horror crossed Aya's face. "No!" she gasped. "Sharat … you can't!"

"What else can I *do*?" asked Sharat, turning to her in desperation. "*One* of us has to get out of here."

Rookh's lips curled. "I'm afraid it's too late for bargains," he said. "Mohini has come up with a far more entertaining solution."

235

Sharat felt his stomach twist in revulsion. "What does she want?" he said.

"You and your tiger are to meet again in the ring," Rookh told him. "Only this performance will be much more interesting than it ever was at the circus. This time it will be a fight to the death."

With a click of his fingers he summoned the demons. "Take the boy to the workshop!" he ordered.

The horrible creatures cackled as they seized Sharat and bound his arms to his body.

"You won't get out of that, tiger boy," jeered one of them.

Sharat felt a wave of panic as the demons dragged him towards the door. "Wait!" he called. "What about Aya? What will happen to her?"

Rookh's face was hard. "The girl stays here until either you or the tiger are dead," he said.

Sharat and Aya's eyes locked in horror.

"No!" Aya gasped.

"I'll come back and get you. I promise," cried Sharat, but before Aya could answer, the metal door slammed shut behind him.

There was a dangerous smile on Rookh's face as he stepped towards the stone bench.

"So, *this* is little Aya," he said, his voice soft with threat.

Aya shrank away in horror. She'd been hoping he'd forgotten her. "You know who I am?" she managed to ask.

"I do now," said Rookh. He glanced contemptuously down at the mangled Mazaria that lay lifeless on the floor. "You gave yourself away when you played your mother's instrument."

Aya's heart wrenched, but despite everything that had happened she no longer felt scared of Doctor Rookh. Slowly, she lifted her head, and for the first time she dared to look him straight in the eyes.

"What are you going to do with me?" she demanded.

Rookh leaned closer. "What would *you* do with a runaway daughter?" he said.

"*Daughter?*" gasped Aya, staring up at him in disbelief.

"Of course," said Rookh. His lip curled. "You're my daughter. Didn't your mother tell you?"

Numbly, Aya shook her head.

Rookh leaned over her. "Just think," he whispered. "You could have been enjoying life as the most important princess in the *Zenana*. Instead you ran away to live in the *sewers*."

Aya could feel his breath on her cheek, but she tried not to flinch in the flickering glare of his diabolical eyes.

"Let me go!" she begged. "What have I ever done to you? What has *anyone* ever done to you?"

Rookh's face closed like a vice. "We're not talking about *me*," he snapped.

Shaking with rage, he lifted his staff. Aya shrank back, expecting the worst. But Rookh had no intention of letting her go that easily. A gust of air whipped up his robes. And before she could blink, he was gone.

* * *

Moments later, Rookh was back in the womb-like chamber that separated his workshop from the mines. Cape swirling, he spun to face the urn that stood waiting against the blood-red walls. He'd caught the tiger and dealt with the brats. Now it was time for the Queen of the Forest to witness her final defeat.

Putting his hand on the stone, his lips twisted.

"So, Casmerim," he murmured. "You thought you could outwit me, but you were wrong."

With a snap of his fingers, he summoned two of his demons. In an instant they stepped out of the shadows.

"Take her out!" he said sharply. "I want her to watch the fight."

The demons hesitated. "Are you sure that's wise, master?" said one of them. "She'll wake up once she sees the light. What if she finds a way to escape?"

"What can she do?" demanded Rookh. "She's still my slave."

"But she's the Queen of the *Jinnis*," the other demon reminded him.

A look of impatience crossed Rookh's face. "Cowards!" he said. "You call yourself demons, but you're as jittery as a pair of old hens!"

Lifting his staff, he pointed it towards the urn and the stone shattered into a thousand pieces.

Casmerim's body tumbled out, as fragrant as ever. She wore only her underclothes, creamy white against her

238

skin, and her luxuriant hair cascaded over her emaciated form.

Eagerly, Rookh stepped towards her, his actions betraying his true feelings, but as he gazed down at the skeletal body at his feet, his expression turned to one of disgust.

"Look at you! You're a ghul now, just like the rest," he sneered. With a quick move he reached down to flip her over, but instead of the sleeping woman he'd expected to find, her skin was icy cold.

Roughly, he brushed the hair from her face. Still she didn't move, but to his horror he saw that her eyes were open. Worse still was the smile that touched her lips. Mocking him.

He stepped back in shock. "No," he breathed. "You can't be dead. Not *now*."

So many times he'd tried to kill her. And so many times he'd failed. Until he'd assumed she was immortal, would always be his plaything, *would one day call him master…*

Rookh pressed his lips together. It was to have been the moment of his greatest triumph, but in an instant everything turned sour. With the Queen dead who would there be to witness his victory? What chance now for redemption? *What chance now for love?*

With a sharp movement he lifted his staff, and a blast of lightning enveloped the Queen's body in a cloak of flames.

"Yes, master! Yes!" cackled one of the demons. "Now she'll *never* escape."

Rookh didn't reply. He knew the demons were right. He was better off without Casmerim. Mohini was a far more *suitable* match. But even as the Queen turned to ash he knew that no matter how hard he tried, he would never be able to erase the memory of that final, taunting, smile.

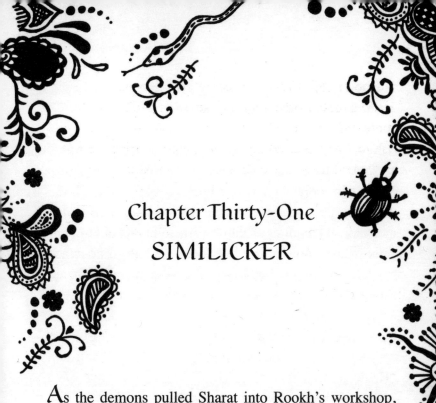

Chapter Thirty-One
SIMILICKER

As the demons pulled Sharat into Rookh's workshop, the air was thick with the smell of despair.

With lanky strides, Neek marched towards them and pinched the flesh on Sharat's arm.

"Looks healthier than most," he remarked tonelessly.

"Just make sure you don't kill him," one of the demons warned him. "He's important."

"Oh, I won't kill him," said Neek. "I just need to make sure he functions properly." With a sure grip he seized Sharat's arm.

"Good luck!" the demons cackled as they left.

Sharat glared up into Neek's expressionless face. "What are you going to do to me?" he asked.

Neek didn't catch his eye. "You're to be prepared to

241

fight the tiger," he said. "Doctor's orders."

Sharat felt a sudden rush of panic.

"No! I'm not fighting Emira!" he said, struggling.

Neek held on tight. "You can't get away, so don't try," he said. "The lickers will get you."

As if in reply, a chorus of clicking swept through the room. With a shudder, Sharat glanced up at Rookh's mechanical creatures as they swarmed in and out of their cells in the dome above. He knew he had to convince Neek to let him go, but *how*? All at once he remembered Suleiman's cheering face as he'd watched the show.

"Does the *Emperor* know what you're doing?" he demanded as Neek pulled him through the workshop.

"The Emperor's out hunting," said Neek mechanically. "He doesn't know a thing."

Sharat's heart sank. He scanned the room, trying to find Emira's cage, but the iron box was nowhere to be seen.

Then, in the midst of despair, he saw a flash of colour and heard a squawk.

"Bite him!" cried a voice. "Bite him and run away!"

Sharat turned his head. A pair of beady eyes and a great curved beak surveyed him from inside one of the cages.

"Pay no attention," droned Neek. "They always want to bite. They also try pecking, kicking, punching, etc, etc, but they can't get away, and neither will you."

Quickly, he opened the cage next to the beady-eyed creature and shoved Sharat in. Then he turned the lock and strode away.

"Wait!" cried Sharat. "You can't lock me up like an

242

animal!" But Neek was already gone.

In dismay, Sharat tried to make himself comfortable, but it was almost impossible. He barely had room to squat. All around him were cages filled with silent, miserable animals – dogs, cats, a squirrel, several monkeys, and a host of mangy birds.

"I told you to bite him!" squawked the raucous voice from next door.

Sharat turned to see who was speaking. There was a shiver of feathers and he found himself facing a big, green parrot. He felt a nudge of recognition.

"Haven't I seen you somewhere before?" he asked.

"Seen me before? Seen me before?" squawked the parrot. He clicked his beak, then his feathers shivered again and changed colour to blaze gold and red.

"You're Uma's bird!" said Sharat in surprise.

"Who's a clever little boy, then?" crowed the parrot. "Ripiraja! Ripiraja!"

"You can talk!" said Sharat. "I mean, you really know what you're saying."

The bird blinked his eyes. "Know what I'm saying?" he asked in an outraged tone. Then he lowered his voice and sidled closer. "Of course I know what I'm saying."

Sharat eyed the parrot. "How did you end up down here?" he asked.

"Got caught!" Ripiraja told him. "Nasty demons! Night-crows. Caaw! Caaaw! Caaaaw!" he crowed. For a moment his beak lengthened and his feathers grew dark. Then he shivered himself back to colour again.

"What happened to Uma?" asked Sharat.

"Ran away! Ran away!" said Ripi.

Sharat shook his head. "I'm glad *someone* got away," he said miserably. "Everyone else I've met in this city is down here. Nara, Aya, and now *you...*"

Ripiraja clicked his beak and his head tilted sideways. "Aya?" he said. "Little girl? Curly hair?"

Sharat nodded. "That's her," he said.

"Where is she?" asked Ripi.

"Stuck in the dungeons," Sharat told him. "She was helping me find Emira."

The parrot looked crestfallen. "Poor little Aya," he crooned.

Sharat's heart wrenched as he thought about his friend. What chance did she have now? "If only there was some way of finding the amulet," he said, thinking out loud. "Aya's still got one more wish."

"What amulet?" squawked Ripiraja.

"It looks like a golden bee, with a big, blue diamond in the middle," Sharat explained. "Uma gave it to me."

Ripiraja's eyes flashed in recognition. "Jinni amulet!" he crowed. "Magic! Magic!"

"That's the one," said Sharat.

"Where is it?" asked Ripi.

Sharat grimaced. "I don't know," he said. "Rookh's taken it."

The parrot grasped the door of his cage with one of his claws and gave it a shake. "I'll find it!" he cawed. "Let me out! Let me out!"

244

Sharat felt a stirring of hope. "Do you really think you can?" he asked.

"I can try!" squawked the bird.

His heart pounding, Sharat's gaze shifted to the latch on the parrot's cage. Quickly, he tried to reach through the bars towards the lock, but his hands were too big. "If only I had some kind of stick!" he said, rattling the bars in frustration.

Ripiraja clicked his beak. "Quick! Quick!" he squawked. "Here comes Neek."

Sure enough, the lanky technician was striding towards them.

Sharat's mind was racing. He had to get Ripiraja out of there. It might be their only hope. Suddenly an idea came to him. He pulled his hands away from the latch.

"Play dead!" he hissed through the bars.

Ripiraja didn't stop to ask why. With a strangled caw, he collapsed on to the floor of his cage, a common green parrot again, but this time his feathers were dull, and his feet stuck rigidly into the air as a nasty odour began to waft from the direction of his body.

By now Neek had reached Sharat's cage. "Out you come, tiger boy," he said tonelessly.

Sharat grimaced. "Before you take me you should do something about that bird," he said, pointing at Ripiraja in disgust. "It stinks!"

The shadow of a frown crossed Neek's face. He shifted his gaze to Ripiraja and rattled the cage. The bird toppled over on to his side.

"Dead?" said Neek in surprise. He frowned. "How did that happen?"

Sharat shrugged. "Maybe you didn't look after it properly," he said. "I bet Rookh won't be too pleased."

A faint trace of worry appeared on Neek's usually placid face. "I'd better dispose of it before the smell gets any worse," he muttered.

Sharat held his breath as Neek unlocked the cage and reached for the parrot.

"I know, I'll feed it to the tiger," he said, looking pleased with himself.

"No!" cried Sharat. "You can't do that… It's … it's diseased. It might make her sick."

"Parrots and tigers don't have the same sicknesses," Neek told him. "The tiger will be happy. They like bird meat." He hurried off, holding Ripiraja tightly in his hands.

Sharat knew only too well how much Emira liked birds from their hunting trips in the mountains. Normally the tiger wouldn't eat rotting meat, but would Ripiraja be able to fool her too? And even if he did, what were the chances of him finding the amulet? Sharat's stomach clenched, but he didn't have long to think about the parrot's fate. As he stared out of the cage he saw someone else coming. It was a girl dressed in yellow robes.

She moved from cage to cage, dropping in bits of food for the animals, and changing their water. Once she reached his cage she gave him a quick glance and shoved a stale chapatti through the bars.

Sharat felt a jolt of recognition. "Nara!"

The sewer-girl stared. Her blind eye was repaired now. A ruby had taken its place and a golden plaque covered half her face. The other eye flashed coldly. Then she recognised him. "Tiger boy," she said with a sneer. "So, he got you in the end."

"What are you doing here?" asked Sharat. "I thought you were being taken to work in the mines."

"I told you I knew how to make myself useful," said Nara. "I've been chosen to serve Doctor Rookh himself." Her face hardened into triumph. "He told me I was unusually talented. He's going to make me his heir."

"That's funny," said Sharat. "He told me the same thing, but it's not much of a job feeding the animals, is it?"

Nara glowered at him. "This is just the beginning," she snapped. She lifted her head in pride. "I won't be staying here for long. I'm going to be a licker."

Sharat felt a chill pass through him. "What do you mean, you're going to be a licker?" he asked. "They're just machines, aren't they?"

Nara shook her head. "That shows how much *you* know," she said scornfully. "The lickers aren't machines. They are all real animals to begin with. Then Neek slowly replaces bits of their body with gold and jewels, until they become immortal." She leaned forward. "That's why the ghuls were stealing children," she said. "Neek uses them for his experiments. *I'm* the first one that didn't die." She touched her new eye proudly.

Sharat stared at Nara in horror. "But if you become a licker, you won't even be human any more," he said. "You'll turn into a machine."

Nara shook her head. "I'll never be a machine," she told him. "I'll always be a girl. A golden girl, living forever in my beautiful golden body."

Just then Neek came back to the workshop. He stood behind Nara. "It's a tricky process," he said. "It took me a long time to get it right. We have to take it one step at a time. Get it wrong, and you've just got a lump of metal and rotting meat."

Sharat's flesh crawled. "What if Nara changes her mind?" he asked. "Can you reverse the process?"

Neek shook his head. "Once you start there's no going back," he said. "If you remove the gold after it's been implanted it tears away the soul, and the specimen dies."

He reached down and unlocked Sharat's cage. "But never mind the others," he said. "It's your turn now."

Sharat stared at him. "Are you saying you want to make me into a licker?" he asked in horror.

"Rookh's orders," said Neek, reaching into the cage.

All of a sudden, Sharat was filled with an overwhelming sense of dread.

"No! Don't! Let me go!" he yelled as Neek grabbed him. But Neek had no mercy. With a vice-like grip, he held Sharat's struggling body out at arm's length as he carried him over to the workbench. Then he pinned him firmly down to the cold surface while Nara clamped his arms and legs so that he couldn't move.

Sharat twisted his head, desperately trying to see what was going on. As he watched, Neek opened a box and pulled out a small disc of gold with slender rays extending from its round body.

"Stay still," Neek told him. "This won't hurt."

"No! Get off!" cried Sharat, wrenching his arms as he tried to get free, but no circus trick could help him now. Neek was already holding the disc over his heart. Then, with a sudden movement, the rays of gold lifted themselves up like a set of spiders' legs and dived down into his chest, embedding themselves deeply into his flesh.

Sharat gasped. For a moment there was a flash of excruciating pain, but it passed almost immediately. Instead, a sense of warmth flooded his body, and all at once he felt more blissfully happy than he had ever felt in his life.

Basking in this unexpected sensation, he looked gratefully up at Neek and Nara, but he barely had time to smile before his eyes closed, and soon he fell into a dreamless sleep.

Chapter Thirty-Two
PRISONER

Aya was left shackled with the sound of rats gnawing in the dark corners of the dungeon and only the ghosts of the ghuls for company, but that wasn't the worst. Doctor Rookh's terrible words had left her feeling sick to the core.

You're my daughter.

Aya had never wondered about her father before. Now, shadowy memories of Rookh's frequent visits to the *Zenana* returned to her. He'd been the only man ever to intrude into the peaceful space her mother had created, bringing anger, violence, and ultimately murder. Her mother had hated him, but that wouldn't have stopped him from making her his wife.

The chains on Aya's ankles clanked as she lifted her

feet off the floor and curled herself into a tiny ball of pain. Hugging her knees, she cried until there were no tears left. Afterwards she lay huddled and still. How she wished her mother was still alive.

With an aching heart, she folded her hands and squeezed her eyes shut.

"Mama, if you're there somewhere, please help me find a way out of this prison," she begged.

For a moment she lost herself in her memories, remembering her mother's laugh and the games they used to play in their little garden.

Just then, she heard a jangle of keys at the door and her eyes flew open in the hope that by some magic her prayer had been answered.

It was Mohini. As she entered the dungeon she slipped the keys into her pocket. She was carrying a wooden platter.

Aya sat up in a hurry and pushed the tears from her eyes. She eyed Mohini with undisguised hatred.

"What do you want?" she asked.

Mohini put the platter down on the stone bench. On it was a clay pot of water and a loaf of bread. "I've brought you some food," she said.

Aya barely glanced at it. "Why bother?" she asked, her voice bitter. "Rookh's only going to keep me locked up in this dungeon."

"Don't worry, he won't keep you here forever," Mohini reassured her. "He just likes to frighten people." She lowered her voice. "Between you and me, I think he was

251

rather impressed by you. You are his *daughter*, after all."

Aya felt her soul shrink. Part of her had been hoping that it was all a horrible mistake. "So it's true," she whispered.

Mohini's mouth twisted. "Of course it's true," she said. "What did you think? That your mother was some kind of saint?"

Aya pressed her lips together in pain.

"That's it," Mohini told her. "Be a good girl and keep your mouth shut. If you're clever, Rookh will give you anything you want."

Aya shuddered. "He doesn't *have* anything I want."

"That can't be true," said Mohini. Her eyes swept over Aya appraisingly. "Wouldn't you like to be a princess? You could have the best of everything – jewels, pretty clothes and as much delicious food as you can eat."

"What, and be a traitor like *you*?" snapped Aya.

Mohini's eyes flashed. "I'm no traitor," she said.

"Then why did you help Doctor Rookh steal Emira?" demanded Aya, glaring up at her.

"I'm not helping him," said Mohini sharply. "I'm *tricking* him."

Aya eyed her with suspicion. "What do you mean?"

Mohini glanced around. Then she lowered her voice. "Rookh thinks that by making Sharat kill Emira he can prevent the Queen's prophecy from coming true," she said, "but Rookh only knows what I've told him. He doesn't know the *real* power of the Sword of Shiva."

Aya shifted, drawn into Mohini's story despite herself.

252

"What are you talking about?" she asked.

Mohini's eyes glittered. "The Sword of Shiva doesn't *kill* jinnis, it liberates them," she said. "At the very moment that Sharat uses it to stab Emira in the heart, a gateway will open in the veil between the worlds to allow her to return to Aruanda, and when that happens, I intend to go with her."

For a moment Aya felt a glimmer of hope. "Does that mean the jinnis will be freed after all?"

"What jinnis?" said Mohini with a sneer. "I'm the only real jinni left in this city. All the rest have turned into ghuls."

Aya stared at her in disbelief. "What about the Queen of the Forest?"

A look of triumph crossed Mohini's face. "She's dead," she snapped. "Rookh's finally killed her. At last."

Aya felt sick. "But she *can't* be dead," she said. "What about the prophecy?"

Mohini's lip curled. "Surely you don't really believe in that silly little rhyme," she said. "Sharat's only twelve years old. How can he be part of a prophecy? Besides, he'll never wake his jinni side now. The Queen was the only one who knew his name."

Aya's heart sank. All of her dreams were crumbling at once. Then another thought occurred to her. "But if Sharat hasn't woken his jinni side, won't using the Sword of Shiva kill him?" she asked.

Mohini shrugged. "Perhaps," she said.

"How *could* you?" gasped Aya in horror. "He's the

Prince of Jinnis!"

Mohini's eyes flashed. "What does *Sharat* know about being a jinni?" she demanded. "He's a filthy mongrel, just like *you*."

Aya stared at her. "What are you talking about?"

Mohini looked at her with disdain. "Sharat's your brother," she said. "For what it's worth."

"My *brother*?" said Aya, stunned.

"Half-brother," Mohini corrected herself. Her mouth twisted in disgust. "Your mother wasn't happy with *one* human lover. She had to have *two*."

Aya wasn't listening. Her mind was racing. Sharat was her *brother*?

With an impatient swish of her dress Mohini stood up.

Aya gave a start. "Where are you going?" she asked in alarm.

"I need to get ready for the fight," Mohini told her. "They'll be starting soon."

Aya felt a flutter of panic. She couldn't let Mohini leave her *now*. "Wait!" she begged. "Don't leave me here on my own!" She reached out and clutched at Mohini's skirt.

Mohini shook her head. "I'm sorry," she said. "You can't come with me."

"But I've got to see the fight!" said Aya, her voice sharp with desperation.

With an impatient move, Mohini pulled back her skirt. "Rookh doesn't want you at the fight," she snapped. "You're to stay down here until he comes to get you."

Aya threw her arms around Mohini's waist. "No ... please ... take me with you!" she sobbed. "I want to go to Aruanda."

"Get off me!" hissed Mohini, sharply wrenching herself out of Aya's grasp. "You're just a sewer-girl. You'd be no use to me in Aruanda. You're Rookh's child now. Take your tears to *him*."

With a toss of her silky hair, she turned away. Then, without looking back, she swept out of the room, and the dungeon doors clanged shut behind her.

With hurried strides, Mohini made her way back to her chambers, pushing all thoughts of Aya out of her mind. Now was not the time for emotions or regrets. Now was the time for action.

"In!" she snapped, barely looking at the new house-marshal.

With a mutter, the door swung open, and closed behind her.

Mohini stripped out of her scarlet gown. Then, wearing only her shift, she moved over to the chest at the end of her bed and opened it to release the spicy smell of cedar, sandalwood and cinnamon. Bending down, she reached in and took out a dress. The fabric unfolded in a cascade of emerald silk: the Queen's dress.

Mohini sighed. It was as good as new. Quickly she pulled it on and clasped a belt around her hips. Then she went to stand in front of her mirror. The woman that looked back at her seemed different somehow. More

regal. And this time there was no trickery involved. Carefully she smoothed the silk.

"Beautiful!" she said.

For a moment she just stood there, admiring her reflection, but then a frown crossed her face. Something wasn't quite right. Putting her hand to her throat she realised that the rubies she'd always worn clashed with the emerald of the dress.

Impatiently, she unclasped the necklace and dropped it carelessly on the dressing table while she rummaged around her jewellery box, but to her frustration she couldn't find anything that matched. Then, just as she was about to give up, she remembered Rookh's latest gift.

When he'd given it to her she'd barely glanced at it, but now her eyes lit up in recognition as she pulled an amulet out of the folds of her old scarlet dress. The Queen's jewel. She'd thought it had disappeared during the troubles, but now, here it was again – a golden bee set with a rare, blue diamond. It was as if she'd been *meant* to have it.

Carefully, she threaded the jewel on to a fine, golden chain, before hanging it around her neck.

"Perfect!" she whispered, a smile of triumph playing on her lips as she admired her reflection one last time.

Chapter Thirty-Three
KEY

As the dungeon doors clanged shut, Aya sat heavily back on the bench. Her heart was beating so loudly she thought it would deafen her, but her eyes were dry. She waited until she was sure that Mohini wasn't coming back, then, slowly, she opened her right fist. The dungeon keys glinted back at her.

"I may be just a sewer-girl, but I know all about picking pockets," she muttered in bitter triumph.

Just then she heard the grinding of metal, and with a start she looked up to see the iron maiden's mad eyes staring down at her. With a gasp she closed her hand, but the iron maiden wasn't interested in the key.

"Food … food … fat … fresh … feast … feed me…" she groaned, eyeing the loaf on Mohini's platter.

Aya's heart skipped a beat, but she felt a shudder of relief. "Yes … yes…" she breathed. "Wait!"

With shaking hands she tried the shackles around her ankles. After a few false starts, the heavy metal clicked open and landed with a clank on the floor. Kicking away the chains, she picked up the loaf and approached the iron maiden with trepidation. In horror she realised that the creature's eyes were *real*.

"Here!" she said, shoving the bread forward. Immediately, a metal claw reached out to snatch the food and the monster began to devour it, drool running down her rust-stained chin.

Aya cast her eyes around the dungeon. There was no time to waste. She *had* to get to the fight.

She ran over to the Mazaria first. Its hands were bunched in two fists and the remains of the wooden drum lay shattered on the floor. Gently, she gathered up the pieces and put them in her bag. Then she looked around for something to use as a disguise and her eyes lighted on the remains of the ghuls; two mounds of crumpled, white fabric.

Nervously, she stuck out her foot to nudge one of the mounds, but to her relief there was nothing there; the ghuls really were gone. With a quick prayer of thanks, she picked up one of the robes and put it on, using the other as a hood to cover her head. Underneath the robes she uncovered two little piles of what looked like seeds. Hardly knowing why, she scooped them into her bag. Then, with a final glance at the iron maiden, she slipped

out of the dungeon, following the way she'd come.

As she hurried along the dark corridors, she was joined by a silent throng of ghuls. Grateful for the cover, she merged with them as they crossed one of the narrow bridges that led over the fiery lake back to the dark island, where the scene had been set for the fight.

The bonfire had been cleared to make way for a ring. Around it, ghuls of all shapes and sizes were being ushered into place by hordes of grinning demons. Aya dropped her head, terrified that the little fiends would recognise her, but luckily they were too busy chattering to each other to pay attention. Keeping her head down, she pushed into the crowd. Only then did she dare look up.

Around her, the ghuls were completely silent and very still, their eyes glinting dully beneath their hoods. Along with the ghuls, Aya caught sight of several children in the crowd. For a moment she thought she recognised a little girl with a golden eye, but the child hurried past with swift, robotic movements.

Craning to catch a glimpse of the ring, Aya saw an area of raised seating with two thrones taking pride of place. Next to that was an ornate golden cage. Inside the cage Emira paced backwards and forwards, a look of fury on her noble face. The cage was crowned with the statue of a golden bird, but Aya didn't have time to take in details. She had to find Sharat.

She didn't have long to wait. Just then, the most awful screeching sound pierced the air and a procession began

to cross one of the spindly bridges. Doctor Rookh led the way, his dark robes sweeping the floor, while Mohini walked behind him, resplendent in emerald silk. Behind Rookh and Mohini was a group of Rookh's generals and political advisors, and following them was a gaggle of women done up in gaudy gowns and ostentatious jewels, their faces painted and their bosoms heaving as they jostled for position.

Once they had all taken their places, Doctor Rookh raised his staff.

"Ladies and gentlemen!" he announced. "This is the moment we have all been waiting for: the triumph of man over nature, of machinery over magic and logic over legend. Soon my power over this city will be complete and the supremacy of the human race will be assured!"

A mixture of cheers and moans filled the cavern. Rookh made a grand gesture.

"Bring in the boy!" he ordered.

Sharat was led into the ring.

His black leggings made him look painfully small and thin. A mask hid his eyes, and a golden medallion gleamed in the centre of his bare chest. He looked neither right nor left but walked straight up to Doctor Rookh.

"Take the sword," Rookh commanded.

For the first time, Aya noticed a table in front of the cage. On it lay the Sword of Shiva. With a sure move, Sharat reached out to grasp the weapon, and lifted it up to cross his chest.

Rookh looked down at the boy standing in front of

him, and smiled triumphantly.

"Present yourself!" he snapped.

Obediently, Sharat turned around and bowed to the north, south, east and west. The ghuls watched silently, their eyes dull, while the humans cheered and the demons shrieked and chattered in delight.

Finally, at Doctor Rookh's command, two of his servants opened the tiger's cage and Emira, released after so many days of captivity, bared her teeth in a terrible roar and threw herself into the ring.

Sharat didn't flinch. Watching the tiger with an air of confidence he began to circle the ring, and then, to Aya's horror, he raised the sword and made ready to fight.

Chapter Thirty-Four
FIGHT

Sharat had never felt happier as he strode into the ring. The golden disc above his heart had taken away all of his cares. He knew exactly who he was and what he had to do. It was all so easy.

He stepped towards the table in front of Doctor Rookh and picked up the sword. A surge of pleasure filled him as he touched the metal. He felt so grateful to his master, for allowing him to feel this great power and joy. At last he could be all he had ever wanted to be, and more. He understood everything now. Of *course* he was the Prince of Jinnis. And now, with Rookh's help, he would soon take the place of the Emperor and be a worthy ruler, both of the underworld, and of the human empire that waited on the surface.

Lifting the sword, he saluted. Then, at last, Emira was released and they began circling the ring.

As Sharat prepared to fight, he couldn't help admiring the beauty of the tiger that prowled opposite him.

She was a rare and spectacular beast, and he knew he had performed with her many times before, but today would be different. Today he was going to kill her. No emotions remained to spoil the fight he was about to undertake, only ruthless determination. He swung the sword to test its weight. It seemed as eager as he was, almost humming in his hand.

Emira reared up, looking as though she would spring out of the ring towards Doctor Rookh, but Sharat was ready. He threw himself in front of her, and the sword sliced through the air. If Emira hadn't moved, he would have cut off her head, but Emira was fast after her years of circus training. Sharat wouldn't have expected any less. She dodged out of the way, and the sword just nicked her ear.

"Ow!" Suddenly Sharat forgot he was the Prince of Jinnis. For a moment he was just a boy again. He reached up and touched his head. It was wet with blood.

"How did that happen?" he muttered to himself, confused. Then he heard Rookh's voice in his head.

"Fight!"

He sprang to attention. Emira was angry now. She had turned around and was coming for him. Again he lifted his sword. It was time for him to prove himself a worthy heir to Master Rookh.

* * *

Emira felt strong and fierce. She knew she should be happy. She had been let out of her cruel prison. Now, here she was again with her boy, surrounded by an audience. Even so, things weren't back to normal. There was something wrong with Sharat. His movements were stiff, he was dressed all wrong, and where was his ring of fire? She growled and looked around. The audience wasn't behaving properly either. Why were all of them so white? And why did they just sit there staring? Emira circled the ring, roaring at the top of her voice to try and wake them up, but they hardly moved at all. It was as if they were half dead.

Then she saw the man in black and her fur bristled in recognition. She would have leapt out of the ring to attack him there and then, but suddenly Sharat was in front of her, a rod of metal in his hand.

Emira could hardly believe her eyes. Sharat was getting in between her and the enemy! Had he not seen the tiny cage she'd been locked up in for so long?

Just then the metal rod sliced through the air towards Emira's face. She dodged to avoid it, but not fast enough – the tip nicked her ear. Hissing in pain she sprang back. Why was her boy trying to hit her? That wasn't how they played the game!

A drop of blood landed in Emira's eye and, as the world around her turned red, her confusion turned to fury.

For years Emira had done what she was told, staying

264

obediently in her cage, performing night after night for nothing more but a leg of mutton and the occasional pleasure of the hunt. She had done this all for the love of her precious little brother, her boy, Sharat. It had always been the two of them against the world. Now he was taking sides against her with the man she hated the most.

Emira spun to face the ring. She watched the boy there. It looked like Sharat, and smelled like him too, but she knew that the real Sharat would never hurt her. This wasn't the Sharat that she had known and loved. This was some kind of a demon. That meant the rules had changed.

Emira roared. The demon wanted to fight, did he? She would show him a fight!

Aya felt sick. She had longed to see Sharat and Emira in the ring, but not like this.

All around her, the ghuls sat watching silently from beneath their ghostly cowls. They didn't react to the drama that was unfolding before them. The only creatures that were enjoying themselves were the demons. Scores of them were jeering and cheering at every move.

Aya glanced over at Doctor Rookh and Mohini.

Mohini was half raised off her throne, her eyes hungry, while Rookh leaned forward in concentration, his staff twitching at every blow.

Suddenly Aya saw things clearly. Sharat wasn't fighting of his own accord. Doctor Rookh was *controlling* him somehow. There was no time to waste. She had to get to him before he killed Emira. Gathering up her courage,

she started pushing through the ghuls, desperately trying to reach the ring.

Sharat was enjoying himself. It was almost like being back at the circus, only this time the fighting was for real! Feeling a surge of excitement, he watched Emira's eyes blaze with fury as she charged towards him. With a flash of gleaming metal his sword sliced through the air, but the tiger was too quick for him, rolling away with a snarl of anger as she whipped out a paw to knock his legs from under his body.

Sharat jumped and Emira missed. Then they both paused for a moment. There was no sign of the friendship they had shared, only the desire to fight and win.

Sharat was just catching his breath when suddenly a sound cut through his concentration. He glanced up to see one of the ghuls waving at him from the audience. Then, as he watched, it pulled off its hood. All of a sudden he realised it was Aya.

Confused, he forgot what he was doing and paused to look. Aya was shouting something. A word, what was it? A name? Sure that it must be important, he strained his ears to catch what she was saying, but just then Emira made her move, leaping towards him with a terrible roar.

In a flash Rookh was on his feet.

"Now!" he cried, thrusting his staff sharply forward.

His body twisting, Sharat's blade shot out and Emira landed on its point.

Without emotion, Sharat watched as the sword in his

266

hand pierced Emira's flesh. For an instant, time seemed to stand still as she hung suspended above him, the silver metal buried up to the hilt in her chest. He braced himself, expecting to be crushed. But Emira didn't fall. Instead, there was an almighty crack, as a bolt of lightning shot out of the sword and hit the ground, lighting up the glassy surface of the ring with an eerie glow.

All at once, the light began to spin, opening up a swirling vortex beneath Sharat's feet.

Emira roared, and time resumed its course. Leaping past Sharat uninjured, she dived straight through the centre of the vortex and disappeared.

As he stared up at the empty space where the tiger had been, Sharat felt a sense of déjà vu. But before he could wonder where she had gone, he felt a sharp pain in his heart and his body slowly crumpled as a fountain of blood erupted from his chest.

"Yes!"

A shriek of triumph rent the air as Mohini leapt down from her throne.

"No!" gasped Aya as Sharat fell bleeding to the ground.

In despair she collapsed on to the bench behind her. It was no use. It hadn't worked!

Clutching the broken Mazaria to her chest, she knew why. It was no good just *saying* a magic word. You had to sing it. Numbly, she watched as Mohini leapt into the ring, her face wild with jubilation.

Just then there was a raucous cry from the golden bird

that had been perched on top of Emira's cage.

Detaching itself, it shot towards the enchantress, its feathers turning from gold to green as it raked its claws across her throat.

"Catch!" it cried, flying past Aya in a blur.

Staring up at the bird, Aya felt a jolt of recognition. But before she could wonder where she'd seen him before, she felt something small and heavy drop into her lap. Looking down, she saw the familiar shape of the golden bee.

All at once her heart leapt. "Alcherisma!" she exclaimed, seizing the amulet.

Moments later a speck of gold flew out of the stone and with a furious buzz the jinni appeared before her. Taking one look at the chaos around them, a look of panic crossed his face. "Are you *crazy*?" he hissed. "Why have you brought me *here*?"

Chapter Thirty-Five
KALKI

As the boy collapsed, he felt a sharp pain in his chest. For a moment all his memories and fears returned with the roar of cheers all around him. Then there was a tugging sensation as though he was being pulled underwater, and all of a sudden the noise stopped.

In wonder, he looked around. He was in a circular tunnel, whose walls were slowly revolving as they flickered with light. The tunnel was twisted, and the pathway ahead rose and fell. Catching his balance, he stepped forward. With a start, he noticed the figure of a woman running up ahead. She was dressed in green with long, black hair.

The boy frowned. His mind was blank, but somehow he knew this woman's name.

"Mohini!" he called, running to catch up with her.

The woman spun around, hair whirling. Her throat was scratched and bleeding, but her face was a picture of jubilation. With a quick glance she looked him up and down.

"So," she said, her mouth twisting. "You made it. I wasn't sure if you would."

"How did I get here?" asked the boy, confused. Visions of fighting, of blood, of despair jostled in his mind.

"You stabbed Emira with the Sword of Shiva, and opened a gateway back to the world of the jinnis," said Mohini in triumph.

"But I was wounded," remembered the boy. "My body collapsed."

"That was just your human side," Mohini told him. "Now you're all jinni. You've left your body and its memories behind."

The boy stared at her. "Does that mean I'm dead?" he asked, suddenly feeling sick.

Mohini shook her head. "Only your human side is dead," she told him. "Let it go. It was worthless, and anyway, you won't need it where we're going."

She carried on down the twisting tunnel, with the boy on her heels.

Just then they turned a corner and up ahead he saw a circle of dazzling light. In front of it, poised to spring, was a white tiger. His heart leapt.

"Emira!" he called.

With a questioning growl the tiger turned her head.

270

Then, as she saw the boy, her growl turned into a purr. She bounded back towards him.

The boy threw his arms around her. "You're alive!" he cried.

"Come on!" said Mohini sharply. "The gateway won't stay open forever. If we don't move now, we'll be trapped between the worlds."

Just then the boy noticed that the circle of light up ahead was beginning to shrink.

"Where are we going?" he asked.

"We're going to Aruanda," Mohini told him. "But we have to go now or we'll never get through!"

"Aruanda!" The boy felt a thrill as the name conjured up visions of a beautiful garden. He hurried on, feeling a tugging sensation as he drew closer to the light, but just then a crystal-sweet voice broke the silence behind them.

"*Kalki! Kalki! Kalki!*" it sang.

The boy stopped in his tracks. Next to him, the tiger stopped too, her ears turned back.

"What was that?" he asked.

"It doesn't matter," Mohini told him. "It's coming from the world of men. You're a jinni. That place can only be a prison to you now."

The boy stepped forward.

"*Kalki! Kalki! Kalki!*" The voice came again, pure and clear.

A thrill of recognition passed through the boy's body. He froze. "Wait a minute," he said. "I know that voice. It's a little girl."

271

"Leave it!" snapped Mohini, as the walls of the tunnel began to close in on them. "If we don't go now, we may never get another chance."

Reluctantly, the boy stepped forward, but just then the voice pierced the air once more.

"*Kalki! Kalki! Kalki!*"

All at once, the boy felt a rush of unfamiliar power flooding his body. "That's my name!" he exclaimed. "I'm Kalki, and that voice is calling *me*… It's Aya!"

Mohini's eyes flashed. "Never mind Aya," she hissed. "I'm the Queen of the Forest and I order you to come with me." She seized his arm.

Emira growled.

Kalki stared at her. "You're not the Queen of the Forest!" he exclaimed. "You're Mohini, Mistress of Illusion. I'm not following *you*."

Giving her a shove, he pulled himself on to Emira's back. Emira roared in approval.

"You fool!" shrieked Mohini as she teetered at the edge of the light. "You have no idea what you're doing. Rookh's a monster. He'll never let Aya go. If you knock him down he'll only rise up twice as strong."

Kalki ignored her, clinging on tight as Emira spun around and flew back up the shrinking passageway. As the tunnel closed behind them, Mohini let out a cry of rage.

Emira shot into the ring, bigger and more ferocious than ever before. Riding on her back, Kalki felt triumphant,

alive, and full of power. He was the Prince of Jinnis! Then he caught sight of a familiar body lying on the ground. Sharat's body. It lay in a pool of blood with Aya kneeling by its side.

Kalki felt a thread tying him to this body and his sense of power vanished as he was sucked back into flesh.

All at once, he couldn't see and he could hardly breathe. For a moment, he thought he had come back simply to die. But then he heard Emira roar and felt a dark vein of strength fortifying his muscles and sealing the wound in his chest. He drew in one ragged breath, then another, and his eyes flew open. He sprang to his feet.

Aya stepped back with tear-stained eyes.

"You're alive!" she gasped.

Kalki's eyes burned. An aura of power surrounded him. At a glance he saw Rookh striding towards him. Quickly, he reached down to snatch up his sword.

"I'll deal with Rookh," he yelled at Aya over the din. "See if you can find a way out."

Aya spun around. To her dismay she was faced with a sea of ghuls. Just then something swooped down from above, landing on one of the ghuls' shoulders with a shiver of ivory feathers. It was the bird from the cage.

Aya stared up at him in recognition. "Ripiraja!" she exclaimed. "It's you!"

"Ripiraja to the rescue!" cawed the parrot as he began to whistle a jaunty tune.

All at once, the ghuls began to follow him, their ghostly feet moving to some long-forgotten dance.

Aya didn't stop to ask how Uma's parrot had found his way into the underworld. Throwing up her hood, she pushed her way through the crowd and stared out at the bridges that spanned the inferno below. Kalki wanted her to find a way out, but she had no idea where to begin.

Emira and Kalki turned to face Doctor Rookh and his army of fiends. In a flash, feathers sprouted from the demons' arms, and they turned into crows. With caws of triumph, they circled the tiger, attacking her eyes and raking their talons across her back, before flying out of reach with cackles of delight.

"You take the crows, I'll deal with Rookh!" Kalki yelled at Emira.

With a roar of pleasure Emira leapt towards her tormentors.

Rookh faced Kalki, his staff raised.

"Let's see what you can do, then, circus-rat," he sneered.

Kalki lifted the sword and swiped, but Rookh was gone.

Just then Kalki heard a raucous caw from above. Throwing his head back, he saw a massive bird, as black as death, overhead. As it dived towards him he smelled the stench of decay.

Without thinking, Kalki took a deep breath, and blew. All at once, the air flew into a gale that blasted the bird towards the side of the cavern, where it smashed with a crunch. Then it disappeared.

274

Kalki's head jerked in confusion. Had he done that? He didn't have long to wonder. As he looked warily around the ring, he heard a blistering roar behind him and with lightning reflexes he spun around to find himself gazing into the jaws of a dragon. With a gasp he leapt aside as a jet of flame nearly engulfed him. The monster lashed its tail and roared.

Kalki stood his ground. He could feel his powers rising up strongly inside him now.

With another roar the dragon lunged and prepared to unleash a second fiery blast. This time Kalki knew exactly what to do. Sucking in his cheeks, he took a deep breath and spat with all the strength he could muster.

A cloud of steam swallowed up the beast and everything around it. For a moment Kalki felt a surge of triumph. But then he found himself slipping perilously on the glassy surface of the island. With a gurgle of revenge the billowing cloud turned into a wave that rose up and swept him right over the side.

Kalki felt himself plummeting down, down and down, through the air and through flickering flames until he plunged into the lake below. As he sank to the bottom there was a shiver of movement in the water nearby. Moments later he caught a glimpse of evil eyes and the glimmer of teeth bared in a terrible deathly grin. Behamot! First there was one … then another … and then he was surrounded!

"Aaaaaahhhhh!" he screamed, his voice escaping in a cloud of bubbles as he lashed out with his sword and plunged it into the mud beneath him, hitting rock.

Suddenly the earth trembled and there was the sound of a great crack. Before he knew it the water all around him had drained away, leaving the monster fish flailing helplessly in the slime.

Kalki scrambled to his feet. Rookh was nowhere to be seen, but just then he heard a roar and looked up to see Emira bounding towards him.

Leaping on to her back, he thrust the sword into the belt around his waist.

"Where's Aya?" he gasped.

Chapter Thirty-Six
ESCAPE

Aya pushed her way through the ghuls, desperate to find a way out, but before she could reach one of the bridges a girl with a ruby eye stepped in front of her, blocking her way.

"Where do you think you're going?" she snapped.

Aya stared up in shocked recognition. "Nara!"

"Do I know you?" demanded Nara, glaring at her fiercely through her good eye.

Aya slipped the hood off her head. "It's me," she said.

"Aya!" Nara exclaimed. Her face softened. "My little princess."

"What are you doing here?" asked Aya.

Nara's face became fierce again.

"I was kidnapped by ghuls to work in the mines."

"Oh." Aya didn't know what to say. "I'm sorry."

"Don't feel sorry for me," Nara snapped. "I'm happy here. I'm working for Master Rookh now."

"You can't work for him! He's the man that killed my mother," gasped Aya. She took Nara's hand. "Run away with me!"

Nara was looking at Aya with an expression of scorn. "Run away?" she said. "Where would I go? Back to the sewers?" She shook her head. "This is the best place I've ever been in my life."

Aya didn't have time to argue. "Then help *me*," she begged. "I've got to get away. I'm Rookh's daughter. He'll make my life hell down here."

Nara's mouth twisted. "A princess even in the underworld," she said, her voice bitter. "Everything is just handed to you on a plate, isn't it?"

"I don't *want* to be a princess," cried Aya in desperation. "You're welcome to take my place. Just show me how to get out of here!"

Nara hesitated. She eyed Aya shrewdly. Then she made up her mind.

"You can't go through the usual gates," she said. "They'll be guarded."

"Is there no other way?"

"Only one," Nara told her. "Through the workshop. The hole in the dome leads into the secret passageways under the city." She pointed out one of the bridges. "It's that way."

Aya clasped her hand. "Thank you!" she said.

Nara pushed her away. "I don't need your thanks," she said, avoiding Aya's eye. "Just get out of here. There's only room for one princess in this kingdom."

Aya glanced around as Nara hurried away. Behind her the ring had turned into a battlefield. The ghuls, something in them woken by Ripiraja's singing, had turned on the demons, lifting them into the air with skeletal hands to hurl them into the fiery abyss below the obsidian island. Aya felt a rush of hope, but the fiends simply turned into crows as they fell, and then rose soaring into the air to repeat their attack.

Keeping her head down, Aya dodged her way to the bridge Nara had pointed out. Before she could get there she was surrounded by demons.

With a cry of triumph they seized her. "Back to the dungeons!" they cackled, but just then there was a terrible roar as Emira came bounding over, and the demons scattered, shrieking as they turned into crows to escape. Kalki was on Emira's back.

"Did you find a way out?" he gasped.

"We have to find Rookh's workshop," said Aya, turning to run. "This way!"

"Get on behind me," Kalki told her.

At a glance, Aya took in Emira's fierce eyes, fearsome teeth, and bloodstained claws, but there was no time to be afraid. Seizing the tiger's fur, she clambered on and clung to Kalki's waist.

Behind them the night-crows had regrouped and were about to dive.

279

"Let's go!" shouted Kalki.

"Don't go without me!" cawed Ripiraja, shooting over their heads in a streak of crimson feathers.

Emira shot across the bridge like a bolt of lightning, while Kalki beat off the crows with his sword.

They reached the first set of double doors.

The house-marshal's bulging eyes flew open. When he saw them he began to scream, "Runaways! Runaways! Runaways!"

"Shut up!" shouted Aya. "This is the Prince of Jinnis! Do you understand? He's the only one that can set you free!"

The house-marshal sneered. "Prove it!" he snapped.

Kalki lifted his hand and blasted the door with a ball of fire.

"I never did like those house-marshals," he muttered as the ashes crumbled to the floor.

Emira dived over the charred wreckage and ran towards the door on the other side. Behind them they could hear the sound of beating wings.

"Come in! Come in!" said the second house-marshal quickly, opening the doors into the workshop.

"Don't let anyone else in!" snapped Kalki once they were through.

The door slammed obediently shut. Behind them they heard the frustrated shrieks of their pursuers, but no sooner had they stepped forward when there was a buzzing and a clicking from above, and a host of similickers emerged from their cells, their ruby eyes blazing as they sought

out the movement and warmth of living flesh.

"Get out of the way!" said Kalki. "I'll deal with them."

Aya watched in terror as he leapt off Emira's back and ran into the centre of the room.

With a furious buzz the similickers turned towards him, but he was ready. Lifting his sword, Aya saw that the blade was white hot and as the creatures dived for him, the sword moved in a blur, creating a shield of fire that made them ricochet off him and clatter to the floor in a hail of golden rain. Soon the workshop was littered with their mangled bodies, their eyes still blazing.

Emira let out a roar of satisfaction.

Quickly, Aya and Ripiraja released the animals from their cages. The room was filled with baying, howls and chirps as they jumped, flew and scurried to find their own ways out.

Neek, alerted by the noise, came rushing into the hall.

"What are you *doing*?" he asked, his eyes staring and his hands agitated.

"Looks like there's been a bit of a malfunction, fish-face!" cawed Ripiraja.

Neek stared down at the pile of mechanical bodies at his feet. His eyes scanned them anxiously, counting them in a split second. "Four thousand, two hundred and ninety-nine!" he cried. "All broken!" He picked one up and looked at it helplessly.

"Let's go!" gasped Kalki.

Emira bounded towards him, and Aya ran to catch up, but before any of them could make a move, a familiar

281

blast of wind threw them apart. With a swirl of his cape, Rookh appeared before them, his staff raised in triumph.

"Not so fast!" he snapped.

Eyes gleaming, he swung round to face Kalki.

"A most impressive display of your powers," he said, gesturing at the creatures that lay twitching on the floor. "I will enjoy being your master."

Raising his sword, Kalki lunged forward, but Rookh blocked him with his staff. He smiled.

"You can fight me, but you can never win," he said. "I own you now. Have you forgotten?"

Kalki felt a burning in his heart. He looked down in shock. The golden medallion was still embedded in his chest. Just then he felt Rookh's will piercing his new-found strength and a shiver of unwanted pleasure ran through his body.

"Master," he whispered.

"No!" cried Aya. "He's not your master. Remember who you are!"

Moments later, Emira's roar cut through the air like a crash of thunder.

Kalki's face twisted in pain as he tried to resist Rookh's control. "I am not your slave," he choked. "I'm the Prince of Jinnis!"

He dug his fingers into his chest and, with a sharp move, he pulled the golden disc from his flesh, throwing it at his adversary with all his force. Without hesitation the spidery legs lifted up and embedded themselves into Rookh's throat.

282

The result was immediate. Rookh relaxed, and a look of bliss softened his face. Then he closed his eyes and his head slumped back, drawn into a dream of his own devising.

Kalki wasn't so lucky. As soon as he ripped out the gold, he began to bleed, but this was no mere physical injury, it was as if all of his life force had been sucked out of his body. In agony he slumped against Emira. He was no longer Kalki, the Prince of Jinnis; he was only Sharat the circus boy, and he was dying.

There was a crack as the heavy wooden door behind them splintered and they heard the gibbering of demons.

"Let's go!" shrieked Ripiraja. "We've got company!"

Sharat managed to pull himself on to Emira's back and Aya scrambled on after him.

"Which way?" she cried.

"Up here!" cawed Ripiraja as he circled the dome and the hole in the ceiling.

Emira roared as she crouched to spring.

"Hold tight!" gasped Sharat.

Emira's body was as sleek as silver lightning as she leapt towards the dark hole in the dome's ceiling and landed in the tunnel where Sharat and Aya had first seen the similickers. Faint starlight shimmered above, but Emira didn't keep climbing. That way would only lead back into Shergarh and she wanted to get away from the city. With a sniff, she turned into the darkness, picking out the shadows of rats as she ran. Normally she would have

283

stopped to investigate. She hadn't eaten since she'd been kidnapped, but now wasn't the time to think about food. It was time to escape.

Unerringly, she led them through the twisting passageways, unravelling their secrets until they spilled out of the bowels of the earth into the darkness of night. In triumph she turned her head up to face the indigo sky that faded to red in the east. A star twinkled above them. They were free!

Emira bounded across the wasteland towards the northern mountains which were just becoming visible against the brightening sky. Behind them, the City of Jewels rose up out of the plains, with Shergarh as its sinister crown. Sharat saw a cloud of darkness rise up from the centre of the fortress, and it was growing bigger.

"Watch out," he gasped. "The night-crows are on our tail."

Emira was running fast, but the crows were faster still, their infernal wings beating them inexorably closer.

Suddenly Aya remembered the remains of the ghuls that she'd rescued from the dungeon floor.

"I'll stop them!" she cried.

Seizing her bag, she scooped out handfuls of seeds and flung them far and wide as Emira raced along.

For a moment it seemed to have worked. With angry caws the crows stopped to descend on the barren earth, seeking out every last seed, but still more were coming, and soon they were surrounded by thrashing wings,

gouging beaks and ripping talons.

"Take that!" shrieked Ripiraja, attacking from above.

"We'll have to stop and fight!" gasped Sharat, his face pale with the loss of blood.

"No, wait!" cried Aya. "Look! It's dawn!"

As the sun began to rise, the crows' raucous cries gave way to shrieks of frustration. Moments later, their wings shrivelled as they turned back into demons and came plummeting down to earth. With a roar, Emira snapped up half a dozen, spitting them out contemptuously when she was done. Then, with a spring she easily left them far behind.

Aya let out a sigh of relief, but they weren't out of trouble yet. As Emira sped across the barren plains away from the City of Jewels the blood kept on flowing from the wound in Sharat's chest.

"How did we get here?" he whispered, his voice weak. "I can't remember anything."

"Never mind that," said Aya, slipping her scarf around him to bind him to Emira's back. "Just hold on!"

Sharat nodded, but his eyes were dull. Soon Emira's fur was sticky with his blood and his hands lost their grip around her neck.

Desperate to keep him awake, Aya kept whispering encouragement, but it was no use. Sharat was too weak, and at some point on their journey he ceased to hear her, and slipped silently away.

Chapter Thirty-Seven

REBIRTH

Aya was woken by the sound of singing.

She sat up and winced. Her head was pounding and her body ached. All day and half the previous night she had clung to Emira as they fled the City of Jewels, following Ripiraja's lead. She vaguely remembered dropping, exhausted, off Emira's back. Then someone had wrapped her in a blanket and she'd fallen asleep.

Now she rubbed her eyes and squinted to block out the harsh morning sun. She was next to a cluster of grey boulders and above her was a real, live tree.

Her heart beating in excitement, she got up to inspect the tree. In wonder she felt its cool, delicate leaves and as she touched its trunk she almost thought she could feel it breathing. For a moment she just leaned against it as she

got her bearings. Behind her she could see snow-capped mountains, while all around the landscape was made up of green, rolling hills dotted with granite boulders. All at once she realised she was in the foothills of the holy mountains, several days' journey to the north of the City of Jewels.

Curious, she walked past the boulders towards the sound of singing and with a thrill of recognition she saw Uma the witch squatting by a lively river. Next to her was a cauldron bubbling over a fire, and nearby Emira was pacing back and forth, a look of fierce sorrow on her face. There was a body lying between them.

"Sharat!" called Aya. In her excitement she began to run towards them, but as she got closer her heart sank. Sharat's skin was pale and waxy and no blood flowed from the wound on his chest.

Still singing, Uma lifted her head to indicate that Aya should hold Sharat's hand. Obediently, Aya did so, but as soon as she touched it, she knew that her worst fear had come true. Sharat's skin was as cold as ice. He really was dead.

"No," she whispered. "No…" In despair she fell to her knees, but Uma shook her head, and gestured for her to sit up.

"Sing!" she said.

Uma's chant wasn't in any language that Aya had heard before, but slowly she began to pick out words, so she began to sing along.

As Uma chanted she fed the fire and smudged Sharat

with aromatic smoke from a bunch of leaves that smouldered in her hand. Then she picked up a hollow gourd to keep time with the music: *tak tak tak, tah tah tah.*

With a sense of wonder, Aya began to see patterns emerging from the steam that was rising from the cauldron – amorphous beings with fluttering hands, hair like clouds, and staring eyes.

Still singing, Uma lifted the cauldron off the fire and into the river to cool down. Then at last she poured out barely a cupful of dark liquid.

"Hold him up!" she told Aya.

Aya lifted Sharat's limp body as Uma drank the potion down in one gulp. Then leaning over Sharat she put her mouth over his, and exhaled with all her might.

Suddenly Sharat took a gasp of air, and let out a hacking cough that threw his body into violent convulsions.

Emira watched, every muscle in her body tense.

"He's alive!" gasped Aya.

With a graceful move, Emira leapt to her feet and walked over to them.

"He's all yours," murmured the witch, putting her hand on the tiger's back.

Purring, Emira leaned over Sharat, and licked the wound on his chest. Aya looked down in wonder. Sharat was breathing peacefully now, and where there had been a gaping hole above his heart was just an angry red scar.

Uma pushed herself up to her feet. "Let's leave them alone," she told Aya. "Sharat needs to rest."

288

She helped Aya lay Sharat down on the grass while Emira curled up around him to keep him warm.

Finally Uma turned her attention to Aya.

"It seems you've been on quite a journey since I last saw you," she said. "Would you like some food?"

Aya hadn't eaten or drunk since finding the crystal pool. Now her mouth began to water.

"Yes, please," she said.

Taking her hand, Uma led Aya towards her shelter, a small building built out of the same grey rock that littered the landscape. Aya glimpsed a flurry of turquoise feathers. A big bird with a curved beak and clever, beady eyes landed on a tree nearby.

"Ripiraja!" said Aya. She turned to Uma. "He helped us escape."

"So he keeps telling me," said Uma.

"Run away! Run away!" cawed the bird, and with a shiver his feathers turned to shades of scarlet tipped with gold. Aya laughed, delighted.

"Beautiful!" she said.

"Don't flatter him or I'll never hear the last of it," grumbled Uma. "He won't stop bragging about how he found the amulet and saved the day."

"Who's a clever boy, then?" the bird crooned. With a flurry of wings, he hopped up and landed on Aya's shoulder, his claws gripping gently so as not to hurt her.

"Oh!" she cried.

"You're very pretty, too," he whispered coyly in her ear.

289

Uma rolled her eyes. "Watch out. He likes you."

Aya giggled. "I like him, too!" she said. "But how did you end up on top of Emira's cage?" she asked the bird.

"Tricks and magic!" said the bird. "Tricks and magic!"

Aya laughed again as she tickled the parrot between the feathers under his chin.

As Uma stopped to watch them her expression softened. "I'm glad you all came back safely," she said.

Then she began to busy herself around the fire. "Now why don't you tell me all about your adventures?" she said. "And don't leave anything out."

Chapter Thirty-Eight

SEED

Sharat woke up to the sound of Emira purring. He opened his eyes.

"Where am I?" he asked.

Emira's purring grew louder.

Sharat sat up and leaned against her for support. As he moved he felt an ache above his heart and looked down to see a scar on his chest. Suddenly everything that had happened in the last few days came flooding back to him.

"We got away!" he said.

Emira pressed her head against his with a rumble of agreement.

Sharat buried his face in her fur. For a moment he just sat there, feeling the warm, familiar shape of her body. Then he noticed the sound of voices nearby and lifted his

head to look around.

Behind them was a river, beyond that was the crest of a hill, and far below that the flatlands stretched all the way to the horizon.

"We're almost back in the mountains!" he said. He looked at Emira in wonder. "Did you carry me all this way?"

Emira growled gently, her eyes gleaming with satisfaction.

Sharat pushed himself to sitting. "Where's Aya?" he asked.

Emira made a gruff noise as she got to her feet and padded up the hill. Sharat followed her past the boulders and saw Aya and Uma sitting together by a campfire, deep in conversation. Ripiraja perched on a tree nearby, his feathers reflecting the sunset.

Uma had already seen them. She lifted a hand and beckoned.

"Up here!" she called.

Emira padded towards her with a growl of greeting.

Aya's head shot up and dimples appeared on her cheeks. "You're awake!" she exclaimed.

Sharat smiled weakly as he stepped up to the campfire. He was feeling dizzy.

"I'm hungry," he said.

"Sit down," Aya told him with a grin. "There's plenty of food."

Sharat sat next to her and took what she was offering. Then he hesitated. "Emira must be hungry, too," he said.

Uma jerked her head towards the mountains. "There are fish in the river, and plenty of goats in the hills," she said. "Emira can look after herself."

Sharat glanced out over the countryside. "Is it safe?" he asked.

Uma nodded. "Yes, it's safe," she reassured him. "We're not in the Empire any more."

The tiger's tail twitched. It had been too long since her last hunt. She glanced at Uma with a questioning sound in her throat.

"I'll watch him," Uma told her. "Don't worry."

Emira's eyes shone with intelligence as she growled in reply. Then she stalked off to find some prey.

Sharat looked around again. "How did we get here?" he asked. "The last thing I can remember was Rookh trying to turn me into a licker." He shuddered. "He put this golden *thing* in my chest."

"I *knew* he was controlling you," said Aya. "He thought that if he could make you kill Emira he could stop the Queen's prophecy from coming true."

Sharat felt puzzled. "But Emira didn't die," he said. "What happened?"

"Mohini tricked him," said Aya. "She knew that when you stabbed Emira with the Sword of Shiva it would open a gateway back to Aruanda. That was her plan all along – to escape. The trouble was, you weren't a jinni then, so when you used the sword it ended up killing you."

"But it didn't kill me!" exclaimed Sharat. "I remember now. We were in some kind of tunnel. Me, Emira and

Mohini. There was a light at the end. Mohini wanted us to come with her. Then I heard someone singing." He stared at Aya. "It was you!" he said. "You were singing my jinni name. It was Kalki!"

Aya nodded. "That's right," she said. "I called your jinni name and you came back as the Prince of Jinnis and fought Doctor Rookh. That's how we got away."

Sharat frowned. "But how did you find out what it was?" he asked.

There was a strange look on Aya's face. "It turns out I knew all along," she said. "Mohini came to see me in the dungeon. She was the one that told me." She glanced at him shyly. "You're … you're my brother."

Sharat stared at her in wonder. "Your *brother*?" he said.

Aya nodded. "As soon as she told me I knew I had to find you," she said. "My mother always used to talk about my brother, Kalki. I just didn't realise who he was." A sad look crossed her face. "I didn't know who *she* was, either."

Sharat reached down to take her hand. "So you were part of my family all along," he said. For a moment neither of them said anything. Then Sharat cleared his throat.

"What happened next?" he asked.

Quickly she told him about how she'd stolen the key from Mohini and made her way to the fight.

"I tried calling your name," she said. "But it didn't work." She shook her head. "I thought it was all over when you stabbed Emira. Luckily Ripiraja found the

amulet just in time and dropped it in my lap."

There was a shiver of feathers in a nearby tree.

"Ripiraja! Ripiraja!" cawed the parrot.

Sharat's head shot up. "You made it!" he exclaimed. "I thought Emira had eaten you!"

"Eat *me*?" The bird puffed himself up in indignation.

Sharat and Aya laughed, and even Uma smiled.

Aya nodded. "I used my last wish to ask Alcherisma to mend the Mazaria," she said. "That's how I brought you back to life. It was no good calling your name, I had to *sing* it."

Suddenly Sharat let out a gasp. "I've just realised what the Queen was trying to tell me at the end of her dream," he said. " 'Aii!' She was saying Aya's name."

He glanced at his sister. "She must have known you were the only one who could wake my jinni side."

Aya nodded. "Maybe that's why she gave me the Mazaria," she said quietly.

Uma was nodding, too. "It's as if you were meant to find each other," she said. "As if she'd planned it all along."

Sharat felt a pang of longing. "I still can't believe she was my *mother*," he said. "I just wish I'd had a chance to rescue her."

There was a look of pain on Aya's face. "We couldn't have rescued her even if we'd tried," she said. "That's another thing Mohini told me. She's dead. Rookh's finally killed her."

Sharat felt a sharp pain. "Dead?" he said in disbelief.

"But what about the prophecy?"

Aya's lips twisted. "That's all nonsense as well," she said bitterly. "There never was any prophecy. It was just a nursery rhyme after all."

Just then Uma interrupted. "I wouldn't be sure about that," she said.

Sharat and Aya looked at her. "What do you mean?" asked Sharat.

"I found something very interesting in your wound," Uma told him. "Something that prevented Rookh's gold from entering your heart. It may even have saved your life."

Rummaging in her skirts she pulled out a small oval object and held it out for them to see.

Clicking his beak, Ripiraja hopped over and cocked his head to one side. "For me?" he said hopefully.

"No, Ripi, this isn't for you," said Uma sharply.

"What is it?" asked Aya.

Uma had a glint in her eye. "This is something I haven't seen for very many years," she said. "It's a seed from one of the trees that used to grow in the walled garden that once stood at the centre of the City of Jewels."

"A *seed*? But how did it get into my chest?" asked Sharat, confused.

"You tell me," said Uma. "It must have come from something you ate. A fruit, perhaps?"

Sharat frowned. "But I didn't eat any fruit in the City of Jewels," he said. He hesitated. "Unless you count the fruit from the dream."

"What fruit?" said Aya.

"The Queen of the Forest gave me a piece of fruit," Sharat explained. "I ended up swallowing it whole when Rookh dragged me out of the urn."

There was a look of jubilation on Uma's face. "That's exactly what I was hoping to hear," she said.

"What do you mean?" asked Sharat.

"Remember I told you that the jinnis were the spirits of the forest?" said Uma. "Well, *this* is the seed of the Queen's tree. She must have given Sharat the fruit knowing that he was her only hope of escaping Doctor Rookh."

Sharat stared at the witch. "Do you mean that if we plant this seed we can bring her back to life?" he demanded.

Uma's eyes were shining. "Yes," she said.

Sharat felt a rush of excitement. "So I've fulfilled the prophecy after all," he exclaimed.

Uma shook her head. "Not quite," she said. "You won't have fulfilled the prophecy until you've planted the seed and the tree has grown. Only then will the Queen be reborn."

Sharat and Aya exchanged glances.

"Let's plant it now!" exclaimed Aya.

Uma shook her head. "No," she said. "We're still a bit too close to the City of Jewels and we still don't know what's happened to Doctor Rookh. I'd prefer to wait until we reach the mountain kingdoms."

"But how are we going to get to the mountains?" asked Sharat. "I don't think Emira can carry all three of us."

Uma's eyes twinkled. "We'll go with the circus, of course," she said.

Sharat's heart leapt. "The circus?" he exclaimed. "Where are they?"

"They're on their way," said Uma. "We should be able to see them by now."

Pushing herself to her feet, she led them past the boulders to a ridge overlooking a road that twisted up the hillside from the plains below. "Look!" she said, pointing.

Two elephants and a chain of caravans trundled slowly into sight.

Sharat let out a cry of recognition. "It's Tara and Baba!" He turned to Aya. "They're the elephants from the circus!"

Aya looked down in wonder. "It's just like we planned," she said.

Uma turned back to the camp.

"Ripiraja!" she called.

The big bird flew over on silent wings and landed on her arm. "Yes?"

"Tell Lemo that the boy and his tiger are safe," she said. "They can come and fetch us as soon as it's light."

With a squawk of agreement, Ripiraja took off and circled three times before swooping down to the valley below. For a while they just stood and watched the stars coming out as night fell. Soon Emira appeared next to them, groomed and well fed. Sharat put his hand out and caressed her neck.

"We're going home!" he whispered.

Emira sighed happily. Then she leaned against her boy and began to purr.

Chapter Thirty-Nine
REUNION

Sharat and Aya were lying asleep by the fire when they were woken by the sound of trumpeting. Immediately, Emira jumped to her feet and shot off to investigate.

Moments later a voice boomed overhead.

"Sharat!"

Before Sharat could react, he was lifted off the ground and drawn into a warm embrace.

"Where have you been?" demanded the ringmaster. "We've been sick with worry."

Sharat grinned in delight. "I've found Emira!" he said proudly.

Lemo lowered him to the ground. "In future, let me know before you disappear like that!" he said, trying to look stern.

299

Sharat rolled his eyes, but he couldn't stop grinning.

Aya sat up, her hair tousled. She looked sleepily up at them.

"This is Aya," Sharat told his father. "She helped me find Emira. Now she's coming to join the circus."

He and Aya had decided not to share their secret just yet.

"You're most welcome," said Lemo, smiling warmly as he took Aya's hand.

Aya eyed his moustache with interest. "Are you Lemo?" she guessed.

"I am indeed," said Lemo.

"Don't I get a hug?" interrupted a low voice from behind them.

Sharat spun around to see an older man with a weathered face and stocky body.

"Hussein!" he cried, running over to embrace his friend.

Aya threw off her blankets and jumped to her feet. Sharat had told her all about Hussein. "Where are the elephants?" she demanded.

"They're just over there," said Hussein, pointing as he disentangled himself from Sharat.

The elephants were still brightly painted. On their backs were colourful blankets and *howdah*s jangling with bells. Emira had already rushed over to greet them and was winding happily around their legs with a rumbling purr. Tara sniffed the tiger's fur, then raised her trunk to trumpet loudly.

Sharat ran over to join them.

"The small one is Tara, and this is Baba," he told Aya. He grabbed Tara's ear and clambered nimbly on to her back.

Aya stood still as the elephants examined her. Then Tara breathed out and sent jets of air down her neck. Aya laughed and Tara wiggled her trunk with a snort of approval.

Sharat barked an order. Tara bowed her head and flapped her ears forward.

"Hold on to her ears," Sharat told Aya. "You can climb up her trunk."

Aya hesitated. "Won't she mind?"

Sharat laughed. "She minds a bit when Hussein does it. She'll hardly notice *you*."

Aya hauled herself up and sat next to Sharat.

"It's a bit different from riding Emira," he said with a grin.

Hussein climbed on next and sat behind them.

"It's good to have you back," he told Sharat. "We were mad with worry when you went missing."

"I told you I'd find Emira!" said Sharat proudly.

Hussein put out a hand and squeezed his shoulder. "You did very well," he said with a smile.

Next to them, Lemo was trying to heave Uma up on to Baba's back while Ripiraja flew around their heads.

"Call yourself a witch?" he crowed. "Fly! Fly!"

"Quiet, or I'll turn you into a toad!" snapped Uma.

Ripi cackled. "Push!" he shrieked at Lemo.

"You would almost think that bird knows what it's saying," remarked Hussein.

"He's just very well trained," said Uma, with a warning look at Ripiraja as she settled into the *howdah*.

Lemo climbed up after her and at last the elephants set off at a gentle pace while Emira roamed ahead, occasionally diving into bushes for prey.

"I'm never putting her back in that cage again," Sharat called out. "So don't ask me."

Lemo smiled over from his perch on Baba's neck. "I won't," he promised. "From now on Emira is as free as you and I."

Emira growled in approval.

It was a gorgeous morning. The sun was rising into a sky dotted with fluffy, white clouds. Now that they were off the plains the air was fresh and cool.

"Have a banana," said Hussein, offering Sharat and Aya a whole bunch.

When Tara heard the word banana, her trunk reached up over the top of her head and they took it in turns to feed her.

The circus had set up camp in a fertile valley by the banks of a fast-moving river. The whole troupe was waiting for Sharat's return. As soon as they arrived, a girl vaulted on to Tara's back and embraced Sharat warmly.

"You made it!" she cried.

Sharat disentangled himself. He was grinning. "This is my cousin, Risa," he told Aya.

The two girls looked at each other. There was a

moment's silence.

"Hello," said Aya shyly.

"Aya helped me find Emira," Sharat explained. "Now she's coming to live at the circus."

Risa hesitated, then she gave Aya a quick smile. "It will be good to have you here," she said.

Then she turned back to Sharat and gripped his arm in excitement.

"You're a hero!" she said. "We'll have your name up in flares, Lemo says."

"What does Pias think about that?" asked Sharat.

Risa laughed. "He'll get over it."

Then Sharat caught sight of the rest of the troupe. "Come on!" he told Aya. "I want to introduce you to everyone."

As he helped Aya climb down off Tara's back she was surrounded by a crowd of people all clasping her hand and kissing her cheeks.

"I'm Vijay, the snake charmer," said a man with slicked-back hair.

"Fezzik, fire-eater," said a lanky man covered in piercings and tattoos.

"I am Bhim! Magician extraordinaire," announced a small, fat man. "I'm sure Sharat has told you all about me."

Sharat laughed. "Don't worry if you don't remember all that," he told Aya. Then he caught sight of Ram. The boy was standing off to one side looking uncomfortable but when he saw Sharat looking at him he stepped forward.

"I'm glad you're back," he said awkwardly. "It … it was horrible not knowing what had happened to you."

Sharat paused. "I'm glad to be back, too," he said. He turned to Aya. "This is Risa's brother, Ram," he told her. "He's an acrobat."

"Hello," said Aya.

To Sharat's surprise Ram smiled. "Hello," he said.

Sharat glanced around. "Where's Risa gone?" he asked. "I want to tell her everything that happened."

But Lara the horsewoman had other ideas. She came striding over with a purposeful look on her face and grabbed Sharat by one of his ears.

"You're not going anywhere until you've had a good wash!" she declared. "And I suggest you come too, young lady," she said, glancing at Aya.

Before Sharat could protest, she had dragged them off for a bath in two steaming basins of water. Then she took Aya away to give her a new set of clothes, and by the time they were blissfully clean and dressed, the feast was ready. Soon great pots of stew, platters of aromatic rice, spicy vegetables and freshly baked bread were served up by the fire, all followed by the most delicious fruit.

Aya could hardly believe the size of the serving that was doled out to her. Rice, stew, vegetables, bread, and three different kinds of chutney.

"Is this all for me?" she said.

Sharat laughed. "Go ahead!" he said. "You're part of the family now."

Aya grinned, and tucked in.

304

During the feast, Sharat continued to be mobbed by people coming to hug him and offer congratulations. Then, as they sat around the campfire they listened, spellbound, as he gave them a watered-down version of the story, leaving out the part about the Prince of Jinnis. Afterwards, everyone fell silent.

"I'm just so glad you got away," said Lemo, putting his arm around his son. "I never thought I'd see you again."

"You'd better choose your next wife a little more carefully!" Lara called out, her dark eyes shining with mischief.

The performers roared with laughter as they teased the ringmaster. Then they rose to their feet to do what they enjoyed best, which was to sing, make music and celebrate.

Sharat was still a bit weak, and Aya was feeling shy, so they went and sat next to Uma.

Once they had settled down, Sharat turned to Aya. He'd barely had a chance to talk to her all day. "I meant to ask you – what happened to Alcherisma?" he said.

Aya looked thoughtful. "I think he must be free," she said. "After he mended the Mazaria he disappeared."

"Do you still have the amulet?"

With a nod Aya reached into her bag and brought out the golden bee. The diamond glittered in the light of the dying sun, but the speck of gold at its centre was gone.

Sharat laughed. "Well, at least he won't have to grant any more wishes," he said.

Aya held it towards him. "Here," she said. "You can

have it back now."

Sharat shook his head. "No, you keep it," he said. "After all, it's as much yours as it is mine."

Aya's eyes lit up. "Are you sure?" she asked.

"Of course I'm sure!" said Sharat. "It's far too pretty for me."

Aya's fingers closed tightly around the jewel. "Hopefully we can give it back to our mother one day," she said quietly.

For a little while they enjoyed watching the dancing, but soon the music slowed down, as it often did when the crew had drunk too much wine.

Sharat nudged Aya. "What about your Mazaria?" he said. "That might liven things up."

"Oh yes!" said Uma. "I'd like to hear it, too."

Aya didn't need any more encouragement. Carefully, she pulled the little instrument out of her bag and began to play.

With a growl of approval, Emira lay down at Aya's feet and started to purr.

"We'll have you on stage with that thing!" Lemo called out loudly.

Aya flushed, but she carried on playing, and soon it seemed that the earth was keeping time underneath them like the beat of some giant heart.

"Can you feel it?" whispered Sharat.

Aya nodded as she played. "Look at the trees," she said.

"They're dancing with the wind," said Sharat.

"One day I'd like to have a good look at your Mazaria,"

said Uma, her eyes settling watchfully on the silver hands, but before Aya could answer, the clouds began to roll down from the mountains. In an instant the sky darkened. There was a rumble, a flash of lightning and then the heavens opened as it began to rain.

The circus troupe moved their party noisily into the big, orange tent and Emira stalked off to find shelter in the trees, but Sharat and Aya didn't move, happy to be outside.

"Come on! Come on!" Uma scolded them. "You'll make yourselves sick sitting out here." She grasped each one of them firmly by the arm. "Bedtime!" she said.

Sharat tried to pull away from her. "But the party's only just started!" he complained.

"I'm not even tired," said Aya.

Neither of them were used to being told what to do.

"Never mind that," snapped Uma. "You've been up since dawn." Her grip was like steel as she steered them towards Lemo's caravan. "I'll give you five minutes," she warned them. "Then I'm coming in to make sure you're both asleep."

They grumbled as they were pushed through the door. Then they stopped in surprise. Before Mohini had come along, Sharat had always lived with his father. He was used to bachelor quarters, but now the inside of the caravan had been transformed. Fluffy white sheepskins lay on the floor and clean linen was tucked neatly into the two beds on either side of the room. A bunch of flowers decorated the table in the middle and a jug of water and

two mugs stood next to it. There were candles burning in brass holders on the walls.

Sharat's cousin Risa was waiting for them. As they came in she brushed down the beds to make sure they were perfect, and adjusted the vase.

Sharat looked around, then grinned. "Is this for me or for Aya?" he asked.

Risa shrugged. "I thought you might both like a decent night's sleep," she said.

Aya sat down on her bunk. "It's been so long since I've slept in a real bed," she sighed. She glanced up at Risa. "Thank you."

"Don't thank me, thank Lemo," said Risa. "He insisted that you should have his bunk."

She gave Aya a quick smile, then blew out the candles.

"You'll have to tell me the rest of your story tomorrow," she whispered to Sharat as she leaned down to kiss him goodnight.

A little later, Uma popped in to check up on them, just as she'd promised. Then, once she was satisfied that they were tucked up safely in bed, she closed the door and sat herself down on the caravan steps. The rain had stopped now and it was a balmy night.

Emira, back from the hunt, came striding through the darkness and lay at Uma's feet. Moments later, Ripiraja landed next to them with a caw.

Just then Lemo and Hussein came over.

"How are they?" asked Hussein in a low voice.

308

"They should be fast asleep by now," Uma assured him.

"Good," said Lemo. "We'll need to leave at first light if we're heading for Narayan's pass."

Uma nodded. "That's probably wise," she said. "Rookh may be out of action now, but he's sure to come looking for them and the more space we can put between us and the City of Jewels the better."

At the sound of Rookh's name, Emira raised her head and a threatening growl played in her throat.

Hussein put a reassuring hand on her back.

"It's all right," he murmured. "You're home now."

"Are you coming with us this time?" Lemo asked Uma.

"Yes, I'm coming," she said. "There's nothing left for me in the City of Jewels. Besides, those children need an education. They've both been running wild for far too long."

Lemo smiled. "It will be good to have you back." He put out a hand to the old woman. "Come on," he said. "Emira can look after them. Let's find you a bed."

With a grumble, Uma got to her feet.

Inside the caravan, Sharat and Aya were lying in their bunks, but they weren't asleep yet.

"I can't believe we made it," Aya whispered into the darkness.

"I always knew I'd find Emira," said Sharat, "but I couldn't have done it without you."

Aya smiled, but there was something that had been troubling her.

"I wonder what's happened to Kalki?" she said. "Do you think he'll come back when you're grown up, like Vasuki told us?"

Sharat hesitated. He couldn't remember much about being the Prince of Jinnis. "I don't know," he said with a sigh. "I don't want to think about that now. All I want to do now is settle back into life at the circus."

Still, he couldn't help feeling a sense of wonder as he put his hand up to touch the seed that was tucked safely into a pouch strung around his neck. His heart was filled with love as he remembered the Queen of the Forest. His mother. Perhaps one day, when he had planted this seed he would see her again. He hoped so.

In her own bunk, Aya's thoughts had turned unbidden to her terrible secret.

"What do you think will happen to Doctor Rookh?" she asked.

Sharat hesitated for a moment. "Do you care?"

"No!" said Aya, her voice fierce. "I hope I never see him again."

"Then you don't have to," Sharat assured her. "The circus is your home now. We'll look after you."

Aya's reply was inaudible. He heard her stifle a yawn.

Smiling, he turned over, wriggling to make himself more comfortable. It was so nice to be back in his own bunk and tomorrow he would go out hunting with Emira just as he always had. Muttering goodnight he closed his eyes and soon he too was drifting off to sleep.

Outside, the wind blew away the clouds and a crescent

310

moon shone its light on the living earth. For a while a few of the circus crew remained around the camp-fire talking quietly, but it wasn't long before even the stragglers wandered off to their tents.

From her place under the caravan, Emira let out a sigh. All was still. It seemed nothing could disturb the peace of the night. But still the tiger didn't sleep. Instead she sat like a sentinel, her eyes glinting in the moonlight as she turned her head to face the valley below.

Acknowledgements

With thanks to Adrian and Noriko for inspiring me, to Rolando and Laura for teaching me, to Danny Diskin for his advice and encouragement, and to all the brothers and sisters who have joined me on my journey.

I'd also like to thank my agent, Laetitia Rutherford, for her patience and support; Lionel Wigram, whose interest and enthusiasm allowed me to keep on going; my excellent editor, Kirsty Stansfield, for her expert advice and Kate Wilson, Managing Director of Nosy Crow, who made it possible for this book to be published.

Finally I would like to thank all my guides, teachers and protectors, here and in the astral. May you continue to inspire me, and may this story be all that you have shown me it would be.

Om Gam Ganapataye Namaha